THE BLUE CANTINA:

ANNA'S SURRENDER

By Paul Blades

I0671880

Dark Visions Publications
darkvisionspub@gmail.com

Other books by Paul Blades:

Klitzman's Isle
Klitzman's Empire
Klitzman's Paradise
Klitzman's Pawn Parts One and Two
Slaver's Dozen- A Tale of Klitzman's Isle
The Taking of Cheryl Part One
The Taking of Cheryl Part Two: Slaver's Bait
Comfort Girl No. 4
Sacrifice to the Emerald God
The Warlord's Concubine, Books 1, 2, 3 and 4
Dreams and Desires, Books 1 and 2
Carmella Condemned
Carmella's Fate

The Maddy Saga:

Vol. I	Maddy becomes a Ponygirl
Vol. II	The Training of a Ponygirl
Vol. III	Ponygirl Champion
Vol. IV	Ponygirl Summer
Vol. V	Ponygirl Love
Vol. VI	Ponygirl Season
Vol. VII	Ponygirl Gambit
Vol. VIII	Ponygirl Pleasures
Vol. IX	Ponygirl Peril
Vol. X	Ponygirl's Choice Part One
Vol. XI	Ponygirls' Choice Part Two

PRELUDE

In a subterranean lounge in a large, converted mansion on the outskirts of a major, metropolitan, American city, three men sat around a small table, their glasses filled with top shelf booze. They were relaxed, enjoying the show. The men were all either approaching middle age, or had just crossed that amorphous, ill defined border. They were all dressed in sleek, well tailored suits, seemingly, in the dark light of the nightclub, all cut from the same cloth. On their wrists were expensive, elegant wristwatches. Their hair was clean cut and well trimmed as befitted men of substance, with a tinge of grey here and there. They were in a celebratory mood.

On the stage in front of them, highlighted by several strong, small spotlights, about four feet off of the floor, a pretty, young girl, outfitted only in a pair of glittering, sapphire earrings and a pair of bright red high heels, had just begun her routine. A slow, rhythmic beat was being emitted at high volume from the club's sound system playing one of those forgettable tunes that combine a dulsatory vocal track accompanied by an underlay of unidentifiable instruments. The beat was, however, appropriately languorous for the slow, enticing movements that the girl was making on stage. She was standing with her legs spread, her hips undulating and her hands were wandering her body as if on a voyage of discovery.

She was obviously aroused, as the glistening of the gaping slit between her hairless love lips indicated. From time to time, she would point a dainty finger at her stiffened clit and give it a loving massage. Each time she did, her eyelids fluttered and her face slackened. She had the men's full attention.

The nightclub was small, with seven round tables covered by light blue tablecloths and with seats for four or five around each one. The floors and wall were colored a dark navy blue. The short service bar, behind which a heavy set, bearded man dressed in a crisp, light blue sports shirt and a matching tie dispensed drinks, was also blue. Even the small, round paper coasters under the men's drinks were colored a shade of blue. It was as if, when the below ground level establishment had been constructed, there had been a sale on blue somewhere and the designers had taken full advantage of it. Above the bar, in script, were the words, 'The Blue Cantina' in, of course, bold, blue neon lights.

The lighting in the club was low, just bright enough for the men to be able to make out the features of the other men at their table. It was early yet, and only two of the other tables were inhabited, one by a trio of men attired and of similar aspect to the first four. At the other table sat a lone man nursing a neat brandy in a cavernous, elegant snifter. He was tall, a little older than the rest, and seemed put off by the loud, insistent music. A waitress, wearing only a frilly, light blue thong and matching blue high heels, stood nearby waiting for a signal from any of the men to fulfill their desires.

The stage itself was small, maybe about seven or eight feet all around. It had a runway that led back to a large, steel door from which the girl had first appeared. Sitting on a stool next to the door, his presence obscured by the low lighting, was a tall, well built man in his early to mid thirties. He was clean shaven and wore a dark blue t-shirt, jeans and work boots. His demeanor was harsh and observant as if he were waiting for some faltering in the young girl's efforts for the opportunity to spring forth and correct her.

The girl on the stage looked about 22. She had ample, but not oversized breasts, clearly all natural by their easy sway and graceful arc. Her head was adorned with midlength, curly brown hair done up in ringlets. Her lips, painted a deep red to match the shiny polish on her finger and toe nails, were thick and moist. During her routine, she kept them pursed as if inviting their use. On her belly, three or four inches above the top of her excited puss, was tattooed in bright blue ink an ornate, scriptive 'D'.

The song slowed to a finish and the girl paused momentarily until the next one began. The men remained silent during the brief interval, no one wanting to break the lascivious spell that the dancer had exuded into the room. The next song had a sharper, more lively beat and the girl's ministrations to her body and the wriggling of her smooth, enticing hips gained energy.

There was a gleaming steel pole behind her, and she turned her body towards it. Placing her hands on the pole above her head, she spread her legs and slowly slid down it, her well toned rear cheeks keeping time to the rhythms of the tune. Her feet slipped out as her torso went lower and lower, jutting her derriere out deliciously and creating more room between the upper half of her body and the pole. When she was bent horizontal to the stage, her legs spread widely, her breasts swinging lustfully from her chest, she took a small, delicate hand and slipped it between her thighs. As her hips rocked back and forth, she used her hand to spread the engorged lips of her pussy, revealing an expanse of soft, pink, wrinkled skin within. She plunged her two longest fingers in the tiny hole and began to stroke herself wildly.

All eyes were riveted on her frenetic self pleasuring. Glasses found their ways to lips without sight. Several of the men shifted themselves as if making room for their hardened cocks in the pants of their well tailored slacks.

When the third song began, a return to the luxurious beat of the first, the girl reached down to the side of the stage and produced a six or seven inch long simulacrum of a male member. It was pink and had a wide base. She knelt at the front of the stage and inserted it into a slot so that it was standing straight up. Eyeing her appreciative audience, the girl commenced a languorous stroke of the faux penis. She bent over and, holding the bottom with her two hands, spread her tongue and then her lips over it. She was clearly well practiced in the arts of fellatio and her efforts at stimulating the pinkish prong induced several of the men to engage in casual, surreptitious strokes of their stiffened pricks.

But it was the fourth song that they all were waiting for. Its rhythm, like the second, was hard and fast. The pink prong was now wet with the girl's saliva. Looking up at the men, who she could barely see due to the glare of the spotlights on the stage, but who she nonetheless knew were out there, she gave her weighty chest a shake, sending her plump mounds into motion and then, slipping forwards and rising to a crouch, she placed the head of the thick penal substitute at the fulcrum of her thighs and slowly lowered herself on to it.

The attractive, naked, young girl let the object fill her. Her knees were spread widely and the men could see the plastic surface push aside her soft labial lips and disappear within her. Placing her hands on the insides of her thighs, the girl began to thrust herself up and down on the faux cock energetically. Her passions were obviously rising fast. One hand drifted to the apex of her distended crevasse and rubbed furiously at her stiffened clit. The other ascended to her jumping breasts and stroked and pinched her hardened nipples. Her lips were parted and her eyes had closed to slits. Her head alternated from leaning back, revealing her graceful, pale white throat and leaning forward, her curly, brown hair hanging down and forming a curtain around her impassioned face.

The music came to a halt. No new tune replaced it. The room was filled now with the sounds of the girl's developing lusts. She was moaning as she pleasured herself before the men. A rosy aura had spread over her chest above her breasts. Perspiration was beading all over her lithe, shapely, young body.

When the girl's crisis came upon her, she gave out a loud groan. Her body shook and her thighs quivered. She called out "Oh! Oh! Oh!" as her pussy's spasms drove her to ecstasy. She seized her breasts and squeezed them harshly. Her eyes rolled back and her lips spread open to allow her utterances of pleasure to escape.

When the paroxysms of her pussy finally faded, the girl took a deep breath. She looked up anxiously at the audience, appearing to her only as dark, male forms. An appreciative round of applause broke out and her anxious aspect turned to one of relief. She rose from her pinioned perch and removed the cum coated instrument of her pleasure from the stage and tossed it into a bin behind it. Giving the men a respectful bow, she retreated hurriedly back up the runway. She paused before the large, ominous door and placed her wrists together and in front of her, presenting them to the man who sat there on the stool. He took a pair of bright, steel manacles and placed them on her wrists, joining them. She opened her mouth and he inserted a bright red, round ball into it. The ball had long, leather straps affixed to each side and he tied them behind her head.

When the girl was properly outfitted, the man pressed a buzzer next to the door. The door opened from the interior and the girl darted in past it.

One of the men at the first table, the group of four, announced to his friends. "I know which one I want." The other men laughed.

"You may have to wait your turn," another replied.

The tall, elegant, older man had finished off his brandy and risen from his seat. He walked slowly and assuredly to the side of the stage and advanced to a large, oaken door. From his pocket he produced a rectangular piece of plastic that looked like a credit card. He slipped it along an electronic device next to the door and its lock clicked open. He pulled the door towards him and entered.

A moment later, a tall, thin, young girl, not much more than nineteen, with long, strawberry blond hair done up in a ponytail with a bright blue ribbon, emerged from behind the large, steel door. Her mouth was distended by a bright red ball gag. She stopped by the man outside the door and raised her manacled wrists to him. Taking a small key, he unlocked the shiny confinements and then removed her gag. The girl then hurried down the runway towards the stage.

When the music started again, the long legged, naked, blond beauty began her undulations.

CHAPTER ONE

Anna sat frozen in the driver's seat of her leased, red, late model Toyota Camry, the radio off, the motor purring, unable to bring herself to commence the process of shutting the engine. Beneath her fur lined, kid leather gloves her hands were sweating and she gripped the steering wheel tightly as if steeling herself to resist some force that might hurl her from the vehicle unwillingly. She was wearing a short, pleated, tan, cashmere skirt and a tight, burgundy, pullover knit sweater under her heavy, black, cloth overcoat. She had adorned herself with a pair of two inch tall, red high heels, as she had been instructed, and she had on more makeup than she usually wore, having outlined her eyes carefully with dark mascara and painted her lids a subtle, soft blue.

Exactly one week ago, the 29 year old, attractive social worker had come to the elegant mansion belonging to Miles Devlin with a trepidation that was only imperceptibly less intense than now. She had been in desperate straights, but had no where else to turn. Just that morning she had discovered that Carol, her best friend and the second in command of the charity that Anna headed, had absconded with approximately $225,000 belonging to the social service agency. As executive director, Anna was ultimately responsible for everything that went on at the Center, a residence home for young girls who had run or been cast away by their families and society. The Center provided them with a loving, warm environment to recover from abuse and neglect and gave them schooling, job training and a hope for a better and more fulfilling future. The money had been the quarterly grant from the county welfare agency and without it operations would come to a grinding halt. The girls who lived and trained there would be cast out into the street or sent back to their abusive homes. It was a disaster of the first magnitude.

Anna had founded the Center five years ago, when she was 24, and it was the centerpiece of her life. She knew what the girls had suffered, having run away from her own dysfunctional home when she was sixteen. Life had been hard, and she had skated precariously amongst the temptations of drugs, alcohol, exploitative men and the easy way out of prostitution, go-go bars and promiscuous sex. Anna had been lucky. After a few false starts, she had been taken in by a kindly, older woman who had found her a job waitressing at a local diner, guided her through the process of getting her G.E.D. and then an associate's degree at the local county college. Anna had gone on to get a B.A. as a social worker at State.

When the old woman died, she had left Anna her large house and about $150,000. Anna started the Center in the house soon afterwards and, through determination, luck and lots of hard work, had gotten the agency recognized as a bona fide charity by the county welfare board. The Center now housed, at any single time, between twenty to thirty girls ranging in age from sixteen to twenty-one. There was counseling, schooling and job placement. Not all the girls went on to lead productive lives, but a high percentage of them did, moving on to good jobs or colleges armed with a better vision of themselves as worthy of respect and love.

But all of that was set to come tumbling down with a huge crash. Carol had vanished without a trace. She was a few years older than Anna and had had a similar life experience, sexual abuse at home, beatings, an alcohol ridden family, and had run away at fifteen. She had not been as lucky as Anna and had descended into a life of drug abuse and prostitution. They had met while Anna was interning at a local drug rehab facility and had hit it off right away. When Anna told Carol of her dreams about founding what in the old days was euphemistically referred to as a 'home for wayward girls', Carol had excitedly agreed to join her once she finished rehab.

But Carol's addictions had reared their ugly heads again. Anna had first noticed it about two months ago when Carol started coming in later and later, tired and disheveled. Anna had found a pint of vodka in her desk drawer. She had demanded that Carol take a drug test, but the tall, thin, blond haired woman had refused. Then, one morning, she had not come in at all. She failed to answer her cell phone or respond to text messages or emails. After three days, Anna went to Carol's apartment to find she had gone. It was with a gnawing, terrible foreboding that Anna had conducted an informal audit of the Center's books and found that Carol had absconded with all of their quarterly grant money, over $225,000.

Anna had cried, heartbroken that her friend had betrayed her and disconsolate at the thought that her life's work, the Center, would probably have to fold. The worst thing about it was that Anna had endorsed the check that Carol had used to embezzle the funds and she knew that she would be implicated, if not in the actual theft, at least in accusations of incompetence and reckless negligence with the Center's money. There was no way that she could come up with that kind of cash. There was only one hope: Miles Devlin.

Devlin had been one of the Center's most enthusiastic supporters for years. In addition to his sizable annual contributions, he had helped obtain the financing for the addition of a new wing on the old house that Anna had inherited and had created a scholarship fund for the girls which was contributed to by many of his bigwig friends. Anna had had some reservations about receiving Devlin's largesse. His reputation was a little darker than shady. Although he represented himself as a wealthy investor, there were rumors about his underworld connections and alleged mob ties. He was young, a little over forty years old, handsome and suave. He had short, jet black hair and a fit, masculine build. He oozed charm. He had appeared at one of the Center's fundraisers about a year after it opened and Anna had eagerly accepted him on the Board of Trustees about six months later. Shortly thereafter, the Center received its first County grant and the hand to mouth existence of the agency came to an end. He was now president of the Board and was involved in every major decision.

Last Friday, Anna had telephoned Devlin and told him that she needed to talk to him urgently. She had arrived a little after seven o'clock that night and was ushered into his private office, a sumptuous, lavishly decorated retreat inside his luxurious mansion. She had sat in one of the comfortable, elegant chairs in front of his large, finely polished, oaken desk and blurted out her troubles. Devlin took in her message of tribulation calmly, but with a severe, disappointed wrinkle in the brow of his handsome, vital face.

"And what do you expect me to do about it, Anna?" he had asked finally. His voice was stern and Anna shivered at his disapproving tone.

With tears in her eyes, Anna had pleaded that the wealthy benefactor replace the lost funds. She promised to repay him, forgo her salary, work a side job, anything to keep the Center from failing and to forestall her personal disgrace.

"I'm sorry, Mr. Devlin," she eked out. "I know it's my fault. I should have known better than to give Carol all that responsibility. But there's nothing I can do now. The Center will have to close. I don't want to imagine what will happen to the girls. There's no place else for them to go. Can't you do something to help?"

"Listen, Anna," Devlin replied, leaning back in his large, black, leather chair, a frown of disapproval on his face, "I'm not in the habit of rewarding negligence or embezzlement. You tell me that Carol took the money. That's what you say. Your signature is on the check and it was cashed at your bank. I don't know whether you're telling me the whole truth or not. Maybe you're using Carol's disappearance to cover up your own crime. Did you owe somebody a lot of money? Do you have a gambling problem or something?"

"I swear to you that it wasn't me, Mr. Devlin," Anna answered, panicked. It was worse than she thought. Maybe she would be arrested. She might go to jail. Her stomach quailed at the thought. Her throat grew tight and her hands began to sweat.

There was a lull of deadly silence in the room. Then Devlin spoke again.

"I want to tell you something, Anna. I don't know who you think I am. I'm sure you've heard all the rumors. Helping out on your charity was a good way for me to get a little favorable PR. I don't give a fuck about your wayward girls or any of your problems. I can tell you that it will be a great embarrassment to me when this all comes out. I will make sure that you are prosecuted to the full extent of the law. Your Center cost me a pretty penny over the years and now to have my name dragged through the mud will undo all the good I got from it. It makes me want to toss you out on your ear. I could call the sheriff right now and you'd be in the county lockup in a half an hour. It's probably the only way for me to escape this mess without the newspapers using me as a fall guy. I can see it now: 'Alleged Mobster Implicated in Charity Scandal.' That's what the headlines will say."

The distraught woman had sat through Devlin's tirade with a building sense of dread. She broke into tears. "Oh, please don't call the sheriff, Mr. Devlin! I didn't take the money, I promise you! I wouldn't do that, the Center is too important to me!"

Devlin let the unhappy woman cry for a few minutes. When Anna looked up, she could see the wheels turning in his head.

"Okay, Anna," he said finally. "What's in it for me?"

Anna tried to stifle her sobs. Her glimmer of hope was tinged with confusion. "What do you mean, Mr. Devlin?" she asked hesitatingly.

"I mean, 'What's in it for me?' You expect me to shell out over 200 grand. What do I get in exchange?"

Anna looked at the man, perplexed. "I told you that I'd pay you back somehow, Mr. Devlin. It'll take a long time, but I promise you'll get all your money back, with interest, if that's what you want."

"Bullshit," Devlin spat out at her. "It would take you a hundred years."

"No it won't, Mr. Devlin! I'll mortgage the house!"

"You can't get a mortgage on the house. It belongs to the Board of Trustees now. I doubt that that group of stuffed shirts will look on your defalcation with amusement. Anyway, it's already mortgaged to help pay for the addition, or did you forget that?"

Anna felt her heart sink. He was right. She fought back a renewed cascade of tears.

"There is one thing you've got that I want, Anna," Devlin told her in a cold, insidious voice.

Anna looked at the callous man with surprise. "What would that be?" she asked, tremulously.

"I think you know what it is," Devlin returned.

The pretty, shapely social worker felt a chill run through her. Devlin, although his actions towards her had always been above board, had asked her out on a number of occasions. She had politely demurred. Many times, at cocktail parties or other benefits for the Center, she had felt his eyes wandering her flesh and she had gotten goose bumps and a sickly feeling. Devlin always appeared with a languorous, beautiful, young woman on his arm, rarely the same one. Anna, like many women, had a sixth sense about men, and she had him pegged as a lecher from the word 'go'. She had often joked to Carol about it, who had responded, "But a good looking one." That didn't matter to Anna. She hadn't dated much since college. She had learned to like sex, but the men she had met had not inspired her that burdening herself with a lover was something that would add much to her life. Looking at the leering face of her charity's principal benefactor, she hoped that she was wrong about what he had implied.

The attractive social worker stiffened in her chair. "No," she said brusquely. "I don't know what you mean."

"That's too bad, Anna. You could have saved yourself a whole world of shit. And me too. It seems that your precious Center isn't all that important to you after all. Now, I suggest that you get out of my house and go and get your affairs in order. The sheriff will be at your house in about an hour. You can wait there for him or you can take it on the lam. They'll probably catch you sooner or later, but you could give them a good run."

Visions of herself being led from her apartment in handcuffs, the headlines the next day in the local paper, appearing at the courthouse shackled in front of the newspaper cameras, filled Anna's head. All that she had worked for would be gone in an instant. The girls at the Center would probably all be on the street in a week. She would never get a job in social work again. Her resolve not to surrender herself to the salacious suggestion of her benefactor weakened.

"What is it that you want, Mr. Devlin?" she asked, trying desperately not to give in to her revulsion or her despair.

"Stand up and turn around," Devlin ordered churlishly.

Anna bridled at the suggestion that she model her body for the man, but she knew that she had no other hope for avoiding calamity. Biting her lip, she rose to her feet and turned slowly in front of the evil man's desk. She had come directly from work and was wearing a knee length, dark brown, woolen skirt and a loose fitting, satin, tan blouse. Her shoes were low cut and businesslike. Her long, black hair was tied up behind her head in a chignon. As she turned, she felt her firm, ample breasts sway slightly inside her modest, stiff brassiere. Her stockinged thighs made a little hiss as they rubbed against each other. She couldn't believe that she was doing this! No matter how bad the ramifications of public exposure of her difficulties would be, wouldn't prostituting herself be even worse?

When the circle was completed, Anna looked back in the face of the man. His eyes were drinking in her flesh appreciatively.

"You don't know how many times I've thought about fucking you, Anna," he said. "You were always just out of reach. I knew that you despised me in spite of everything I did for the Center. I'm going to enjoy having you suck my cock."

Anna sat back down in her chair. "Please don't make me do this, Mr., Devlin!" she pleaded desperately. "I'll do anything else! Please!"

"I tell you what, Anna," the man answered, "I'll give you one week to think about it. But let me make the deal perfectly clear. I want a full, signed confession. I don't care if you took the money or not. I want our, 'relationship', let's call it, to be ironclad. Don't bother to put a date on it. I'll just fill that in later if you ever break our deal. Second, you'll be my toy for one year. You'll do whatever I say, whenever and wherever. From now on, you'll spend your weekends here at my mansion. You can go to work during the week, but you'll come here on nights that I want you. You'll dress the way I say, you'll never talk back or disrespect me. When the year's over, I'll give you back your confession and we'll call it even."

Anna was stunned at the man's cruel demands. She would be his whore for a whole year! Her hands tightened into little fists. She cursed Carol, cursed Devlin, cursed fate. Maybe it would be better to get her humiliation over with, take her medicine. She didn't have to decide tonight. He had given her a week. Maybe she could come up with something. She looked at Devlin coldly. "How do I know you'll live up to your part of the bargain, assuming I agree, which I doubt very much? How do I know that you'll give me the confession back?"

"You'll just have to take my word, Anna. The fact is that I'll probably get tired of you long before a year's out anyway. You're good looking, but you're no Venus de Milo. I've fucked a hundred cunts prettier than you, and more willing too. I'm just doing this to teach you a lesson. Don't think you're so all high and mighty from now on. I've seen how you looked at me. You think that I'm dirt, a fool to be milked for his money. This is payback, bitch. Every time I fuck you, I want you to realize who's the lowlife now. So, be here by seven o'clock next Friday night or not. It's up to you. If you do come, I want a signed, written confession, in your own handwriting and you better come looking like you want to fuck me, high heels, makeup, the works. Do you understand?" He waited until he was sure that his conditions had fully sunken into the mind of the frail, unhappy social worker. "Now get out," he spat at her.

Anna spent the next week in agony. She had gone home and, after drinking a quarter of a bottle of scotch, cried herself to sleep. Each morning, she forced herself to go to work, dragging herself out of bed, standing listlessly in her shower while the hot water streamed over her nude body. Every day, at the agency, there were a hundred little details to deal with. There were counseling sessions to attend with the girls, minor and not so minor disciplinary matters, screening candidates for admission. This was always a difficult task as it required a fine balance between girls who were so far gone that there was little hope for them and girls who really just needed some counseling and a bus ticket home. There were always more applicants than beds. Since Carol was not around, Anna had to take up the slack of her work as well, putting together the scheduling of the staff, processing invoices and purchase orders, drafting correspondence that had to get out.

The worst part was having to carry her secret all alone. Normally, she would have confided her deepest fears and worries to her friend, Carol. They had spent many a night in deep conversation about their pasts, how their abuse had damaged them, how it felt so good to be better and living a life of helping others avoid the same fates. Since Carol was nowhere to be found, she had to bear her fear and shame alone. Sure, she had friends, other social workers from other agencies around the county, one or two men that she had met and become friendly with. But how could she tell them about what was happening, that money had been stolen, that she was considering prostituting herself to save the Center. If she agreed to Devlin's nefarious deal, there was no way that she would want anyone to know. The money problem would be solved. If she didn't, everyone would know anyway as she was carted off in a police car and her reputation destroyed forever. No, she had to bear her torment alone, much like she had done in the past, too ashamed and fearful of the consequences if she asked anyone for help.

On Tuesday, Wendy, one of the older girls in the center, a sprightly redhead, had a mini crisis when her job prospect rejected her at the last minute. Anna considered the girls in the Center as family. It was difficult for her to watch the pretty, 19 year old cry. She knew that if the Center closed, there would be tears all around as the hopes of her chances for recovery and to lead a decent, productive, rewarding life would evaporate. She calmed the young girl down as best she could and tried not to have her despondency about the Center's future add to the girl's dismay.

"Don't worry, Wendy, something will work out for you. I know it," she said as she held the girl in her arms in her office, her sobbing face nestled in her shoulder. "We all experience setbacks. It's how we deal with them that makes the difference."

When the tiny, shapely, red haired girl left, Anna went into the bathroom down the hall from her office and had a cry of her own.

On Thursday, she had finally accustomed herself to the decision she knew that she would make all along. She called Devlin's office to tell him she would agree to his terms. Devlin either wouldn't or couldn't talk to her and his secretary indicated she would relay the veiled message back to her boss.

That night, Anna had gone out shopping. Her wardrobe was generally conservative as befitted the director of a social service agency. She charged the $200.00 cashmere skirt and the $150.00 woolen sweater as well as the $120.00 bright red high heels. As the shop girl rang her up, she wondered where she would ever get the money to pay for it all. She stopped at the fancy lingerie store at the mall, but was unable to bring herself to purchase any of the expensive, revealing underthings displayed there. It was too much for her to deal with, the image of her exposing herself to the jaundiced eye of the perverse tycoon. He would have to be satisfied with what she had on hand. She did purchase a set of cheap, gold plated earrings, little golden circles that would dangle from piercings in her ears, to make herself look just a little prettier.

Now, sitting in the driveway of the huge, foreboding mansion, Anna regretted not buying something sexy. She had seen the beautiful, model quality women Devlin had dated and doubted that they had any reticence about showing him their lace clad bodies. Devlin held all of the cards. What if he fucked her and then decided that she wasn't attractive enough to keep his end of the deal? Now that she had decided to go through with his perfidious contract, all her hopes were on its success. Keeping the Center alive was more important than anything else. There had been a short period, after she had run away from home, that Anna had exchanged her body for the means of life, shelter, food, clothing, and she knew what it was like to fuck someone who you inwardly despised. Then her rewards had been the basic necessities of life. Now, her reward would be much greater. She would sacrifice herself for a short while so that dozens of young women wouldn't have to spend their lives in misery. It was just sex, after all.

Drawing on her deep, inner reserves of strength, Anna forced herself to open the car door and step outside. She saw her stocking covered leg extend from the car seat to the ground and her short skirt ride up her thigh, flashing the trim, bronze skin above her stocking. She knew that she had great legs. She felt a sudden surge of sexual power as she pushed the car door closed. She would make the best of a bad situation and convince Devlin that she was the best fuck he had had in a year. There was a time, not so many years ago, that men had paid good money to slide their hands along her soft, inner thighs and gain access to her point of pleasure, had ogled with desire her round, well formed breasts.

Anna's courage faded the closer that she got to the mansion. The parking lot was big. Three of Devlin's expensive, shiny, luxury cars were lined up like stallions awaiting their master's pleasure: a long, black Mercedes limo, a luxurious, rust colored, Lexus coupe and a shiny, silver Maserati. The house loomed large over her, the broad, arching entrance well lit, the rest of its bulk dark and sinister with lights at only a few of its many windows. The November night was cold and moonless. Tall, eerie looking trees swayed and creaked in the biting wind. The crunching sound made by her footsteps in the gravel of the driveway sounded ominous, and she advanced unsteadily on the front of her shoes, fearful lest she stumble on the fine points of her high heels.

When she reached the wide, granite steps that led up to the doorway, she paused, wrapping her arms around her for warmth. Once she crossed the threshold, she would transform her life. She would become, essentially, Devlin's sexual slave. Maybe she was making a mistake. Her heart was beating wildly in her chest. She held a small, black leather purse in her right hand. She had agonized about the decision of whether to bring a suitcase. In the end, although she had packed and unpacked her carrying bag three times, she had decided against it. There had just been something too final in the thought of preparing for a weekend stay with him. The excuse that she needed to go home and put on clean clothes would give her a respite from her subservience to him, a chance to put some space between what she knew she had to do and her inner self.

Steeling herself for her ordeal, Anna climbed the three stone stairs and advanced to the door. She hesitated only a moment before ringing the bell.

Just as he had a week ago tonight, Devlin's tall, lanky, male servant opened the door. He was swarthy, with jet black hair and a long, suspicious face. He was dressed in a black suit with narrow lapels and a thin, black tie. There were traces of grey around the sides of his head and he looked to Anna to be in his middle to late fifties. Last week, he had hardly said a word to her and he was equally unloquacious now, admitting her with a small, condescending nod.

The entrance hall to Devlin's mansion was laid with shiny, gray slate and surrounded by deep bronze, polished oak paneling. An expansive, red carpeted staircase led to the upper floors of the house. Devlin's office was off to the right. Anna slid off her gloves and handed them to Devlin's servant who waited patiently while she removed her overcoat. He placed the gloves in the pocket of the coat and hung it in a closet embedded in the wall close to the entranceway. He signaled wordlessly for Anna to follow him.

The tall, elegant servant strode across the stone floor towards the entrance to Devlin's office. His footsteps were quiet, highlighting the loud, echoing click-clacking of Anna's heels. He was dressed in a dark, well pressed suit appropriate for his station. Anna wondered, as she followed him, how much he knew about the purpose for her visit. He undoubtedly was well versed in Devlin's playboy lifestyle and she imagined that he had escorted dozens of Devlin's conquests across this large, cavernous foyer. She also wondered how public her upcoming 'relationship' with the servant's master would be. There would be nothing unusual in itself for her to have become enamored of the good looking, dynamic businessman. Eyebrows might rise among the Board of Trustees, but there was nothing unethical in itself for the executive director of the Center to be dating the president of the Board. Things would work out, they just had to.

The entrance to Devlin's study was secured by a large, ornate, dark stained door. The servant opened it and stood back, letting Anna precede him into the room. It was a large room, lit by an elegant, central chandelier and finely chiseled, glass sconces on the walls. The lighting was bright, yet soft. The rug was a thick, gold carpet and the walls were painted a creamy off-white. Facing the front and side of the building were large, arching, French windows offset by long, thick, brown curtains. The room was divided in half with an expansive, leather couch facing the window, a wide and long, glass coffee table in front of it and two over stuffed, fabric covered chairs on either side facing each other.

Behind the couch was Devlin's aircraft carrier sized desk. Devlin, dressed in an expertly tailored, light blue dress shirt and tie, was sitting behind it. His cuffs were bound by gleaming, gold cufflinks. Behind him, on the wall, was a large mural depicting a scene from antiquity. Anna had seen it before and deemed it appropriate for the hedonistic bachelor. It was called, if she remembered correctly, 'The Rape of the Sabine Women', memorializing the ancient Romans' seizure of women to populate their nascent city. The fierce, Roman men, bandits really, were grappling with the buxom, semi draped, protesting women prefatory to hauling them off as captives. Anna had a new insight as to how the women must have felt.

Devlin was on the telephone arguing with someone about pricing and delivery dates. Anna did not see the servant leave and knew that she had been left alone with the fearsome man only when she heard the sound of the heavy door closing behind her. She stood for a moment, watching Devlin's animated face but tuning out the conversation. Her heart was beating wildly and her arms were trembling. She was standing at the corner of the desk and was unsure of whether she should take a chair or await her prospective despoiler's command. Devlin looked up at her, his eyes roaming her body knowingly and then directed his attention back to the call.

"I don't care what your problem is," he said. "You promised me Tuesday and it better be Tuesday or we're going to have to revisit our relationship!....No, I don't understand....Well, that's your problem, isn't it...I'm just going to say this one more time. Deliver the goods on Tuesday or don't deliver them at all! And the price stays the same, got it?" He slammed the receiver down into its cradle.

Devlin looked at his watch and then up at the primly, but elegantly dressed, young woman. "You're five minutes late," he noted with disdain.

Anna was taken aback by his hostility. "I, I'm sorry," she began to sputter. "I was…"

"I don't want to hear your excuses," Devlin interrupted rudely. "When I say seven o'clock, I mean seven o'clock. Understand?"

"Yes, Mr. Devlin," Anna replied meekly. Things were not getting off to a good start. Maybe this was all a mistake, she thought. Her trembling had spread from her arms to her knees and she hoped that the callous man didn't notice it.

"Did you bring the letter?"

"Yes, Mr. Devlin," Anna answered. She could not suppress the tremulousness in her voice.

"Give it to me," he ordered.

The frightened, nervous woman edged her way closer to the desk and reached into her small handbag. She had written four or five versions of the note, trying to set down the terms of the confession that the man had demanded in a way that would at least give her some wriggle room should it be disclosed and setting forth what she hoped would be extenuating circumstances. She had settled on a short and sweet statement: "I, Anna Addunizio, admit to embezzling the sum of $227,475.28 from the Wayne County Young Women's Center." She had signed it but left it undated as per Devlin's instructions.

Anna leaned over the broad desk and handed the note to Devlin. While he perused it, she took a seat in one of the straight backed, padded chairs in front of his desk. As she sat down, she wiped her sweaty hands on her soft, light tan skirt.

Devlin looked up. "Who told you you could sit down?" he asked accusingly.

"N-no one," Anna replied.

"Then stand up while I read this."

"Y-yes, Mr. Devlin," Anna answered obediently.

"And don't give me all of this 'Yes, Mr. Devlin. No, Mr. Devlin,' crap. When I give you an order, just do it."

Anna felt her eyes begin to water. Humiliated at the man's coarse tone and brisk manner, she suppressed her polite reply to his churlish instructions and stood. She gripped her handbag tightly in her right fist as Devlin read the note twice. He put it down on his desk.

"Okay, that'll do," he said with finality. Anna felt like some terrible threshold had been crossed. He looked over Anna's trembling form. "I thought I told you to get all dressed up," he said, disdain in his voice.

"I-I did, Mr. Devlin."

"You don't get it Anna, do you? You're a whore now. An expensive one, I'll grant you that, and maybe, to your own mind, for a good purpose. But you're a whore nonetheless and you've come dressed like your going to a PTA luncheon. I assume that that's the best that you have."

"Yes, Mr. Devlin," Anna squeaked out. She was mortified both at Devlin's coarse assessment of her new status in life and his insulting evaluation of her best efforts to look sexy. This was not starting well at all.

"We'll have to do something about that. Have you eaten dinner?"

Anna was surprised at the question. She had, actually, eaten dinner, a bowl of soup. She had promptly thrown it up. She doubted that she could keep anything down now, although she was hungry.

"No, Mr. Devlin," she answered.

"Okay. We'll eat," the man announced, matter-of-factly. He pressed a button on his phone. A man's voice answered.

"Yes, Mr. Devlin?"

"Is dinner ready?"

"Yes, Mr. Devlin."

"Set a place for Miss Addunizio. She's to be our guest for the weekend."

"Yes, Mr. Devlin."

Devlin began to rise from his chair. Anna felt a surge of courage. "Mr. Devlin, you haven't said anything about the money. How do I know that you'll pay it?"

The sharply dressed man looked at her angrily. "Are you doubting my word?"

Anna courage took a steep dive. "N-no, Mr. Devlin. But the money needs to be deposited by Monday. I have to pay the Center's bills and make payroll."

Devlin sat back in his chair. "You'll get your whore's wages Monday morning, Ms. Addunizio. It will be all cash and deposited in your personal bank account. You will then write a check to the agency. This will ensure that there is proof positive that you took the money. Is that all right with you?" His question was clearly rhetorical, but Anna answered it anyway.

"Yes, Mr. Devlin," she replied.

"All right then," he said. "Come with me. Leave your pocketbook here. You won't be needing it."

Devlin led her from his study back to the foyer and then down the long hallway to the right of the stairs. They entered a small, elegantly appointed room with a dark blue rug and light green, pastel walls. In the middle was a small, mahogany table set with fine china for two. Tall, crystal glasses of water sat at each place setting with sparkling, silver utensils on each side of the elegant plates. Devlin indicated Anna's chair and she sat down. He sat down across from her.

Dinner was surreal after the coarse greeting the man had given her. His servant wheeled in covered dishes on a cart from the adjoining kitchen and served them both. Devlin peppered her with questions during the meal. How old was she? Where had she come from? Where did she go to college? His tone was, if not amiable, at least polite. Anna answered, at first, in short, direct replies, but when the conversation came to the Center and how she got it started, she became more expansive.

The meal started with a fresh, crisp, Waldorf salad and was followed by medallions of veal covered with a light, white wine sauce, small, roasted potatoes with rosemary sprinkled on them and crisp stalks of asparagus. Anna watched as Vincent, she had heard Devlin call his servant by name, poured out large servings of the pleasant, dry, white sauvignon. Devlin encouraged her to drink it down and insisted that she have a second glass. Anna welcomed the softness and warmth the wine brought to her body. It would make what she had to do later just that much easier to have her senses dulled. It also made Devlin seem just a little less foreboding, a little more attractive.

Vincent had cleared away the remnants of their meal and had served Anna a decaffeinated latte at her request. Devlin ordered and received a demitasse of espresso and a snifter of cognac. He leaned back in his chair after taking a long sip and perused Anna's body. The room was ominously silent.

"Okay, Anna," he said after a few moments. "Let me see your tits."

The order was shocking in its callousness, especially after the refined and civilized meal they had just consumed together. Devlin's insulting attitude back in his office had faded from Anna's mind. This brought her right back to reality.

"Here?" she asked incredulously.

"Of course, here," Devlin replied. "Are you stupid or something?"

"B-but, Vincent..."

"Let's get something straight, Anna," Devlin said harshly. "You're my whore. For one year. You do what I say, when I say it. If you're not willing to do that you can get out right now. I have your confession. It's all I need. You're not my lover. You're not my girlfriend. You're my whore and you better start acting like one. If I tell you to strip, you'll strip. If I tell you to suck my cock, you'll suck my cock. Do you understand?"

Anna's eyes had welled up with tears. This was not what she had hoped it would be. She had been deceived by Devlin's brief, polite treatment of her.

Anna's unhappiness was compounded when Vincent reentered the room. He had a small plate of mints and, setting it down on the table, he started to brush up the crumbs from the delicate, lacy tablecloth. When he was finished he stood by the side of the room awaiting his employer's desires.

"I'm waiting, Anna," Devlin insisted. "Don't worry about Vincent. He's seen tits before. And I'm guessing yours aren't anything special anyways."

Anna leaned back in her chair. There was about four feet separating her from Devlin across the small table. This was the moment of truth. Either she complied with his coarse demand or she didn't. There would be no negotiation. Any chance that she would be able to convince the authorities that she had nothing to do with the theft of the Center's funds was lost as a result of her delivery of the confession to Devlin. So it was either suffer the shame and humiliation of being her cruel benefactor's plaything or the scandal of being exposed as a thief.

Stifling a sob, Anna took up the soft, elegant, cloth napkin from the table and wiped her lips nervously. She placed it down and, after casting a troubled look at Vincent, seized the hem of her tight, knit sweater. She took a deep breath and began to pull it upwards. It rose over her breasts, up over her face and then over her head. When it was clear of her long, flowing, black hair, she dropped it to the floor next to her chair.

Anna had firm, ample breasts, not showgirl sized, but more than enough for a handful. She had worn a white bra that covered her nipples and areolas. There was a pattern of fine lace etched on the filled cups and a trace of lace along the tops. Her stomach tightened and soured as she reached behind her to loosen the hook that connected the straps. As she did, she noted unhappily that her breasts jutted out invitingly from her chest. Reluctantly, she let the shoulder straps of her delicate garment hang loose on her arms and then, crossing her hands in front of her, drew them down. Her soft, smooth mounds were revealed to the eyes of the men. She dropped the bra to the floor on top of her sweater and then leaned back in her chair, erect.

Devlin's eyes were drinking her up. He had his snifter of cognac in his hand and he swirled it a couple of times and took a sip. Anna was trying not to cry.

"They're better than I expected, Anna," Devlin said appreciatively. Anna's areolas were wide and smooth, darker than her Mediterranean skin. Her nipples were short and fat. They had stiffened from fear.

Devlin looked at Vincent. "Give her a snifter of cognac," he ordered. "I think she needs it."

The tall, silent servant took a large, round glass from the dark, mahogany china closet along the wall and placed it in front of Anna. The cognac, a forty year old Napoleon, was already on the table and he pulled the cork free, pouring Anna a good two inches of the amber colored liquor.

Anna was grateful for the proffer of the booze. She leaned forwards and took the glass in her sweaty right hand. As she moved, she felt her breasts sway and regretted it. She knew that their movement would draw Devlin's attention and when she looked up at him, her assumption was proven correct. Devlin's eyes were fixated on the round, exposed mammaries.

The unhappy woman took a long drink of the liquor. She wanted to blot out, if possible, her feelings of humiliation and self disgust. It would probably take the rest of the bottle to do the job right, but any little bit helped. It was so strange to be half naked in this cultured, well appointed room, Devlin's servant standing obsequiously on the side. It was like some kind of movie and she was an actor in it. Could she play the roll of a brazen whore? She had to.

Devlin was staring at her almost unnaturally. "Take another drink," he ordered. Anna compliantly absorbed a large mouthful. The liquor burned as it went down, but it sent a welcoming numbness to her brain.

"Finish it up," Devlin instructed her. Anna brought the elegant, curved glass to her lips and, leaning her head back, let the balance of the cognac pour into her mouth and then down her throat. She closed her eyes as it went down in an attempt to blot out the reality around her, but she could not erase the vision of her exposed breasts, rising as she tilted her head backwards, and then falling again as she lowered the glass and opened her eyes.

"You can go," Devlin instructed his servant. Vincent gave a nod and quietly left the small room. The door to the kitchen swung closed behind him.

When Vincent was gone, Devlin turned his attention back to his whore. "Come here and suck my prick," he said coldly.

His words hit Anna like a fist. This was not what she had expected at all! Suppressing a sob, she slowly rose from her chair. Here was the moment of truth, the moment that she had been dreading. But it was better to get it over with than to be dangling on a precipice all night wondering how and when her initiation as Devlin's slut would begin. She felt wobbly on her high heels as she crossed the short distance between her and her owner. "It's all for the Center," she told herself, tying to steel herself for the unpleasant task ahead. "I have to do this. There's no other choice."

Devlin had turned his chair and had his legs spread as she approached him. His eyes were focused on Anna's naked, swaying breasts. Without preliminaries, Anna knelt between his widespread thighs, his shiny, black, hand tooled shoes on either side of her. Resting herself on her heels, girding herself for her odious duty, she reached towards Devlin's lap, took hold of the fly to his well pressed, black slacks and lowered the zipper. Once it was open, she freed his tumescent cock from the slit in his boxers and eased it out.

Before addressing Devlin's long, fat meat, Anna gave a last, supplicative look up at the man in whose power she had put herself. She didn't really expect absolution from her obligations, but hope springs eternal. Seeing only the man's lust filled face and his hard, fierce determination, Anna lowered her head into the man's lap and took his hardening tool between her lips. She gave an unconscious, but audible, moan of self disgust and misery as the tube of flesh crossed her lips and entered her mouth.

Devlin emitted a sigh of satisfaction as Anna closed her soft, warm lips around his manhood. It rose quickly to its full length and hardness. Anna let the meat fill her, until the tip brushed against the entrance to her throat and then pulled her head back slowly, tightening her lips' grasp around the insulting pole, letting them flow over the smooth, flat glans and then suckling at the meaty head. She placed her right hand around the stiff shaft and paid homage to the fatty helmet, tracing her tongue across the tiny slit at its top. Her stomach roiled at the taste and smell of the man's arousal. She wanted to get this over quickly, but she didn't want him to be critical of her efforts. Until the money was actually paid into the bank account of the Center, the agency was still at risk. Once that was done, maybe she would change her mind about the whole thing. What would Devlin be able to do about it, sue her? She tried to think of herself as giving a $225,000 blow job. Maybe she was a whore, but she was, as Devlin had said, an expensive one.

Alternating between servicing the head of Devlin's fat prick and sliding her lips up and down its shaft, teasing it with her tongue, Anna felt a slight tingling in her loins. Devlin was a handsome, sexy man, not some slob in the back room of a bar. She knew that sometime tonight he would fuck her and she began to wonder what it would be like. It had been a long time. Could she assuage her shame at her forced prostitution by experiencing pleasure? Her body felt loose and warm from the cognac and she began to get into the rhythm of her task. She had sucked cocks before. By the time she left her oppressive, abusive home, she had been well taught. There wasn't much difference between the duty she was performing now and the duties that she had performed then. Maybe some. Now she was a full adult and had learned what true sexual pleasure was. It had taken years of therapy, but she had put her unpleasant experiences behind her. She had lived through that and she would live through this.

Devlin had placed his hand on her head and he was running his fingers through Anna's long, jet black, silky hair. She could feel his movements under her, his hips shifting slightly, his knees widening. He was moaning steadily, calling out softly for her to, "Keep sucking! Slower! Do that again!" She sensed that his climax was close and the thought that she had produced such passionate responses in the man gave her a strange sense of pride. Her free hand drifted over her thighs and she pressed her knees closed tightly together, squeezing her warming conch. She was chagrinned that sucking Devlin's cock was stoking her passions. Her naked breasts had hardened and she felt them sway and tremble as she worked at her master's rigid pole.

Anna didn't think twice as the fat cock in her mouth began to jerk and pulse, spilling Devlin's creamy seed within her. She swallowed it dutifully, ignoring its piquant taste, the feel of the hot meat slithering over her tongue and across the tender nerve endings of the roof of her mouth. She increased her tempo at his loins. Devlin moaned loudly and grunted each time his cock sent another spurt of his essence into her. His hand had tightened in her hair and his firm grip pulled at their roots, causing the young woman to moan in pain. She did not stop, though. She matched each jet of Devlin's sperm with a hard, rapid descent of her mouth on his prick until, finally, the counterthrusts of the man's hips began to wane and his hold on her hair began to loosen. When she sensed that the aftershocks of his orgasm had subsided, she quickly pulled her lips free. She had done it. It wasn't so bad now that it was over.

"What are you doing?" Devlin asked angrily.

Anna looked up at his face with surprise. The taste of his spume was still reverberating in her throat.

"I didn't tell you to take your mouth off of my cock! Put it back on until I tell you!"

Anna felt a surge of sorrow pass through her. She had just given the man the best blow job she knew how and he was no more appreciative than if she had been the lowliest whore in the lowliest brothel. Her lips curled in a frown and she started to cry. Devlin took hold of her hair and leaned over so that his face was inches from hers. "Do what I tell you, cunt!"

Dismal at her treatment, Anna leaned forward and subsumed the man's softening tool between her lips. The flaccid instrument lay lifeless on her tongue. Her hands rested lightly on Devlin's thighs and her chest heaved with suppressed sobs. "Put your hands behind your back," the man ordered her. "Don't ever touch me unless I tell you to."

Unhappily, Anna brought her hands behind her. She was arched over, and the only point of contact between her and her cruel benefactor was her mouth on his cock.

The couple remained as they were while Devlin finished his cognac. The cock began to resume its form and Anna dutifully gave it encouragement with her tongue, trying hard to suppress her revulsion. Her back began to ache and she spread her legs slightly to give herself some ease. Tears had escaped from her eyes and she felt them rolling down her cheeks. She would have to endure three days of the man's abuse before the money was safely in the Center's account. How would she ever make it, never mind a year? But she had survived worse. Maybe the man would tire of her like he said. She was not the Venus de Milo, as he had reminded her. She was pretty enough, a long, narrow nose, smooth, graceful lips and dark brown, soft eyes. Her face was roundish, but not circular. She had a long neck, well formed, taut thighs and a flat belly. But the model types she had seen him with were the true beauties, long, languorous legs, high cheek bones. Sex just dripped off of them. He would lose interest in her quickly, she knew that. Until then, she would do what he said, take whatever pleasure she could, and then, somehow, sometime, after she had gotten her confession back, exact her revenge.

Devlin's cock had resumed its hardness and Anna had recommenced her adoration of it with her lips and tongue when Devlin spoke to her again.

"You know, Anna, I knew you'd be back. You're a natural whore. But you have a lot to learn about sucking cocks. I just didn't get the feeling that you meant it. It was like getting a blow job from my Aunt Nellie. You're going to have to get a lot better."

Anna gave out a sob as she took in the man's insults. Did he mean it or was he just trying to hurt her? If he was, it was working. Anna felt demeaned and worthless. If she couldn't give a satisfactory blow job, how would she keep the dissolute man satisfied? Would he kick her out on Sunday evening and tell her the deal was off?

Anna heard the door to the kitchen opening and closing and the heavy tread of Vincent's footsteps come into the room. She was mortified that he would see her slavishly serving his employer's cock, half naked, her hands crossed behind her like some kind of captive. But that's what she was, wasn't she. She was the horrid man's captive for the next year. What difference did it make if the butler knew it? The way Devlin had been treating her, it would be readily apparent anyway. Yet the idea that the man could see her face buried in Devlin's lap, was watching as she slowly rose her head up and down over his cock, shamed her.

Devlin spoke out. "Vincent, I want you to take Anna to her room. I've got some more calls to make and I'll be up later. I want her stripped and kneeling on the bed when I get up there."

"Yes, Mr. Devlin" the tall man replied.

"Okay, slut," Devlin said, addressing Anna. "Get up and go with Vincent. Do what he tells you."

Sorrowfully, but happy to be freed from her demeaning posture, Anna let Devlin's hard cock slip from her lips and stood. She looked at Vincent's face for a sign of his contempt for her, but, to her surprise, detected none. He was the perfect servant, expressionless, polite, sure of himself. Her jaw was sore from her extended efforts on Devin's cock and she stretched it and licked her lips before bending down to retrieve her blouse and bra.

"You really are a stupid cunt, Anna," Devlin declaimed sharply. "Did I tell you to pick up your clothes?"

Anna looked back at him dolefully. "N-no," she murmured.

"Then why did you do it?"

"I, I thought that…."

"Don't think, Anna! Just do what I tell you! And put your hands back behind you! I didn't say to release them, did I?"

Anna was trembling with unhappiness and fear. It was clear that her whole being was committed to the despicable man's control. She dropped her clothes back to the floor and eased her hands back behind her.

"Okay, now get out of here," Devlin commanded.

CHAPTER TWO

Like a dispirited prisoner, Anna followed the tall, quiet servant into the hallway and then to the broad, curving stairs that led to the upper floors of the mansion. The tippy tap of her bright red high heels as she crossed the stone floor of the entrance hall were silenced as she began to ascend the carpet covered steps.

She was ashamed at how docilely she was following Devlin's callous commands. She thought of running back down and fleeing out the front door to her car, but suppressed the impulse. Would they stop her, or let her escape? Her coat was in the closet, so she didn't need her blouse. Then she remembered that her keys were in her pocketbook in Devlin's office. God knows what he did with it. No, she wouldn't run. In for a penny, in for a pound. She had already demeaned herself, shattered her illusions about her integrity and self worth. What was she to do except ride this thing out?

Anna hoped desperately that there was no one else in the house. This big a place couldn't be run by only one servant. There had to be maids, kitchen help, maybe a head housekeeper. She couldn't stand the idea that one of them might emerge from somewhere and see her swaying, jumping, naked breasts as she climbed the stairs, her obsequious demeanor, the servile way she was following Devlin's servant.

No one disturbed them, however, as they rose steadily to the second floor. Anna had assumed that her bedroom would be on this floor, but she was wrong. Vincent proceeded to mount a second flight, narrower and covered with rubber treads. It wasn't on the third floor either and Anna followed the servant unhappily, her wrists criss-crossed behind her back obediently, as they ascended to the fourth and top floor of the mansion.

While the second and third floors were decorated with the same thick, bright red carpet as the stairs, the hallway on the fourth floor was uncovered and Anna's heels made clicking sounds that echoed in the empty passageway as she walked along the bare wood. The hallway was dimly lit by several naked, low watt light bulbs down the length of the ceiling, and the undecorated walls, colored a light green, were faded as if it had been some years since they had been painted. Anna had imagined herself as being treated like an honored guest, but here she was being led to what she conceived as being the servant's quarters.

Vincent stopped at the third room down on the left. He took a chain that led from his right pants pocket to a loop in the waist of his pants and eased it out, revealing a small set of keys. The doors on this floor were heavier and thicker than the doors to the rooms that they had passed on the other floors and, as she watched Vincent unlock it, a feeling of trepidation passed through her. Vincent entered the room first, flicking on the lights from a switch in the hall.

The room was about fifteen by twenty and had a large, queen sized bed in its middle. It was covered by a soft, gold comforter and had large, fluffy pillows at its head. The walls were painted a dark red and had a carpet that matched. There was a large dresser against one wall and night tables on either side of the bed with tall, shaded lamps on top of them. A wide mirror hung on the wall opposite the bed with ornate, gold plated, rococo framing around it.

Compared to the bare, stripped down décor of the hallway, the room seemed elegant. It was out of place on the remote fourth floor of the mansion. Anna wondered what purpose it served. Had Devlin had it made up especially for her? Why was her room so far distant from the rest of the house? Why was there a heavy, solid, wooden door?

Vincent closed the door behind them and locked it. He spoke to her for the first time, his voice monotoned and businesslike.

"Take off your clothes."

Anna looked at the man with horror. She had heard Devlin's command that she be naked as she waited for him, but she hadn't considered that she would have to denude herself in front of his servant. Wasn't she to be left with any self respect? Would she be expected to fuck him as well? That was going a little too far. But the door was locked and they were on the fourth floor of the mansion. Vincent was much bigger than her 5 foot 5 inch frame. And there was the money. She had already invested one blow job in it. What would Devlin do if she refused?

A wave of fear swept through the young woman. No one knew she was here. If she had been smarter, she would have left a note somewhere. She hadn't thought that she might be kept a prisoner. As it was, Devlin could just make her disappear. He could keep her captive here for as long as he wanted. When he got tired of her he could kill her and dump her body in some swamp or something. Her confession would be explanation enough for the police as far as her disappearance was concerned. For the first time, real, piercing fear joined her feelings of intense humiliation and shame.

Seeing Anna's hesitation, Vincent repeated his instruction. Tearfully, Anna began to comply. She lowered the zipper at the side of her skirt and then slid the garment over her hips. She placed the expensive garment neatly on the bed.

She had worn a pair of dark, sheer, self supporting stockings and the lacy tops encircled the upper reaches of her brown thighs. Anna was half Italian, on her father's side, and she had inherited his olive colored, brownish Mediterranean skin. She had also inherited his hairiness and she was more than chagrined at having to expose her bushy, black pubic covering to the servant. She had shaved her legs and underarms before coming here, but she had never shaved her pubes, limiting herself to once in a while trimming its wilder excesses.

The abundant growth of hair created a small mound under her plain white, bikini panties and peaked out on the sides. Revealing her sex to this strange man seemingly made of iron was one of the last things on earth that she wanted to do. But she knew that she had to do it. What choice did she have? She hooked her thumbs in the waist line of her panties and eased them over her hips and down over her knees and feet.

In her nervousness, Anna had forgotten to remove her bright red high heels. They were bound to her feet by little straps that crossed her instep and she crouched down now to loosen them. As she did, she felt the cold, hard eyes of the servant on her naked skin. She shivered as she thought of what he might do to her. When she had freed her feet she was able to pull her panties off over them and she laid them on the bed atop her skirt. A moment later, she had removed her sheer, silk, black stockings and they joined her other clothes on the bed.

The tall, expressionless man pointed to a doorway on the other side of the room. "That's the bathroom," he intoned. "Use it."

Anna shuffled off obediently. It was tiled in baby blue, had a glass enclosed shower and a large, dark blue vanity and sink made of marble. Anna went to close the door but, to her surprise, saw that there wasn't one. She blushed as she realized that she would have to pee while the man was in the next room and could hear her. Her embarrassment became acute when he came and stood in the doorway.

"I can't pee while you're watching," she dragged up the courage to protest. Vincent looked back at her expressionlessly. She waited for him to leave the doorway, but he just stood there silently. She realized that it was a lost cause. He would just stand there until she went. His eyes peered at her remorselessly. Her nakedness made her feel vulnerable, quelling her urge to refuse the tall, dark servant's command. She gave in.

The unhappy, young woman released a long, hard stream of fluid into the bowl while Vincent watched. It had taken a few moments before she was able to force the flow from her body, but she closed her eyes and tried to pretend that he wasn't there. The noise of the water striking water resounded through the small room. When it ceased, Anna gratefully wiped herself and cast the tissue into the bowl. The toilet made a loud, angry sound when she flushed it.

Standing at the vanity, washing her hands, Anna saw her face in the mirror over the sink. Her eyes were puffy and reddened and her mascara had run. She looked a mess. Her nakedness was reflected back at her, somehow making it seem all the more real and distressing. Using a wet tissue, she carefully dabbed away the black lines and smudges that descended from her eyes. She really didn't care how she looked, but Devlin might and she didn't want to hear any more of his caustic, demeaning abuse if she didn't have to.

Vincent retreated from the doorway and Anna exited the bathroom. The servant leaned over the bed and drew the comforter down its length until the smooth, pastel green sheets beneath it were fully revealed. After pulling the top sheet down to the foot, folding it on itself carefully so that it lay there neatly, he pointed to the bed. "Get on it," he ordered.

Ashamed at her meek submission, Anna complied nonetheless. Vincent instructed her to kneel with her thighs spread wide apart and to return her hands behind her back. When she was posed to his satisfaction on the firm, comfortable mattress, he spoke to her.

"I am Mr. Devlin's servant. It is my responsibility that all of Mr. Devlin's orders are carried out to the letter. I do not like to have to give instructions twice. This time, I will let it go."

The tall man paused so that his revelations could sink in. Anna wondered what would happen if she was slow to obey him again. She felt helpless and vulnerable as she knelt naked and exposed before the powerful man, her hands submissively hidden behind her. "How did I get into this mess?" she thought unhappily.

"You will stay in that position on the bed until Mr. Devlin comes to use you. I will not say what will happen if you disobey. You will find that out on your own. Do you understand?"

Anna almost swooned with fear. She didn't want to speak, but was afraid that remaining silent would enrage the unnaturally calm and collected man. "Y-yes," she finally muttered.

"When you answer me, you will say, 'sir'. Do you understand that?"

"Y-yes, Sir," Anna eked out.

The cold demeanored man gathered up Anna's clothes from the foot of the bed. Anna wanted to protest, but she feared whatever retribution he had promised her for disobedience. Dismally, she watched him take them with him as he left the room. Her heart sank as she heard the lock turned shut.

Anna listened to the sounds of the man's retreating steps as he returned downstairs. The heavy door muffled the sound, but it was still audible. Once it had faded away, the room was stone cold silent and Anna shivered with fear. She was grateful that the man had left the light on. It would have been hell to have to wait here in the dark for the arrival of her abuser.

She was in a mental state that she knew well. Many a night as a young girl she had lain in her bed listening in dread for the sound of her father's footsteps on the stairs. Her mother was usually passed out from gin. She could hear the television on downstairs and her father rummaging around the kitchen or living room looking for something to drink. As long as the TV was on, she knew she was safe. It was when it was turned off and she heard the heavy booted footsteps begin to ascend to the second floor that her heart would begin to beat wildly.

As then, the sound of Devlin's steps on the stairs and in the hallway would be the harbinger of the arrival of her tormentor. She knew that somehow she had to get out of there. The room had a small window and Anna looked at it anxiously, wondering whether she could open it and climb down and escape. She fought the urge to get up from the bed to go and look. She had an idea what would happen to her if she were caught: she would be beaten. Maybe they would tie her up so she couldn't move. The very thought of being bound and unable to use her hands or legs was terrorizing to her. She knew from her past life what it was like, having been tied to her bed on nights when she struggled too much. She hated the familiar feeling of powerlessness that was overwhelming her.

Anna was just about to crawl off of the bed so she could inspect the window when she saw the small camera mounted on the wall above the mirror. It was one of those web cams, small and unobtrusive. There was a little red light under it which, she assumed, meant that it was on. Someone was watching her. The very thought of it made her skin crawl. Even if they were not watching now, the camera was probably making a video of her, a video that could be easily checked to see if she had been disobedient. She looked at it forlornly. She realized that when Devlin came to fuck her, he would get it all on tape. The idea that their impending fornication would be rendered into a permanent record, available for the enjoyment of anyone who could get a copy, sickened her.

She closed her eyes and took a deep breath. She mustn't cry, she mustn't. Her face would get all messy again. Besides that, and more importantly, she needed all of her psychic strength to get through the night. Devlin was going to come here and, what did Vincent say? Use her. That was it. Not fuck her, not see her, not sleep with her, use her. She realized that she was just a thing to be used by the hard millionaire. She was going to be his toy; that was what he had said. She hadn't realized the full import of what he had meant at the time. She did now.

Anna opened her eyes, trying to calm herself and take stock of her predicament. She caught sight of herself in the mirror opposite the bed. She was a vision of loveliness. Her long, black, wavy hair descended down past her shoulder blades. Her full breasts were presented proudly. She could see her camouflaged sex between her outspread legs. Her belly was firm and tapered down enticingly to the fulcrum of her thighs.

During the next hour or so, Anna's eyes returned again and again to her disconsolate figure in the mirror. She was tired and lonely and afraid. She tried to not look at her reflection, but, unless she closed her eyes, which made everything worse, the silence, the helplessness, she was forced to take in her abject form, displayed brazenly for the camera above it.

Anna jumped when she first heard the sound of heavy, determined steps on the stairs and then in the hallway outside her room. She heard the key enter the lock in the door. It swing open and she saw immediately that it was Devlin. He was still dressed in his finely tailored shirt and tie, his black, sharply creased pants and his imported shoes. He had a drink in his hand, cognac. Anna wished forlornly that he had brought some for her.

"So, how are we doing, Anna?" Devlin asked as he let the door swing shut behind him. He turned and locked it, placing the key in his right front pants pocket. "Are you comfy?"

Anna was unsure whether he expected a response. Comfy? He had to be kidding. She had been kneeling for a long, long time in abject fear and her muscles in her back and legs ached. She was tired and thirsty. She fought of the urge to cry.

Annoyance sprung up in Devlin's handsome face. "I asked you a question, whore," he said angrily. "I expect an answer."

"Y-yes, Mr. Devlin," Anna replied, her voice soft and shaky.

"You are a stupid cunt, Anna," he said coldly. "You don't know when to talk and when to shut up, do you?"

"N-no, Mr. Devlin," Anna answered, sure this time that he expected a response.

"Well, you're going to learn, aren't you?"

"Yes, Mr. Devlin."

"Before I fuck you, Anna, I want to get a good look at you. Get up from the bed and come over here."

The frightened, humiliated woman suppressed her natural urge to respond to her treatment with a string of outraged expletives. There was no telling how he would react to that and she was clearly his prisoner and at his mercy. She remembered how angry the man had gotten when she had removed her hands from her back without permission earlier. She kept them there now, inching her way over to the edge of the bed. Clumsily, she threw first one leg and then the other over the side and stood. Her breasts swung back and forth at her erratic movements. It only took a couple of steps before she was a few inches away from the callous man.

She cringed when she felt his hands take possession of her breasts. His fingers felt like poisonous leaches as they pressed into the soft, resilient flesh. Her limpid, brown eyes were captivated by his starry, blue ones. There was some kind of power emanating from the man that she felt impossible to resist or challenge. His thumbs began to toy with her nipples and she felt a tingling in them that she desperately wanted to suppress. His hands then lowered to her hips, assessing their roundness. They were hot and Anna desperately wanted them to leave her.

"Turn around," he ordered.

Anna turned slowly so that her back was to him. She felt his hands wander over her firm rear globes.

"You've got a nice ass, Anna," he said as he rubbed it. "It was the first thing that I noticed about you. And then that haughty, 'Don't you dare even think of coming on to me,' look you gave me. I knew that I had to have you right there and then. When was the last time that you got laid, Anna?"

Anna was mortified at the question. It was no business of his. But she knew that she had to give some kind of answer. "I-I don't remember," she managed to murmur.

She felt one of Devlin's hands leave her rear globes and then felt it come back down harshly. The sound of the slap echoed off of the walls of the small room. It stung intently. "Owwwwww!" she called out.

"That's 'I don't know, Mr. Devlin.'"

"Y-yes, Mr. Devlin," Anna responded. She felt like she was going to break down any moment. Her rear burned where the man had struck it.

"Owwwwwww!" she cried out again as Devlin gave her ass another fierce slap.

"That wasn't a question, Anna. That was an instruction. Do you know the difference between a question and an instruction?"

"Y-yes, Mr. Devlin," Anna answered, desperate to avoid another insulting, painful blow.

"Okay then," the cold, harsh man said. Suddenly, there was another cruel slap to her behind. Anna shouted out in pain and her tears began to flow. What had she done now? Devlin answered her unspoken question.

"That was for lying, Anna. Everybody remembers the last time they were laid. I got laid this morning, and once after lunch too. So let me repeat the question. When was the last time that you got laid, Anna?"

Anna forced out the answer. "About a year ago, Mr. Devlin."

"A whole year without a cock. That's a long time, Anna. Do you frig yourself often?"

Anna didn't want to answer, but she knew that she had to. "Not often, Mr. Devlin."

"When was the last time, Anna?"

"About two weeks ago, Mr. Devlin."

"Did you use a vibrator?"

"N-no, Mr. Devlin."

"Just your hand?"

"Y-yes, Mr. Devlin."

"You'll have to show me how you do it, Anna. Would you do that for me some time?"

The thought of saying no never crossed the unhappy young woman's mind although she could think of nothing less she would like to do. "Yes, Mr. Devlin," she croaked out.

Devlin reached around Anna's chest and seized her breasts, pressing his strong, muscled chest against her back. Her hands were crossed at a level just below his belt and she could feel his heavy manhood through his pants. She moaned with frustration and fear as the man's cruel hands manipulated her firm, round flesh. She wanted to turn around and push him away, flee from this well appointed room that had become her prison, but she knew she wouldn't, couldn't. She was too afraid of what would happen.

"I'm going to fuck you now, Anna," Devlin announced. She could feel that his cock had grown hard and firm behind her. "Be a good girl and get on the bed while I get undressed."

A wave of unhappiness flowed through Anna's body as she realized that she had no way to stop the ruthless man. The thought of his cock in her pussy made her want to wretch, but the sooner it started, the sooner it would be over. She leapt at her warder's command and crawled back onto the large mattress, reassuming the position she had been in when he had come first into the room.

She watched unhappily as Devlin undressed. He took off his shirt and tie first, revealing a tight, well sculpted, hairless chest. She heard his shoes hit the floor as he kicked them off and watched as he loosened his belt and pulled off his pants. When he was naked, he got on the bed and told Anna to, lie down.

Quivering with fear and unhappiness, Anna stretched her naked body down alongside the fit, handsome man. At his instructions, she removed her hands from behind her back and put them over her head. Devlin ran his hand down the soft skin of her torso and over her thighs. He leaned over and took one of her nipples in his mouth and began to suck on it gently, bringing an unwelcome sensation to her loins.

As the lips pulled at her teat, his tongue teasing it, his hand slid across her belly. His warmth commingled with hers, triggering a shudder in her body. She wanted to relax, knew desperately that she had to relax. Everything depended on satisfying this demanding, jaundiced man. She closed her eyes and tried to imagine him as someone else, or that she was here voluntarily, that she was attracted to him, that they were lovers, anything. She felt the hand drift lower and his fingers mingle with the curly thatch that covered her mons. Knowing what he wanted, she spread her legs to give him access.

"You're wet, Anna," he said as he slipped his fingers the length of her crevasse. She was wet. She didn't now how it had happened, but she was grateful. She gave a little moan as she felt the man's fingers slide between her soft, engorging labia and enter her.

As he stroked and caressed her moistening slit, Devlin resumed his oral caresses to her breasts. He bit and teased them, licked her nipples and then pulled them into his mouth to give them long, hard suckles. His body was hot next to hers and Anna began to feel the beginnings of passion.

Devlin took his time in preparing the young woman for her ravishment. He ran his hands up and down her inner thighs as if assessing his new possession. She raised her knees and spread them widely as his touch enflamed her. His mouth left her breasts and she felt his tongue washing along her upper chest to her neck and then up over her chin. He circled his free hand over her head and turned it so that she was facing him. When his lips touched hers, Anna gave a deep, impassioned sigh and opened them, welcoming the hot, agile tongue that entered her mouth.

Her body was ablaze with need when Devlin's hand lowered her knee next to him and then crossed over her leg with his body. She felt his hardened cock brush across her hip. The head of his cock explored the entrance of her womb, sliding up and down the length of her slit and making her moan and raise her hips to encourage him. She felt its bulbous head part her excited love lips and then slip within her.

"Ohhhhhhhhh!" Anna moaned as the thick meat began to traverse her needy canal. If she had to be fucked against her will, this was the way to go, she thought, as Devlin's cock plowed back and forth along her pussy's electrified walls. He was an expert cocksman and he rubbed the top of his prick along the apex to her pussy, agitating her hard, enflamed clit. He alternated his strokes, long, slow, languorous ones that made her squirm with desire and short hard ones that made her heart pound and her body yearn for more. She pressed her thighs tightly against his hips and her tongue danced with his in her mouth. "Oh! Oh! Oh!" she murmured through her filled mouth at each of the man's hard, demanding thrusts. Her hands were still above her and she desperately wanted to clasp her owner's hard body tighter to hers, to feel his chest crushing her breasts, but she dared not move them without his command. Higher and higher into lust he drove her. Her breath became short and she felt the tell tale signs of her impending crisis.

Suddenly, with a groan of disdain, Devlin withdrew his cock from Anna's yearning slit. He raised himself on his elbows, separating their torsos. "Don't you know how to fuck?" he asked her rudely.

Anna was too astounded to speak. Her head was dizzy with her arousal. What was he talking about?

Devlin rose from Anna' body and dragged her off of the bed, throwing her on the floor. She landed with a loud, 'clunk", giving out an astonished protest. Her heart was pounding with fear and shame.

"Are you a complete fuck up?" Devlin yelled as he posed himself ominously above her.

"N-no, Mr. Devlin! No!' Anna replied frantically as she cowered fearfully on the floor beneath the callous and angry gaze of her master. What had she done wrong, she asked her self again.

"You fuck like a fish!" Devlin shot out at her. "I thought you might be dead!"

Anna wanted to plead with the enraged man but knew that would only make him madder. His words struck her like blows from his fists and she began to cry. She was stunned at how quickly the tone of the room had changed from impassioned fucking to violence and degradation.

Devlin ordered Anna to rise and stand next to the bed. "Put your hands and forehead on the mattress," he instructed her churlishly.

Anna, too distraught to do anything else, obeyed him instantly. She bent over, her breasts dangling below her chest, her ass upraised in presentation position. She heard the sound of leather running along cloth and she knew that he was removing his belt from his pants. She gritted her teeth and closed her eyes, realizing, to her horror, that she was going to be beaten. It hadn't happened to her for well over ten years, but she remembered what it felt like and she remembered the shame and worthlessness she felt when it was over.

Devlin stood behind the bent over, defenseless woman. Without saying a word, he slammed the wide leather of his belt across her tender, exposed rear globes. Anna whined with unhappiness and pain. The fiery sensations coursed through her. She wanted to get up and run away, but she knew there was nowhere to go. When the second blow landed, she whined even louder, determined not to cry out or beg for surcease. It was the third blow that did it, seemingly harder than the first two, as if the man had been intent on forcing her to give in to the humiliation and pain. "Ohhhhhhhhhh!" she yelled out. "Please stop! Please!"

Her supplication for mercy did not avail her. A fourth and a fifth lick of the fiercely wielded belt crossed the tender skin of her rear and she began to sob. Her rear burned where it had been struck. "Ohhhhhhhhhh! Please stop! Please!" she called out.

Devlin stopped after the fifth blow. "You're a piece of shit, Anna. You don't know how to suck cock and you don't know how to fuck. What do you know?" he barked at her angrily.

From behind her sobs and tears Anna managed to reply, "I don't know, Mr. Devlin. Please don't hurt me any more! Please!"

"Get up on the bed, cunt!" Devlin ordered. "On all fours like a little doggie!"

Anna scrambled into position. Her breasts swaying beneath her torso, and she locked her arms and held her back straight, spreading her legs.

"No, the other way," Devlin said harshly. "Facing the mirror."

Anna turned herself around as instructed and Devlin took a position behind her on the bed. She felt his hot hands take hold of her burning rear globes. Without ceremony, he thrust his hardened cock into her gaping slit. Anna gave out as sob as she felt the offensive instrument fill her, sliding easily along the walls of her purse.

"I see you're still nice and wet, Anna," he mocked her. "You must like being beaten."

Anna swallowed her objection and what was left of her self esteem as the man began to slap his thighs against the back of hers, riding her hard. Her heavy breasts swung back and forth at each impact of the man's member. His thick pole scoured the interior of her hot cleft, reigniting her lusts. Anna cursed herself for enjoying the man's brutal assault. She felt his hand in her hair and her face was rudely lifted up.

"Look in the mirror, Anna. This is how we'll fuck until you get better at it. You're just a hole to be used. Look at your tits jumping around. You look like a cow."

Anna moaned with shame as she was forced to watch her own cruel ravishment in the mirror. What was worse was knowing that it was all going to be on tape, for Devlin's enjoyment and whoever he let see it.

Despite her dismal unhappiness at her cruel treatment, Anna felt her juices begin to rise once more. Something about the man's treatment of her struck at her core, releasing long pent up feelings. Yes, she was a whore. Yes, she deserved to be treated like a fuck toy. The harder the man fucked her, the more excited she became. "Oh! Oh! Oh!" she called out. She could see in the mirror the passion in her face, her breasts swinging wildly, the man's hand entangled in her hair, the swaying back and forth of her little, golden earrings. She could also see the grimacing, determined face of her owner as he sought his pleasure within her. "Oh, god! Oh, god! Oh, god!" she exclaimed as her pussy began to convulse and contract. "Oh, I'm coming! I'm coming!" she yelled out as the hard pulses brought ecstasy to her flesh.

Devlin just kept going on and on, ignoring her ejaculations of pleasure. She felt her need rising again and began to cry, wanting desperately for the pleasure to stop. She despised herself for her wantonness. She didn't want to come, didn't want to respond to the relentless, hot, thick prick that was traversing her inner passage. She came again and her whole body seemed to explode in pleasure. She tried to form words to express the overwhelming sensations, but could only moan deep and loud.

As her pussy's convulsions continued relentlessly, she saw, in the mirror, the face of her abuser strain and his eyes roll back. His pounding at her rear became more intense and he gave out a mighty groan. When she felt his cock jerk and spasm in her tunnel, the spread of his warm discharge within her, she came again. As her pussy throbbed and pulsed, she noticed her face in the mirror. She did not recognize the strange, frantic face of the woman staring back at her.

Shame flooded the unhappy young woman as her pussy's convulsions slowed and Devlin eased his piece from her plush, messy hole. Devlin did nothing to ease her dismay.

"You're going to have to get a whole lot better at fucking if you expect to make it through the whole year, Anna," he said as he removed himself from the bed. He retrieved the glass of cognac he had placed on the top of the dresser near the bed. He took a long pull at it. Anna could see her juices reflected on his soft, but still tumescent cock. She remained kneeling on all fours on the bed, afraid to move, while the man dressed.

When Devlin had finished, he stood in front of the unhappy young woman and took her cheeks in his hand, lifting her face so that she was looking directly into his. "Having fun yet, Anna?" he asked her.

Anna didn't know how to answer. Would she be punished for lying? She hated the cruel man's abuse of her, his caustic critique of her sexual skills, the way that he had rudely used her. On the other hand, she hadn't had an orgasm like that for years, maybe never. Was something wrong with her? All in all, though, it had been a miserable experience and she decided to answer the question truthfully.

"N-no, Mr. Devlin," she murmured.

Devlin laughed. "That's too bad, Anna. But it did seem a moment ago that you were having fun. You sounded like a choo-choo." He laughed at his joke. "Maybe you want to call the whole thing off. It's not too late. You could go downstairs, get your clothes and go home. I promise not to call the sheriff until the morning. That way you can get a good night's sleep before you're hauled off to jail. Or maybe you can make the state line before morning, disappear. I'll let you have a couple of hundred bucks for gas. Is that what you want?"

Anna cringed at the thought of jail. "N-no, Mr. Devlin," she whined. "I'll get better, I promise. Don't call the sheriff, please,"

Devlin released the unhappy woman's face and, reaching under her, took hold of one of her dangling breasts. He squeezed it playfully. "You know, Anna, once the money is put into your account on Monday, there's no going back. People don't welsh on me. If you think jail is bad, I know some people who could make your life very unpleasant and for a much longer time. So if you have second thoughts, you better make up your mind before Monday morning."

Anna's lips formed into a frown and she suppressed a sob. The man's hand on her breast was a stark reminder of what her existence would be like for the next twelve months. But the Center was her whole life. Her mind was a jumble of confused emotions. She looked up at her tormentor. He had a self-satisfied grin on his face. Why not? He had already gotten his revenge for her disdainful treatment of him. But she was strong. She could take whatever he dished out to her. She wouldn't be in his power all the time. She had her apartment and her work. She would make them her islands of retreat and when she was here, under his thumb, she would think of those places and the fact that she would soon return to them.

Devlin's hand left her breast. She had not answered his taunt, but it hadn't called for an answer. He poured the remainder of his snifter of cognac back into his throat and then ordered her to lie down on the bed. He pulled the covers over her.

"Goodnight, Anna. I'll see you in the morning."

He walked to the door and, after taking the key from his pants pocket, unlocked the door and left. A moment after, the big door slammed shut and the lock clicked closed. The lights in the room went out. She listened carefully as his footsteps retreated down the hall and then descended the stairs.

It took a long time for Anna to fall asleep. Her body was exhausted and felt like a wrung out dishrag, but her mind was going a hundred miles an hour. The lamps on either side of her bed were apparently connected to the switch in the hall and at first, when they were extinguished, the room had descended into darkness. A faint glow came in through the small window from the lights outside and, when Anna's eyes adjusted, she could just make out the dark shapes of the furniture in the room around her.

She could feel Devlin's discharge leaking from her still burning quim and she wanted desperately to go into the bathroom and clean herself. She looked up at the camera, barely visible in the slight light, its little, red indicator glowing brightly. Was she allowed out of bed? What if she had to pee during the night? Or in the morning? Was she supposed to just lie here and await permission?

A wave of misery flowed through the young woman as she thought of how just a little more than a week ago everything had seemed like it was going just right. Now she was immersed in a world of unhappiness and strife. Why had Carol done it? They were best friends. She could have gotten her help. If she needed a respite and a few weeks in rehab to get her head on straight, that could have been worked out easily. Anna cursed herself for believing that her life was secure and safe. She curled her body up into a ball and began to cry. Was saving the Center worth this misery? Maybe she should follow Carol's path and immerse herself in a self destructive life of alcohol and drugs. It would lead to unhappiness and death. She knew that. But wouldn't death be better than living through what confronted her now?

She thought of Devlin's coarse, callous use of her, his repeated insults, his demeaning attitude. It seemed almost as if he had the key to her subconscious, knew just how to treat her to make her unhappy and submissive. There were few coincidences in life, and she realized that his name, Devlin, was appropriate for his character. He was a devil, cruel, callous and carnal. She wondered about the rumors of his underworld contacts and how much of it was true. Everything that had happened since she came into his office a week ago screamed that it was. And his threat tonight about a fate worse than jail, would he make a threat like that unless he had the ability to carry it out?

Anna had lain in the bed fitfully trying to let sleep overtake her for about half an hour before she heard footsteps coming back up the stairs. Devlin's footsteps had been quick and determined. These were more like Vincent's, slow and calculated. She cringed at the thought that he was coming to deliver her back to her tormentor or, even worse, that he had decided to take a piece of her for himself. But the steps passed by her door and she heard the sound of another door down the hall being opened and closed.

A few minutes later, the door opened and closed again and Vincent's footsteps returned. This time they were accompanied by what sounded to Anna like high heeled shoes striking the hardwood floor of the hallway. Did Devlin have another woman in residence? Was he holding someone else in bondage? Or was it a servant, a maid or a cook, or Vincent's wife or girlfriend? The fact that there was another female in the house was both comforting and disconcerting. It would be horribly shameful to have to display her abject status before another woman.

On the other hand, the fact that another woman was in apparent residence on the remote fourth floor of the residence meant that maybe Devlin would not keep her prisoner here, that her presence might be known by someone, making it more difficult for Devlin simply to order her disappearance. She suppressed an urge to get out of bed and hammer at the door, calling for help.

Anna listened to the sound of the footsteps fade away. In the returned silence, she resumed her unhappy ruminations regarding her plight. After many long minutes of fretting and ruing her fate, she finally passed off into a fitful sleep.

* * * * * * * * * * * * *

When Anna awoke, the light had just begun to break into the room through the small window. She looked around uncertainly, at first unsure of where she was. It only took a moment for her to remember. A wave of despondency flowed thorough her. It was Saturday and she would spend the entire day in Devlin's power. What would it be like? He couldn't spend the whole day fucking her, could he? When he wasn't, would she spend her time locked up in this room with nothing to do but look at her naked body in the mirror?

She had to pee desperately. She looked up at the camera. Maybe she could sneak off and no one would notice. It looked outside like it was about 6 a.m. The man couldn't have a twenty four hour sentry watching over her, could he? Anna decided that the risk of discovery was better than suffering indefinitely the pressure on her bladder and maybe ending up pissing her bed. Looking carefully at the camera, as if she could detect whether someone was watching, she slid the covers off of her body and dashed into the bathroom. She didn't know if the camera had an audio component so she dropped a heavy wad of toilet paper into the bowl to cover up the sound of her fluids emptying into it. It seemed to take forever and she pressed down hard to speed up the flow. After the last few drops trickled out, she wiped herself, washed her hands quickly, and rushed back to the bedroom to slide under the covers.

About a half hour later, she heard footsteps climbing the stairs and then the lock turning in her door. It was

Vincent. He was dressed as he had been the night before and he was carrying a long, thin whip. Anna felt a stab of fear press into her heart. She sat up with a start and backed herself against the headboard to the bed.

"You have been disobedient, Miss Addunizio," Vincent stated coolly after he had locked the door behind him.

"I'm s-sorry," Anna bleated out. "I had to go to the bathroom."

"Lie down on the bed, face up," Vincent ordered her coldly.

"P-please don't hurt me," Anna pleaded. "I won't do it again. I promise."

Vincent swung the long, thin lash across the bed, striking the frightened woman across her body. She flinched when she saw it coming and it bit into her upraised arm and the thigh that she had pulled up to protect her belly and breasts.

"Ooooooooouuu!" she screamed. "That hurts! Please! I'll lie down! I'll do it, please!"

Vincent held the long quirt in abeyance as the panicked woman complied with his order. When she was flat on her back, her legs extended, he ordered her to put her hands at her sides. She looked up at the cruel man fearfully.

"I'm going to give you one lash for getting out of bed without permission. There will be a second one for refusing to obey my order. The third one will be for not calling me 'sir'. If you move or try to interfere, you will get another. Do you understand?"

Tears were flowing from Anna's eyes. Her heart was pounding in her chest at the prospect of the impending, excruciating pain. She wanted her body to disappear, rued her very existence as she contemplated the torment and humiliation of being whipped. She knew that she had no choice but to submit to the steely eyed servant. Though she wanted desperately to get up and run, to hide in the bathroom, under the bed, in the long closet that sat along one wall, she forced herself to remain as ordered: subservient, compliant and shamefully vulnerable.

Her mouth was dry and she found it difficult to form words. "Y-yes, Sir," she managed to say, her voice tremulous.

The first blow crossed the tops of Anna's plump mounds, just above the nipples. Anna closed her eyes when she saw it coming and tensed her body. The kiss of the whip sent searing pain through her. She arched her back and screamed, "Aaaaaaoooooough! Oh my god! Ohhhhhhhhhh!" She looked up at her assailant pleadingly. Her eyes were awash with tears. When she saw the man's hand raised once more, prefatory to another blow, she tightened her fists by her sides, struggling with all her might not to jump off the bed to avoid it. The lash made a fierce snapping sound as it crossed her flat, taut belly.

"Aaaaaaoooooough!" she cried again. Instinctively, she raised her knees and curled her torso. "Oh! Oh! Oh! Don't hit me again! Please, Sir! Please!" she cried out. She looked into the determined, indifferent eyes of the servant and knew that begging was useless. She quickly resumed the position Vincent had demanded and then closed her eyes again when she saw the whip descending. This time, it crossed the tops of her thighs. The fire-like pain burned into her and she screamed once more, "Aaaaaaooooo-oough!"

Anna's whole body trembled with the aftereffects of her whipping. Her chest heaved with her sobs. The places where the lash had landed burned with pain. She looked up at the servant dolefully, hoping to see some evidence of compassion for her suffering. She saw none.

The tall, indifferent man placed the whip on the bed and went over to the dresser. He leaned over and opened the bottom drawer. When he rose, Anna saw that he had two lengths of leather cord in his hands. Anna knew what they were for.

"Please don't tie me up, Sir," she begged through her sobs. "I won't get out of bed again. I promise, Sir." She hated herself for her abjectness, her cowardice before the tall, cruel servant, but his punishment of her had brought her across the line from a self reliant, strong willed head of an important social service agency to a trembling, terror filled adolescent. She was self conscious of her nudity, her helplessness, her isolation from the world. They could do anything they wanted to her up here and no one would ever know.

"Roll over," the man ordered, ignoring her.

Anna, afraid of adding to her punishment, obeyed. When she was lying on her belly, she resumed her pleas.

"I can't stand to be tied! Please don't tie me up, please, Sir, please!"

"Put you hands behind your back," the man said.

Anna obediently, if reluctantly, crossed her wrists behind her. When she felt the leather strap encircle them, she pressed her head into the mattress and sobbed. Vincent wrapped it both lengthwise and crossways, securing her wrists tightly. A feeling of intense sickness flowed through her as she felt the knot tied off and her arms confined. "Ohhhhhhhhhhh!" she moaned. She felt her ankles crossed and the leather tightly secured around them. The sensation of her imprisoned limbs was horrifying to her. It brought back terrible, disabling memories. She knew that begging for release would not change her fate, but she couldn't help herself.

"Please, Sir, please, don't leave me like this! You don't understand! I can't stand it! Please!"

The man had returned to the dresser and when he stood up Anna saw that he had something else to add to her misfortunes. It was a leather belt with a large rubber ball attached. Anna recognized it immediately. She had worn one before, many years ago. "Ohhhhhhhhh!" she moaned. "Don't gag me, please, Sir, please!" The thought of her mouth confined was abhorrent.

"Since you cannot learn to remain silent, you must wear the gag," Vincent said.

Anna pressed her face into the mattress. "No! Please!" she yelled into it. "You don't understand!"

The tall, powerful servant took hold of a skein of Anna's hair and lifted her head. With his other hand, he pressed the ball of the gag against her lips. Anna gritted her teeth, denying the admission to the infernal instrument. Vincent spoke in a stern, even tone. "If you don't open your mouth, I will take you down the hall and give you a real whipping. Do you understand, Ms. Addunizio?"

Sobbing with misery, fearful of what the harsh words of her assailant implied, a sickening despondency spreading through her body, Anna nodded her head and parted her lips. Vincent forced the large, spongy ball into her mouth. It plopped past her teeth and pressed down her tongue, filling her oral cavity. Anna's head was jerked back as he tightened the strap behind it. Her lips were drawn into a grotesque grimace. She moaned in misery as Vincent let her head fall back down to the mattress. He left the bed and Anna heard him fiddling around again at the dresser. She turned her head to look and saw him with a heavy, black bag in his hand. She let out a muffled moan as she realized that he was going to hood her. She did not struggle as the man draped the hood over her head. What was the sense? But her whole body tensed in protest and her limbs squirmed in their confinements. She closed her eyes as it was drawn down over her face. She felt a string pulled at its base, tightening it around her neck.

"I will be back in two hours, Miss Addunizio," he told her. "I expect I will find you where I have left you. I suggest you use the time appropriately to commit yourself to obedience." The heavy 'thunk' of the door closing sounded to Anna like the slamming of the door to a prison cell.

Panicked, Anna's mind roiled in protest. She twisted and turned her wrists fruitlessly to try and free them. She pulled at her crossed ankles futilely. When she opened her eyes, to her dismay, all she saw was utter darkness. She bit down hard on the soft, large intruder in her mouth and shrieked and moaned. Anna felt like she was being drawn to the edge of insanity. The impossibility of her predicament, given all that she had done to bury her past, the rewarding, productive life she had built for herself, fueled her manic efforts to break her bonds. After many minutes, when her psyche finally accepted the uselessness of further resistance or protestation, she let her head fall to the bed and cried.

The time dragged along slowly. Two hours was a long time to be naked and bound, unable to see the advancing light through the window to measure time. Intermittently, Anna continued to struggle at her confinements. What she would do if she got them loose, she didn't think about. Her revulsion at being trussed and helpless was so strong that it overwhelmed all rational thought. After a while, though, the hopelessness of her efforts came home to her. She had to endure the cruel, offensive bindings for as long as her masters wanted. A huge, empty pit in her stomach, she finally surrendered to their power over her.

Although she hated being helpless and bound, the gag in her mouth was even worse. It was a continual, hateful presence. She could lie still and ignore, for a few minutes at least, the fact that her hands and legs could not obey her will, but the large, spongy ball in her mouth, suppressing the frantic, hysterical cries of protest she cast into the empty room, was a continual reminder of her powerlessness. Her jaws began to ache from their extension. She felt herself drooling from the corners of her mouth, unable to exercise the muscles of her tongue to swallow.

Anna tried every posture imaginable. She lay on her belly for the longest time, turning her head right and left in an effort to assuage her discomfort. She lay on her right side, her knees scrunched up almost to her chest in a fetal position. After a while, she turned her torso and discovered that she could not lie on her back for long, even though this was the best position to alleviate the flow of her saliva down her chin and neck, as she was able to tilt her head backwards and let the moisture slide down her throat. The crossing of her wrists just above her waist dug deeply into the small of her back, causing it to ache.

It was an odd and terrifying sensation to be so blind and helpless in what she knew was a well lit, conventional room. She tried to remember its appointments, the dresser, the side tables, the lamps, the color of the walls. Then she recalled the camera up near the ceiling. She realized that her supine, naked, bound form was being recorded. It felt like the whole world was watching her through the callous, electronic eye. Every time that she moved, drew her knees to her chest, rolled from one side to the other, shook her hooded head, her mind recorded a vision of herself as she imagined she appeared.

She tried to remain still, but the distress that she felt ate at her, making her body restless. She alternated closing and opening her eyes under her hood, but neither state was satisfying nor gave her relief from the dreadful darkness that surrounded her. She held herself stiff and motionless for the longest time, counting out a cadence, trying to calculate the passage of the interminable minutes. "One thousand, two thousand, three thousand...," losing count quickly as her despair and the impracticality of counting down two full hours overwhelmed her. "One hundred and twenty minutes," she thought, "more than seven thousand seconds."

At each passing one, she felt herself sinking further and further down into a dismal trough of self pity, felt her veneer of confidence and self respect ebbing further away. Her body had been stolen from her. Every form of self expression, all of her ability to take action, to effect the world around her or her own fate in it, had been taken away. She was as helpless as anyone could be and had no options other than to await her deliverance at the whim of her masters.

Somehow, Anna was able to drift off to sleep. She was startled from a disquieting dream when she heard the sound of what she assumed were Vincent's steps coming up the stairs. She couldn't remember its details, but the remnants of the dream's horror hung on as she heard the footsteps coming closer to her door and then the lock turn.

She was lying on her left side, facing the door when the man entered. Her heart fluttered as she considered her hoped for liberation. She had given long and careful thought to her predicament and had determined to listen carefully and do everything she was told. Now that the man was here in her room, she redoubled her resolution.

Anna felt the bed sag slightly as the man sat down on it next to her. Was he here to free her or to torment her? She realized that she was wholly in his arbitrary power. If she made the wrong move, did the wrong thing, her torment could be extended, or, if her controller chose, made even worse.

Anna felt the man's hand slide down her proffered, naked, right hip. It was hot and strong. The contact was welcome, a break from her long, uninterrupted isolation. She assumed it was Vincent, but she was not sure until she heard him speak.

"Have you learned your lesson, Ms. Addunizio?" the servant asked. There was a slight tinge of sympathy in it, almost as if some part of him rued the necessity of punishing her. Anna nodded her hooded head and murmured a sad, muffled, affirmative reply. The strong hand lingered on her body, caressing her sensitive flesh from her knee to her hip. She felt pressure on her hip and she obediently followed its urging and turned to her back. The hands of the servant passed over her taut, nervous belly and seized her plump, defenseless mounds, stroking and massaging them. Anna initially felt revulsion at the man's intimate touch, but the warmth of his hands and the leisurely, knowledgeable way that he manipulated her orbs soon became comforting and turned to mild excitement when he pinched and pulled playfully at her stiffened nipples.

The hands left her breasts and slowly dragged along her belly and across her thighs. Anna thought of the markings the man had put there and the pain she had suffered at each determined, remorseless blow. Was whipping going to be a steady part of her life under Devlin's dominion? He had whipped her last night, slapped her with his belt. That had been nothing compared to what Vincent had done to her, a mere annoyance in comparison. But both had been insulting, demeaning, stripping her of dignity and stressing her powerlessness.

Apparently having satisfied himself, Vincent raised her feet and untied her ankles from each other. He got off the bed and ordered her to sit up and to bring herself to the edge of the mattress. Anna felt his hands on the strings to her hood and was relieved when it was pulled free. She blinked her eyes in the bright, morning light. She remembered that it was probably only around 8:30 or so. She had a long day in front of her and her stomach quailed as she pondered what it would be like.

Anna expected Vincent to remove her gag and to untie her hands, but he had other ideas. "Get up," he ordered her. Anna dutifully, if unsteadily, rose to her feet.

"Do you have to use the bathroom?" He asked her coldly.

Anna, realizing that she might not get the chance again for a long while, nodded dutifully. Vincent made a gesture with his hand signaling her to go and she complied without reservation. He stood at the door while she peed and, afterwards, had her spread her legs so that he could wipe her. Anna felt a surge of shame as he dragged the toilet paper across her love lips, pressing down to absorb the last drops of her discharge.

The man washed his hands and then brought Anna back into the bedroom and had her sit back down on the bed. The only items of her clothing that were left in the room were her high heeled shoes and he buckled them on her feet. "Get up and follow me," he said, matter-of-factly.

The unhappy young woman stood behind the suited servant as he unlocked the door. He didn't mean to have her walk through the mansion bound and naked, did he? Her mind revolted at the thought. She knew, though, she had no choice if that was what he intended and, when he opened the door to let her pass, she stepped out of the room that had been her prison.

Walking down the narrow stairs behind Devlin's servant, Anna was filled with dread and unhappiness. She had caught a glimpse of what she looked like in the mirror in her room. Her long, black wavy hair was disheveled and tangled. Her makeup was smeared and her eyes looked black. The shiny gold earrings that dangled from her ears, the only remnant of her adornments that they had permitted her to retain, looked incongruous and mocking as they emerged from her tangled mass of black hair.

If she had any hope she could regain some of her self respect and dignity before her next confrontation with the craven master of this house, it was shattered by that glance. She felt dirty and soiled and she dreaded being presented to him naked, bound and gagged. If he thought of her before as a lowly whore, a sluttish slave, her appearance now would strikingly confirm his opinions.

Anna stepped carefully down the stairs. She didn't wear high heels that often and her lack of practice on them was compounded by the fact that her hands were bound behind her. Her shoes made loud, echoing sounds as she placed them carefully on each tread. Vincent was moving quietly in front of her.

She expected to be brought down to the ground floor and was surprised as they reached the second floor to see Vincent turn to his right and go down the hall. They passed several doors to what Anna supposed were bedrooms and entered a double doorway at the end of the hall. The room they passed into was bright and surrounded by windowed glass. It was decorated in light, elegant furniture, a glass table with straight backed chairs around it, a couple of lounge chairs, large potted palms. The rug was a flowery print that reached to within two feet of the walls of the room, exposing evidence of the polished wooden floor underneath.

To her dismay, she saw Devlin sitting in a comfortable, light blue arm chair on the left near the windows. He was dressed in a soft, fluffy, white, terry cloth robe that reached to his knees and had brown, leather slippers on his feet. He was reading a newspaper and had a cup of coffee on a small, glass table next to him. His legs were crossed and Anna could see a patch of darkness between his thighs where his sex resided. Vincent brought her to a position a few feet in front of him and stood by her side, awaiting his master's pleasure.

Devlin lowered his paper and let his eyes wander across Anna's naked flesh. She was conscious of her bound hands behind her and the round, spongy ball that peaked out from her widened mouth. Devlin nodded to his servant and Anna listened to the soft tread of his feet as he left the room. When the door closed, Devlin smiled at her and went back to reading his paper.

While Devlin read, Anna stood trembling in front of him. Nervously, she took the opportunity to look out of the windows behind her master. She had only seen the mansion at night and she was awed by the view. The building sat high on a hill and she could see for miles over the leafless trees that surrounded it. Off in the distance, there were the tops of the tall buildings of the city.

She tried to estimate where the Center was from where she stood. The sun was to her right and she knew that she was looking north. The Center was on the city's outskirts, somewhat south and east of it. She felt some comfort that she could see the world outside of the mansion, that it still existed. It made her more hopeful that Devlin would allow her to return to it. At the same time, she realized, she was not the same person who had entered Devlin's mansion last night, who had tidied up her desk in her office in the Center, making little notes about the things she needed to do on Monday when she returned. The recollection of her naïveté regarding what her time with the Center's principal benefactor would be like reminded her that all she was doing, all that she suffered, was so that the Center could continue. Her resolve to take all that Devlin could dish out returned.

Devlin finally put down his paper and leaned over, picking up his coffee cup. It was made of elegant china, gold rimmed. He took a sip and put it back down in the delicate saucer and then looked up at her.

"Good morning, Anna," he said, almost cheerfully. "Did you sleep well?" The sound of Devlin's voice shattered Anna's resolve to be strong. Tears welled up inside her. She nodded dolefully at the man's pleasantry and murmured a stifled, "Yes, Mr. Devlin." The sound of her strangled voice made her swoon with shame.

"I see that you've been a naughty girl," the man continued. "Did you learn your lesson?"

Anna was not sure whether the man was referring to her bound hands, her gag, or the red stripes that she wore across her breasts, belly and thighs. Probably all three. Her unhappy answer sounded like "eh, i-er eh-in," and barely escaping her gagged mouth. The very reminder of her sufferings made tears flow from her eyes and her body tremble. She tried desperately to control herself, but she felt like she was coming apart right in front of the man.

"Come here, Anna," Devlin ordered. His voice was soft and sympathetic. He opened his arms invitingly. Anna stepped cautiously towards him. He indicated that she should sit on his lap and she carefully maneuvered herself so that she could sit on his left thigh, her bare legs between his, her naked shoulder leaning against his strong, upper arm. He wrapped it around her and pulled her towards him.

"Poor little Anna," he said soothingly. "You've had a very hard time, haven't you?"

Anna felt a well of sorrow flow through her. She nodded dolefully. Yes, she had had a very hard time. It was incongruous, but she felt relief and the lifting of her anxiety as he uttered the kindly words. She began to cry and Devlin pulled her head into the nape of his neck and held her tight. As she sobbed, he murmured soft, soothing words to her. "Go ahead and cry, Anna. You'll feel better. That's it, let it out. Let it all out."

A dam broke in Anna's heart and all of her unhappiness flowed free. She hadn't cried like this since she was a teenager. The man's strong arms felt soothing around her. His soft, cotton robe felt warm and comforting on her naked skin. She was chagrinned that she was making such a display before him, but nothing she did could ease the flow of tears or sobs.

Devlin ran his hand over her head, stroking her hair. After a long time Anna felt her control over her emotions returning. The hand that caressed her head was welcome. She felt it fiddle with the strap behind her head that held her gag in place and then it loosened. Devlin urged her head up and drew the large, spongy ball from her mouth placing it on the table next to them. Holding her head in his hands, her face turned towards him, he placed an affectionate kiss on her lips and then kissed her cheeks, her chin and even over her eyes. "That's a good girl," he whispered to her. "That's a good girl."

When Devlin's lips returned to hers, Anna felt the man's hot breath. When his tongue slipped along the surface of her lips and then prodded at the opening between them, Anna parted her lips and accepted the man's hot, lust driving tongue inside. As their tongues intertwined, she felt his hand wander over her breasts and belly, caressing and stroking. He cupped one breast after another in his hand, squeezing them gently, kneading them softly, bringing a wave of pleasure to her. His hand descended as his lips left hers. While his fingers pried at the entrance to the gates of her moistening cleft, pushing aside the thick array of curly, black, pubic hair that disguised it, he seized a nipple with his lips and began to suckle at it, playing with its tip with the tip of his tongue.

The emotionally drained young woman reveled in the passion that the man was raising in her. She pulled at the bound hands behind her, wanting to wrap her arms around the man who was stimulating her naked flesh. After ensuring that her sex was soft and moist, Devlin pushed her thighs further open, caressing the soft inner skin on both of them. He passed his hand over her hip, along the side of her torso and over her belly. Lust erupted within the naked, bound woman everywhere the hand passed. It was like she was an instrument he was playing and he was a virtuoso at passion. When his fingers slipped between her love lips and entered her, scouring the hot, inner surface, Anna moaned with lust. When his thumb began to stroke gently against her hardened clit, she groaned and shifted her hips, spreading her legs wider, melting into her master's arms.

Devlin used his hand and his lips to drive Anna deeper and deeper into her excitement. He brought her to the edge of completion twice, only to slow his caresses, withdraw his hand from her needy quim, and resume stroking her trembling thighs. Anna gave out long, deep throated moans when he finally allowed her to come. Her body rocked in the man's arms as pulse after pulse of exquisite pleasure flowed through her. Her bound hands writhed behind her. She could feel her pussy's walls clamp down tightly on the fingers inside it. Her electrified love button screamed as

Devlin's thumb continued to torture it to ecstasy. Her cries of pleasure echoed through the brightly lit room.

As her orgasm subsided, Devlin loosened his grip on her body. Anna's heart was pounding and her breath was labored. A warm contentment had spread all through her. It felt odd that the rude, callous man of the night before should be capable of bringing her so much pleasure. For a while, he allowed her to rest in his arms and absorb the glowing aftereffects of her powerful climax. After a minute or so, his voice pierced her reverie.

"Was that nice, Anna? Did you like that?"

"Yesssssss, Mr. Devlin," Anna sighed, letting her satisfied body rest against him.

"I want you to suck my cock now, Anna, and try to do a little better than yesterday.'

His instructions jolted her from her listlessness, a reminder that she was his to command. She slid her body off of his lap and took a kneeling position before him. While yesterday she had been appalled and insulted by his rude demand, now she was almost grateful for the opportunity to bring him pleasure, for the opportunity at redemption. Anna looked up at the man, her brown eyes soft and watery. He was smiling down at her appreciatively. He spread his thighs wider, brushing aside his robe. Anna leaned forwards, capturing his hardened prick between her lips.

The bound woman took her time in servicing Devlin's thick, long cock. She could feel the heat of his thighs on the sides of her arms as she brought her mouth up and down on it, concentrating on the soft textured hardness as it passed over her lips, its salty taste. The bulbous head dragged over her tongue as she pushed her head down as far as she could go, feeling the smooth helmet push against the entrance to her throat. She could hear the man sigh, his breath getting deeper and deeper as she caressed him. His hips pushed back against her when she descended his stiff pole with her lips and withdrew as she slid them back up, her tongue washing it. She nibbled at the cock's tip until Devlin moaned and then brought her mouth down again, time after time. There was something about her obsequious serving of him that felt right. He was a powerful, self assured, domineering man and she was nothing but a lowly servant of his lust. Her pussy still glowed from his manual administration of passion to it and the sensation of his thick meat in her mouth made her lust rise again. She remembered how the thick, rigid wand had driven her to ecstatic convulsions the night before and, to her shame, her pussy seemed to yearn for its presence once again.

When she felt his passions about to erupt, she slowed her efforts to prolong his delight. He sighed and moaned, his hips shifting, his hands wandering over her head and over her shoulders. When she resumed her efforts, he groaned and his body tensed, receiving the hot moisture of her mouth and tongue.

Finally, she let him come, his piece jerking and spasming in her mouth, his bitter, salty spume flooding her. She felt entranced as she drank it, as if the pulsing manhood had cast a spell over her.

Remembering her instructions from the night before, Anna kept her lips locked on Devlin's softening wand until all of his juices had ebbed from it and he gave her a signal to rise. He ran his hand over her head. "That was a little better, Anna," he said. "There's hope for you yet."

Devlin picked up an intercom from the table next to him and pressed a button. Vincent's voice came over it and he instructed his servant to return to the sun room, as he called it, to retrieve their 'guest'. He made Anna lean forward and, to her dismay, reinstalled her gag. He returned to his newspaper.

Anna knelt at the man's feet, her bound hands resting in the small of her back, until Vincent entered the room, about two minutes later. He stood next to her, awaiting instructions

"Anna," Devlin said, looking up from his paper, "I want you to get all cleaned up and then you can come down and have breakfast. We'll talk about the rest of your day then."

Anna, having been dismissed, rose obediently to her feet and followed Vincent from the room.

CHAPTER THREE

Anna stood under the shower, letting the hot water calm and soothe her body. The red lines where Vincent had struck her stung at first when the water hit them, but had quickly faded from her notice. She wondered whether she would ever feel clean again. Her crying jag with Devlin and the ease with which she had succumbed to his manual excitation of her lusts disturbed her. She had not felt such an authentic release of her pent up emotions in many years. The pleasure she had received while sucking on his tool seemed strange and perverse.

Vincent had told her she had a half hour to clean herself. She shook herself from her torpor and applied the luxurious soap that had been supplied with the bathroom to her body. She washed her privates thoroughly, eliminating the evidence of her bouts of passion from her curly pubic hair. As she ran her hands over her flesh, she marveled at its sensitivity. She squeezed and caressed her heavy breasts, receiving a twinge of desire in her place below as a result. When she ran the soap over her nether lips, her hand stayed longer than necessary, rubbing her little nub of pleasure gently until she felt a familiar burning in her crevasse.

After washing, she dried her body with the plush, oversized towel that had been provided. She looked at herself in the mirror over the sink while she dried her hair with the blower that had been supplied as an amenity in the bathroom. Devlin thought of everything, she mused, as she ran the hot air over her locks while running a brush through them with her other hand. There was even a fresh, new toothbrush for her to use, still packed in its plastic case. She was looking at her face, examining it closely to see if the shift in her personality was reflected there. The cheap, gold plated earrings that she had bought, the only part of her attire that she had worn on Friday night when she came to Devlin's mansion still left to her, other than her high heels, glinted in the bight light. She had removed her dried up makeup before the shower and her face was devoid of supplementation. Her lips were just a little paler and her skin just a little less rosy. Her eyes, which had been carefully adorned with decoration before coming to Devlin's mansion, shone nicely in their natural setting.

Although she was alone in her room, Anna did not feel alone. Her masters, Devlin and Vincent were there even if only in her mind. She thought of the ever present eye mounted on the wall of her room and was thankful to be, if only for a little while, free of its gaze.

The young woman had committed herself to follow Vincent's instructions to the letter. She had cleaned herself thoroughly, wiped the polish off of the fingernails of her delicate hands and was making sure that her hair had a nice curl to it as she dried it. But it was his other instruction that disturbed her. He had told her to shave her pussy before he came back and had pointed out the small pair of scissors, the shaving cream and the plastic, disposable razor she was to use. He was very specific, telling her that she should leave a thin, short line of hair around the entrance to her womb, long enough so that it would not chafe or irritate, but short enough so that it would appear like a dark outline to her sex. The worst part was that he had ordered to do it while sitting on the bed.

When her hair was dry and brushed, Anna filled the small bowl she had been provided with warm water and brought the implements necessary to her task into the bedroom. She glanced briefly on the eye in the sky, ruing the show that she was about to put on for it. She hated the thought of there being a record of her demeaning task, but she knew well enough the punishment for disobedience.

Maneuvering herself onto the bed, her back against the pillowed headboard, Anna spread her olive brown, trim thighs widely apart. She was sitting on one of the pillows so that her sex would be raised and prominent and had placed a towel under her so that the remnants of her adult growth would not land on the bed. Someone had made it in her absence and she wondered who. She was sure there were other people around, although she had not seen them yet. She dreaded being confronted by witnesses to her defilements.

Avoiding any further glances at the cold, remote, anonymous audience up on the wall, she picked up the scissors and began to snip away. Soon, her mound of curly, black hair had been reduced to a short sea of soft grass. She applied the shaving cream to her loins and, taking the razor in her right hand, began to remove everything but a thin band around her slit. The area above her cunny was easy. She felt a pang of remorse as she saw the proof of her maturity disappear. The area around her pussy was a little more difficult, and she used her left hand to pull the skin tight on either side of it while she made sure that she removed the hairs that crept up the inside of her thighs and adorned the slopes of her nether lips.

Like many women, Anna had never made a point of taking a good look at the crevasse between her thighs. She had seen pictures of pussies, of course, on the internet and in magazines that her father and, later, some of her so called 'boyfriends' had had. Seeing her own was much different. When the shroud of curly hairs had been removed, she took a moment to examine the well defined lips, the wrinkled entrance to her canal, the seeming surfeit of skin that surrounded it. She had been carefully examining it when she remembered the camera on the wall and, blushing with shame, quickly went back to her task.

The last step was the application of a skin cream to her loins. It smelled nice and was soothing to her slightly irritated skin. She took her time applying it, working it deeply into her denuded flesh until it felt smooth and soft.

When her pussy was trimmed as ordered, Anna put the shaving things back into the bathroom and returned to the bedroom. She stood, as instructed, at the end of the bed, facing towards the camera, her hands folded behind her and her legs spread. The long, wide mirror on the wall reflected her from her head to her knees and she could not help but stare at her clearly visible love lips, admiring their clean lines and the trim of black hair that surrounded them.

Vincent came into the room a few moments later. He was carrying her clothes from the day before, at least most of them. Gone were her panties and bra. He had brought her smooth, tan, cashmere skirt and her expensive, burgundy, knitted, sweater blouse, her long, black, sheer stockings. Devlin had stated last night that she looked like she was dressed for a PTA meeting. Maybe he was right. She knew that she would have to find things more revealing and provocative if she was to satisfy her master, the man who owned her body and soul for the next twelve months.

The butler ordered Anna to turn towards him and show him her pussy. He gazed at it for a moment and then reached out his hand and rubbed his palm over her bare skin. He seemed satisfied. He ordered her to get dressed.

The trip back downstairs was much different than earlier. Although her breasts swung free underneath her blouse and she was more than conscious of her bare sex beneath her skirt, Anna felt more composed and at ease. They went down to the second floor and returned to the sun room.

Devlin was already seated at the table. To Anna's surprise, there was a young woman sitting next to him. She had long, flowing brown hair, down almost to her waist. Her body was slim and languorous, her face pretty. She wore a dark red dress with a sharp 'V' neckline, revealing the edges of her small, rounded breasts. She and Devlin were laughing about something.

Devlin was facing the door and was the first to see Anna enter.

"Come in, Anna. We just started. I'd like you to meet Elaine, my friend."

"Hi, Anna," Elaine said merrily. "Mr. Devlin has told me all about you."

Anna wondered what "all about you" meant. She hoped it didn't mean what she thought. Devlin quickly proved she was, unfortunately, right.

"Did you shave your pussy, Anna?" he asked nonchalantly. He might have been asking her if she had brushed her teeth.

The young woman blanched at replying to her owner, as she had gotten used to thinking of him. The woman, Elaine, was staring at her as if she too had an interest in this information. Remembering Vincent's whip and the fact that the money to bail out the Center had yet to be paid, Anna managed to whisper a muted response to the question. "Y-yes, Mr. Devlin," she replied.

"Let me see. Lift up your skirt," Devlin ordered. He was dressed in a yellow, knit sports shirt and sharply creased tan trousers. He had a hand on a tall, large, round wine glass with orange juice in it. From the fact that a champagne bottle sat in a bucket of ice to his right, Anna deduced he and Elaine were drinking mimosas. Anna suppressed a sob and let her hands fall to the edge of her soft, brown skirt. How many people were going to be in on the fact of her subservience to the callous businessman, she worried fretfully. Was there no limit to what she was going to have to endure? She had been feeling good after her shower and being allowed to dress. Relatively good that is. A dark shadow seemed to have formed over her life and being clean and wearing clothes was, in itself, not enough to dispel it. Having to display her finely trimmed quim to this strange woman negated all of her efforts to regain some equanimity about her predicament. She wondered if Devlin had shown Elaine the videos from her room. She prayed that he had not.

Hesitatingly, slowly, Anna's fingers grasped the hem of her skirt and began to raise it. Blood rushed to her face as she experienced the shame of being a thrall to the wealthy man, her black knight. The hem gradually passed her upper thighs. She recalled the long red line that lay across them, a virtual declaration of her subservience. As she brought the hem of her skirt up to her belly, Anna defensively brought her thighs together and crushed her denuded slit between them. When the skirt was fully raised, Anna closed her eyes to block out what was happening, what she was doing.

"Anna," Devlin said, "you have to spread your legs, we can't see it. Be a good girl now and show us your cunt."

The unhappy girl moaned and steeled herself for obedience. She moved her thighs apart so that her pussy would be revealed in all it splendor.

"Very nice, Anna. You did a very good job. I'm pleased," Devlin commented. "What do you think Elaine? Doesn't Anna have a pretty pussy?'

"Very pretty, Mr. Devlin," the young girl answered. "Good enough to eat."

The attractive woman's comment made Anna quail with distress. She hadn't considered whether Devlin would force her to have sex with other women. From Elaine's comment, she had to believe that that indignity was somewhere down the road for her. She knew men had a thing for girl on girl sex, and she often wondered why it excited them so. It did nothing for her. Pictures of it she had seen made her feel creepy. There had to be some barriers to sexuality, didn't there? If you couldn't go into the women's locker room without worrying whether someone was looking at you lustfully, where could you go?

Anna was intensely conscious of her naked sex as she stood before the table in front of Devlin and the woman. Her hands were sweating and her fingers trembling.

"Come over here, Anna," Devlin ordered. "I want to feel it."

Anna, opening her eyes, obediently stepped closer to him and presented her naked pussy. She flinched as his hand took possession of it. It wandered over the bare portions of her loins and then caressed the narrow, fuzzy strips of hair that were left. In spite of her dismay, Anna felt a twinge of desire as his hot hand captured her sexual mound. A wave of lust passed through her as he traced a finger along the length of the divide between her bearded love lips. She was staring out the window at the bright day, concentrating on a single tree that was swaying slightly in the mild, late autumn wind.

The room was silent and she could hear her own breathing becoming labored and needy. Devlin's hand was working her puss and she knew that her moisture had come when she felt his fingers slide inside her. He alternated between running them along the soft, slick walls of her interior and massaging the bud at the top. Anna closed her eyes again as she felt her lust build. Her knees weakened and, for a moment, she felt like she was going to fall. She gave a deep sigh that she regretted as soon as it came out. Devlin laughed. "You're such a slut, Anna. You've really surprised me. If only you knew how to fuck."

Devlin's words pierced Anna cruelly. Was he going to leave her nothing? She fought back her tears.

Devlin, having satisfied himself, removed his hand from Anna's sex and wiped it on a napkin. "You can sit down, Anna. Vincent will be here in a moment with our breakfast."

Anna, her mind dazed from lust and shame, stepped back and lowered her skirt. She cast a glance at Elaine, who was looking back at her with great interest. Anna lowered her head to try and avoid her gaze and took a chair opposite her.

"Have a mimosa," Devlin said cheerily. He poured some orange juice into Anna's glass and topped it off with champagne. Anna, taking Devlin's suggestion as an order, picked up the glass and took a long sip. It was cold and tasty, and the sensation of having the slightly fizzy beverage pass down her throat helped to calm her. Her pussy still burned with desire and she brought her thighs together to try and quell it.

Vincent appeared, rolling in a small cart. He came to the table and placed covered dishes in front of the three diners. When he lifted the cover off of Anna's plate she saw a fluffy omelet, a side of small, home fried potatoes, browned to perfection, and a sprig of parsley.

Elaine and Devlin chatted happily throughout the meal. Elaine tried to engage Anna in conversation a few times, but Anna's answers were short and evasive. She had eaten a few bites of her breakfast, but was really just playing with it. Devlin, noting her reticence at eating, spoke up.

"Anna, you have to eat. If you don't eat, I'll have Vincent whip you. Do you understand?"

Anna shivered at the thought of Vincent's whip and was mortified for the elegant young woman who sat opposite her to hear that she was subject to it. She pursed her lips to hide a frown and then answered dutifully, "Yes, Mr. Devlin." She started to force the meal down.

Once breakfast was finished, Devlin pushed his chair back from the table and gave out a sigh. "Vincent's a magician in the kitchen, don't you think, Anna?"

In fact, the omelet had been just the right combination of a tart cheese, sautéed, finely chopped green and red peppers and small pieces of ham. It felt good to have something inside her stomach, despite her lack of appetite. She looked up at her master and nodded affirmatively. "Yes, Mr. Devlin."

"Anna, I'm going to be busy this afternoon. Elaine is going to take you shopping, get your hair done. She's going to pick out some nice, sexy things for you to wear. I want you to cooperate with her. Okay?"

The news that she was to be let out of the mansion, if only for the afternoon, surprised and gladdened her. The thought of being in the company of the svelte beauty who knew of her shameful and abject surrender to Devlin did not. She looked at the woman and then back at Devlin. "Yes, Mr. Devlin," she answered.

The two women rode toward the city in the back seat of Devlin's limousine. Elaine prattled on busily and, gradually, Anna began to engage in conversation with her. Elaine let her know all the parties she had been to lately, the fancy stores she was taking her to, how nice Mr. Devlin was. "We'll get you some really pretty things," she said, stroking Anna's arm. Anna shriveled at the contact, remembering Elaine's comment about eating her pussy.

It took some courage, but Anna finally asked the question that had been on her mind since she had seen the long haired beauty in Devlin's sun room. "What's your relationship to Mr. Devlin?" she asked.

Elaine's eyes made an involuntary, evasive movement. "Oh, we're old friends," she answered. "I work for him sometimes."

"Are you working for him now?"

"Well, not really. Well, maybe. It depends on how you look at it."

"How do you look at it?" Anna pressed.

Elaine looked at Anna sternly. "Listen, honey, the less you know about Mr. Devlin and his business the better off you are. Mr. Devlin did me a favor. A big favor. And so I do him favors. That's all there is to it. He still helps me, gets me modeling jobs. I'm in line for a big commercial. He knows a guy who knows a guy. That's all."

Anna wasn't satisfied. There was one big question she needed to know the answer to. "Please, I don't want to pry into your relationship with Mr. Devlin. But I have to know something. Will he keep his promises? Will he keep his word?"

Elaine gave Anna a sympathetic look. She saw Anna's teary eyes and smiled warmly. "Mr. Devlin's a businessman. He lives on his word. If he doesn't live up to his promises, no one will do business with him. He's always kept his promises to me. Is that what you wanted to hear?"

It was what Anna wanted to hear, but was it the truth? The fact that the girl seemed to have a light, breezy relationship with the millionaire was somewhat comforting. The fact that she easily and without question accepted Anna's bondage to him was not. If Devlin had his hooks in Elaine like she did her, wouldn't she lie for him?

Anna looked up to the front seat and saw the driver's eyes peering back at her through the rear view mirror. He had heard their conversation, she was certain of it. Surely Elaine wouldn't say anything bad about Devlin in his presence.

The driver was a short, barrel chested, Hispanic man, somewhere in his mid thirties. He was dressed in a dark business suit that accentuated his broad shoulders and fitness. His face was round and he wore a seeming two days growth of black beard on it. His hair was long, down to his shoulders. When he had stood by the limo, holding the door open so that the women could enter, Anna thought that she detected a bulge under his jacket that might be a gun. He had given Anna a lascivious look when she had gotten into the car and it had disturbed her.

"Let's have some more champagne," Elaine suggested merrily in an attempt to break the somber mood that had arisen in the limo. The car had a small refrigerator mounted behind the front seat and a little closet for glasses. Elaine pulled out a bottle and some long, thin, fluted stemware. When she popped the cork, a load of fizz erupted from the top and dripped onto the limo carpet. Elaine just laughed.

Anna's head was still somewhat woozy from her mimosas of this morning, but she accepted the bubbly anyway. It was better to be numbed than to have to think about what was happening to her. Tomorrow was Sunday and then there would be Monday. By this time Monday, the money would be back in the Center's account and she would have saved it. She would decide then what to do.

They were expected at the salon and were given a royal greeting. The tall, fey hairdresser took some time in deciding what do to with Anna's "mess" as he called it. His discussions were with Elaine, not with Anna, as if she were a pet that had been brought into a grooming shop. Finally the man decided on a midlength cut that came down to just the middle of her neck. When he was done, Anna had to agree that the results were stylish and looked good on her. It was long enough so that you could still appreciate the wavy richness of her locks, but short enough so that the flesh of her smooth, soft neck could be seen.

The next stop was the lingerie shop. Elaine brought Anna into the dressing area and instructed the shop girl to bring several sets of bras and panties for their perusal. Anna balked at stripping naked so that the lingerie could be held up against her skin and so she could try on the bras, but Elaine insisted. "Listen," she said. "Mr. Devlin gave me clear instructions. If you don't want to cooperate, that's up to you. But I wouldn't want to be you if you don't."

Succumbing to necessity, Anna disrobed and stood there stark naked in the small, windowless cubicle while the 18 year old or so shop girl brought them armfuls of panties and bras. She was chagrined to show the young girl her neatly trimmed pussy and was ashamed of the long red stripes that ran across her breasts, her belly and her thighs. She saw the girl look at the evidence of her debasement with more than mild curiosity. Her momentary expression of alarm gave way quickly to a businesslike, pleasant, mien.

Elaine favored lavender, a deep red and black to offset Anna's dark skin. Anna blushed as the shop girl held panty after panty to her shaved loins to see how the colors matched her flesh. She tried on several pairs of silk stockings, carefully pulling them up her thighs so as not to damage them.

"You've got great legs," Elaine complimented her. Anna had always worn either pantyhose or self supporting stockings and felt uncomfortable putting on the garter belts that she was shown. Elaine brought her to one of the full length mirrors to let her see herself. She was wearing a black garter belt and dark, black, sheer stockings. The bra, which covered only the lower half of her breasts and pushed them together to form a tight cleavage, was black as well. Elaine made her put on her high heels so she could see how it looked. When she stared in the mirror, she saw someone who she didn't recognize. The woman was pretty, seductive, almost like one of those girls in lingerie ads or in soft core men's magazines. Elaine stood close to Anna, letting their upper arms make contact. Her hand came to rest lightly on Anna's left rear globe. "You look marvelous, honey," she said. "Mr. Devlin will like it a lot."

Anna agreed. The straps of her garter belt framed her trimmed pussy perfectly. Her breasts were pushed up in presentation position and her legs looked long and sensuous. She looked eminently fuckable. Embarrassingly, she could see that her nipples had tautened. The hand resting lightly on her rear was hot and disturbing. She caught Elaine's eyes peering into hers in the mirror and shivered.

Elaine settled on ten sets of undergarments and bought ten pairs of sheer stockings in varying shades to go with them. The next stop was a dress shop. They knew Elaine there as well.

They spent about three hours in the dress store. Elaine picked out a number of short, sheath dresses with thin straps. No way would Anna ever have bought them for herself. They were prohibitively expensive, but that wasn't it. Their thin fabric clung to Anna's body like a second skin. Their bodices were loose and suggestive, plunging deeply so that the tips of Anna breasts were just barely covered. She knew that if she leaned over she would be giving everyone quite a show. The hems reached just a few inches below the crux of her thighs. Anna wondered how she would ever be able to sit down in them without exposing her sex.

Elaine also selected three strapless dresses of varying shades and two long gowns with slits that ascended practically to her hip. By the time they were done, Elaine had purchased twelve dresses in all. The ones that were most disturbing to Anna were pastel with long bodices that ended just below her hips and had short, flouncy skirts. She looked just like a teenager in them. The thought of reliving her teenage years was horrific to Anna. In fact all of the dresses, even the gowns, seemed to make her appear much younger than she was. Anna didn't know what instructions Devlin had given Elaine as to what kind of dresses to buy, but she sensed that the whole intent was to make the age difference between her and Devlin seem greater than the twelve or so years that separated them.

Before they left the dress shop, Elaine insisted that Anna wear one of the adolescent style dresses.

They stopped for a quick bite to eat at an elegant downtown restaurant. Conscious of her short, revealing skirt, the tight, uplifting bodice of her dress, the way that it clung skin-like to her curves, Anna felt all eyes on her, even as she strode in behind the languorous, svelte form of Elaine. They ate a couple of light salads and drank a few glasses of wine before resuming their assault on Devlin's pocketbook. They went to three different shoe stores and bought ten pairs of pumps and high heels. The last stop was a beauty salon where an elegantly coiffed and expertly made up female sales assistant produced several shades of powders and eyeliners that would be complimentary to Anna's new wardrobe. Anna was surprised how much she enjoyed being fussed over and agreed that the shades that she had been using in the past were not nearly as complementary to her skin and hair color as the ones the woman selected. When the makeup lesson ended, a stylist painted Anna's finger and toenails a deep, almost maroon red. Elaine picked out a sultry smelling, imported perfume for her.

Anna felt transformed when they got into the limousine to return to Devlin's mansion. She had left a moderately attractive young woman, dressed conservatively as appropriate for her age and station in life and was returning looking like a high class, juvenile harlot. She had to keep her knees closely together to stop her skirt from riding up her thighs and she was self-conscious about the exposed portions of her breasts. Elaine seemed subdued as compared to their journey out as if she too dreaded a return to the Devlin mansion.

It was a forty five minute ride back to Devlin's estate from the city. The closer they got to their destination, the larger grew the knot that had formed in Anna's stomach. The selection of the huge wardrobe at Devlin's expense underscored the commitment she was making to him. With each dress, each dainty undergarment, each bright, snappy high heeled shoe that Elaine had added to the pile of loot, Anna had felt a piece of herself slip away. Now dressed in her new finery, she felt like she had sold herself in exchange for the habiliments of luxury. "No," she thought. "It's all for the Center, the girls. I don't need these things, don't want them." But somehow she felt that the haute couture dresses, the lacy, delicate underthings, the expensive and refined haircut she had agreed to, would all be added to her tab and serve as further justification for Devlin's sense of ownership of her.

Looking out of the window of the sleek limousine, watching the countryside speed by, Anna reminded herself that she could just walk away from all of this if only she had the courage to face the consequences, the shame of exposure, the possibility of jail. If she knew that somehow the Center would continue, that someone would step up and save it by replacing the money that Carol had stolen, she could accept whatever she had coming to her. After all, the Center came first. But that was the tipping point in all of her equivocations. There was little or no hope that the Center would be able to survive the negative publicity. All of those young girls now resident there and all of the many ones to come, would be left to fend for themselves in a hostile, exploitative world. No, it was better that she suffer in their stead, that she serve as the sacrifice for their betterment. What was one person's life and well being compared to all the others?

Casting her eyes up to the front seat, Anna saw the eyes of the driver in the rear view mirror. Was she right to assume that she still had a choice? If she were to get out of the limo when they reached Devlin's and get into her car and drive away, would the coarse looking, muscular man drag her inside anyway? Would Elaine utter a single syllable of protest as she screamed and struggled for her freedom? She doubted it. And then she would face Vincent's whip and the more drastic, unnamed punishments he had threatened her with this morning. Anna turned away from the vision of the chauffeur's beady, sinister eyes in the mirror.

What was she thinking about? She didn't even have her car keys. They were in her handbag in Devlin's office or wherever he had put it. She hadn't wanted to leave the mansion without it, felt naked without the reassurance of its contents, but had been too afraid to ask for it before they had left. The small bag held her keys, her identification and served as a kind of emergency kit for all the small crises that could pop up during the course of a woman's day. Without it, she felt defenseless, like the little girl that she seemed to be becoming, dependant on others for everything. She needed her handbag and could not flee without it. She would have to go inside the mansion when they got there and face whatever torments Devlin had in store for her tonight. She closed her eyes and leaned back in the soft, cushioned seat, her heart sick at her predicament.

Anna's stomach rolled over as the limo pulled onto the gravel parking area in front of the mansion and stopped in front of its ominous entranceway. The bags containing Anna's booty and the clothes that she had worn this morning were in the trunk and, after opening the door so that Anna and Elaine could step out, the driver went around to the back of the vehicle to retrieve them. The dresses had been shipped ahead by the dress shop.

Vincent was waiting at the door and escorted the two young women into the library to the left of the entrance. It wasn't really a library, although there were several lines of unread tomes along the walls. It was more like a lounge, with several overstuffed, leather couches, easy chairs and a large entertainment center. Like Devlin's office, it had large, arching windows that looked out on the driveway and, on the side, over the vast, spreading lawn of the estate and towards the tree covered hills that lay beyond. It was dark outside, a little after 7, and the view out of the side window was overcome by the night.

In the front, Anna could see the parking paddock and the resting vehicles in the bright lights that flooded the area. She thought of her red Toyota Camry they had passed on the way in and how wonderful it would be to run to it and flee. Vincent told the women that Mr. Devlin would be with them shortly and that they should wait here. The driver dumped the packages into the room and left.

Elaine went over to the bar at the side of the room, poured herself a drink and then plopped down on one of the easy chairs. Anna was too afraid to follow suit. Vincent had told her to stay where she was and she had learned to treat his instructions literally. So she stood near the entrance to the room, her hands at her sides, her palms sweaty and her heart beating wildly, waiting for the appearance of her master.

Devlin came in a few minutes later. He was dressed in a stylish, glossy suit and tie like he was prepared to go out. He smiled when he saw Anna and took one of her hands in his and led her to the middle of the room.

"Ah, Anna," he said, "you look marvelous. Turn around so that I can see all of you."

Anna, letting her hand slide from Devlin's, stepped back from him and twirled around slowly. She recalled the night a week ago when she had done the same thing, not fully realizing what subservience to the man would entail. She had been chagrined and humiliated then. Now she felt only fear.

"You've done very well, Elaine," Devlin remarked as his eyes consumed Anna's expensively decorated frame. Anna could detect the seeming ever present undercurrent of lust in his eyes. "You look like such a sweet, young thing, Anna, but we all know what a little whore you really are. It's a compelling contrast."

Anna cringed at his insult, but suppressed her protestation.

"When I came in your hands were at your sides, Anna," Devlin continued. "You know full well that I want your hands held behind you at all times unless I've given you permission to use them. Vincent will punish you for that later as a reminder. Now put your hands behind your back like a good, little girl."

The news that Vincent would whip her again sent a stab of fear through the young woman even as she obeyed her master's command. She didn't remember him saying that, although she had to acknowledge that it was implicit in all that had happened to her since last night. She held back her tears, her hands poised behind her.

"I got her a lot of things, Mr. Devlin. I think you'll like them. What you don't like we can send back," Elaine commented. She had raised her posture from her sprawl on the couch although she had not stood when Devlin entered the room. It appeared that the rules that applied to Anna did not apply to her.

Devlin merely nodded in response. "Take off your dress, Anna, I want to see what you've got on underneath," he told the young woman.

Anna had been practically naked almost all afternoon in front of Elaine but stripping in front of Devlin while she was in the room was another matter altogether. She did not consider refusing despite her chagrin. She was back in her prison now, subject to the callous man's will.

Sliding the thin straps of her flowered, earth toned dress off of her shoulders, Anna let them fall to her sides. The loose, revealing bodice fell down as the tension was released, exposing the dainty, strapless bra she was wearing. Her nipples rose just above the tops of the uplifting cups. She shimmied the dress down her hips and let it fall to her ankles. As she leaned over to pull it free of her shiny, black high heels, she felt her breasts sway slightly in their confinement. Once she had stepped free, she placed the dress carefully across the back of one of the large, plush easy chairs and brought herself to attention before her master.

The matching bra and panty set were colored a pastel lavender with lacy frills. She was wearing a black garter belt that held up a pair of sheer, light tan, silk stockings. She had seen what she looked like in the mirror at the lingerie shop when she had put them on and she knew that she presented a comely, delectable vision to the man, an invitation to his lust. Her knees felt weak and her body shuddered as she dreaded what he would do next, what his next command would be. Her fears were confirmed when he told her to come closer and approach him.

Her hands joined behind her back, feeling Elaine's eyes piercing her from behind, Anna took a position inches away from her tormentor. She flinched slightly as his hands rose to seize her breasts.

"You look lovely, Anna," Devlin said as he began to massage the young woman's firm, ample globes. He pinched her fear stiffened nipples, softly at first, and then harder and harder until Anna gave out a little squeal. Her involuntary protestation produced a sardonic chuckle from the man. He placed one of his hands behind her head, drawing her face to his and seized her lips with his own. Anna felt his hot, thick tongue slide into her mouth as his free hand continued to worry her breasts and nipples. His clothes brushed up against the naked skin of her belly and their thighs closed together.

Anna felt a surge of lust erupt within her mixed with the shame of being so used in front of the other woman. Her hands, free to move, but locked behind her by the iron will of her master, writhed in a futile expression of her humiliation. She could feel her heat rising as Devlin's tongue scoured her mouth. His strength and power were sparking her desire. He was a handsome, attractive man, one who, had circumstances been different, she might have welcomed to her bed. His hard hand had a grip on her hair, holding her helplessly in place as he enjoyed her subservience. His free hand abandoned her breasts only to slide wantonly over her taut, bare belly and over the tops of her thighs.

Ann's heart was beating wildly when Devlin released her. If she thought that he was finished with her, she was wrong.

"Take off your bra and panties," he said churlishly.

Anna suppressed a moan of unhappiness. He was going to fuck her. She knew that. The thought of him piercing her with his inflamed, thick cock, making her moan with unwanted pleasure before the other woman, made her stomach churn. A wave of sickness spread through her. Seeing the stern confirmation of his command in her master's face, Anna moved to comply with his humiliating order.

Reaching back for the clasps of her dainty brassiere, her mind filled with a familiar misery, Anna unhooked it and let her breasts fall free. She laid the garment on top of her dress which was folded over the nearby chair. Her panties were beneath her lacy, black garter belt and she had to loosen the snaps that held her sheer, tan, silk stockings aloft before she could slide them down over her thighs and knees and step out of them. Keeping her eyes pointed at the thick, plush rug beneath her high heeled feet, Anna snapped the dangling straps of the garter belt back in place. Her panties lay on the floor next to her. Before she had the opportunity to crouch down and put them on the back of the chair, Devlin stepped forwards and reassumed command over her body.

She had known that the purpose of the accouterments that Elaine had purchased for her that day was to drive men's lusts and she realized as Devlin regained possession of her loose, heavy breasts and placed his lips once more upon hers that they had achieved their goal. Devlin pressed his body firmly against hers and she could feel his steel hard cock beneath his pants. Passively, she allowed the man to explore her mouth and now naked breasts, all the while trying desperately to fight back the sensations of lust that he was arousing in her.

He encircled her torso with his strong, right arm and took hold of her wrists which she had dutifully placed behind her. His other hand wandered over her belly, caressing the smooth, taut soft skin. Her heart fell as she felt the hand slide inexorably lower and lower until it intervened between her parted thighs and took possession of her naked, trimmed mons. The heat of his hand stirred her passion as he cupped the precious mound. She gave out a muffled, muted moan when she felt a finger trace the length of the divide between her engorging labia. It came to rest upon her stiffened clit and Anna felt her knees weaken as it toyed with the lustful appendage.

Anna had her eyes closed, trying to imagine herself anywhere else besides the center of the well appointed, well lit, civilized room. Her lips remained parted and she drew in a deep breath when Devlin's lips moved from hers and descended to take hold of her hardened, rigid nipples, one after the other, sucking on them intently, making her moan. She tottered on the edge of giving in to the lusts that were arising within her, ignoring the why and the how of what was happening to her, casting aside her reticence at exhibiting her wantonness before the burning eyes of the beautiful, young woman behind her. Devlin's hand probed deeply into her moistened crevasse, causing her to sigh.

"Turn around," she heard him say suddenly. She was shocked from her enthrallment. He placed his hands on her slender shoulders and guided her body until she was facing away from him. Elaine was sitting in her chair, lust in her own eyes. She had a thick tumbler of scotch in one hand while the other rubbed along her pretty thighs over her slinky dress. Devlin urged Anna forward until she was standing just in front of the beautiful, sultry woman. "Lean over and put your hands on the arms of the chair," he commanded coldly. Anna felt ashamed and depraved to be exhibiting her lust in front of the other female. She leaned over obediently, her heavy breasts swaying away from her body. Her face was inches away from Elaine's.

Anna heard the sound of Devlin's zipper lowering behind her. Her back was arched and her rear presented to the callous man. She felt a harsh slap on her exposed behind. "Spread your legs, stupid," Devlin said.

Cringing at the demeaning remark, shamed at her obsequious obedience, Anna complied with the rude command. Her ass stung where it had been struck. She spread her legs widely so that her quim would be rendered convenient for the man's penetration. She felt his hand caress her rear globes and then repossess her steamy slit, rubbing softly along her sensitized love lips, stroking softly her hardened and needy nub of pleasure.

"Kiss her and play with her tits while I fuck her," Devlin ordered Elaine. She had been staring into Anna's impassioned face with yearning of her own. She lowered her glass down to the table next to her and placed her hands on either side of Anna's head, caressing her hair and looking sweetly, but lustfully into her eyes. Anna had never been kissed by a woman, not in that way at least, and part of her revolted against it now. She trembled as Elaine's lips moved closer to hers and parted slightly, her tongue washing over them in anticipation. The hand in her loins was insistently driving her lusts and when her lips met Elaine's and the younger woman deftly slipped her long, languorous tongue into her mouth, Anna moaned with passion.

Elaine's lips pressed hard against hers as she explored her mouth. Her hands, gentle, soft, female hands, descended to Anna's naked shoulders and then slipped under her torso. Anna moaned again when they took hold of her free swinging mounds and began to caress them, gently, but firmly, massaging their bulk and then deftly, exquisitely, teasing her fat, rigid nipples.

Devlin's hand left her yearning sex and she felt the head of his cock probing at its entrance. She was overwhelmed with the combination of lust and shame that she felt as she awaited her impalement. Devlin's hands took their place on her hips and his cock began a slow, steady advance along her tender canal, causing a wave of pleasure to pass through her. He sank to her depths, fully inside her and began his motion. His cock dragged along her exposed point of lust, thrilling her. She moaned deeply into Elaine's energetic mouth and her body shook. The thick rod worked its way determinedly along her hot canal driving her further and further along the path towards ecstasy.

The subservient young woman was driven into a frenzy. She sucked hungrily at the tongue that filled her mouth and pressed her breasts into the hands that was pleasuring them. She rocked her hips against the thighs of her invader, encouraging his cock to move more quickly back and forth within her. The stiff pole relentlessly scoured her pussy's walls, dragging across her engorged, electrified clit. All her reservations about submitting to the man's rude, obscene demands passed away, subsumed by her growing lust. The hands that gripped her hips tightened and she heard the man who owned them and her groan lustily. When his cock began to jerk and spurt within her, it pushed her over the top and initiated the throbs and convulsions of her cunt.

"Mmmmmm! Mmmmmmmmm! Mmmmmmmmmm!" she called out as she came. Part of her pictured her obscene display in the cultured room, her nakedness compared to the finely clothed bodies of her assailants, her long legs, her upwardly pointing ass made more delicious by the lift of her high heels. But it was only a momentary flash of visualization, as her mind succumbed to the exquisite sensations of her climax.

Anna felt the rocking of Devlin's hips slow. The convulsions of her pussy faded into small, exciting echoes of her orgasm. Elaine reduced the tempo and intensity of their kisses and eased her massage of her naked, free swinging mounds. Anna gave a soft sigh as the cock that had driven her lusts softened and slipped from her slit.

CHAPTER FOUR

Anna's heart continued to beat wildly even as the lips and mouth that had been exciting her left her body. Elaine gave her a last, loose lipped, soggy kiss that sent a warm pulse of pleasure through her. Devlin was running his heavy, strong but soft hands over her rump and her naked back. The heat of his touch kept her body on a soft burn. She looked into the lust filled face of Elaine. The pretty model was stroking Anna's face with her left hand and had taken repossession of her glass of scotch with her right. She took a long sip of the amber liquid, keeping her eyes firmly fixed on Anna's.

Anna's body shivered with apprehension as to what Devlin might make her do with the younger, svelte woman. The taste of her lips was still on Anna's mouth and she felt shamed at the pleasure that the woman's tongue and hands had brought her. Devlin's hands circled round her torso and took hold of her dangling breasts, squeezing them firmly, his fingers pinching at her still stiffened nipples.

"You have a sweet cunt, Anna," he said. "It's too bad you don't know how to use it better. I think I'll have to get you some lessons. What do you think, Elaine, could you give my new whore some pointers?"

"Most certainly, Mr. Devlin," Elaine responded, an impish smile on her pretty face. "I'd be glad to."

"Would you like that, Anna? Would you like Elaine to show you how to fuck?"

Anna's mind revolted at the thought. She knew that Devlin expected an answer to his question. But should she answer it honestly or lie? Would he punish her for saying what he would be sure to know was a falsehood, or give him another way to shame and humiliate her by saying 'no'? But what was the truth? Elaine had shown her what a woman's knowledge of female pleasures could bring her. The thought of Elaine's tongue in her mouth, her soft, gentle hands flowing over her body gave her pussy a little twinge. Devlin's continued massaging and teasing of her breasts didn't help. But she wasn't a lesbian! She felt shamed at how the woman had made her feel.

Deciding that admitting her revulsion at girl on girl sex was better than being punished for lying, Anna responded to her owner. "No, Mr. Devlin," she murmured. She cursed herself for being unable to disguise the building passion in her voice as the hot hands on her breasts began to reignite her lust.

Devlin laughed. "Good girl, Anna!" he exclaimed. "You know better than to lie to me. But what you want isn't important anymore. If I want you to suck on Elaine's cunt you'll do it. Understand?"

"Yes, Mr. Devlin," Anna answered. Her stomach quailed at the thought of putting her mouth on a woman's sex. She could see the gleeful anticipation in Elaine's eyes. "Oh, god," she thought. She feared that he would make her do it now. What would Devlin do if she refused? There would be no money for the Center, that was for sure. But would he call Vincent in and have him whip her until she complied? Her passionate response to Devlin's fucking of her and the comfort she felt as his strong, hot hands wandered her body, extending her post coital bliss, had pushed from her mind where she was, what she was doing.

Suddenly, it all came back to her. Naked and prone in Devlin's elegant library, she was reminded of how he had debased her. She was his plaything, at least until Monday. Each step in her defilement at his hands had made it easier to submit to the next. She had invested too much to not let the game play out. Once the money had been deposited into the Center's account, things would be different. She could run or she could submit to the humiliation and shame of arrest for embezzlement. Until then, she was at Devlin's mercy.

Devlin's hands left Anna's burning breasts and he gave her a playful slap on her behind. "Get up, Anna, we're going out for dinner. I want you to wash out your pussy and put your dress back on. No sense staining it with my leaking cum. There's a bidet in the bathroom upstairs. Wash yourself out good and then come back here. And be quick about it. I'm hungry."

Anna stood and obediently placed her hands behind her back. Devlin had rung for Vincent and the butler appeared at the door to escort Anna upstairs. Dressed in only her garters and stockings, she followed him docilely into the hallway and up the long, wide, carpeted stairs to the second floor. He led her to a large, well appointed bathroom with a small bidet in the corner. Reluctantly, she turned on the water and, after removing her stockings and garter belt, squatted over it while Vincent stayed and watched.

The spray was warm and comforting and she closed her eyes to blot out the sight of the tall, fearsome man as she introduced the nozzle to her quim and let the water enter her. She tried to blot out the thought of Devlin's strange, callous butler, but his presence loomed over her. She could not drive from her mind Devlin's promise of a punishment to be experienced later and the fact that it would be delivered at this man's hands. A stone formed in her heart as she recalled the sharp, fierce pain he had induced in her that morning and she shivered.

There was a bar of creamy, scented soap next to the bidet and she lathered it in her hands and washed the outer lips of her sex conscientiously. When she had rinsed herself off, she opened her eyes again to see the butler staring at her coolly. She bit her lips to prevent tears coming to her eyes at her humiliation and fear. She stood and dried her loins with a large, fluffy towel and then, after redonning her scanty finery, followed Vincent back to the library.

When she entered it, her hands pressed together behind her, she saw Elaine squatting in front of Devlin. His cock was in her mouth and she was pleasuring him languorously. She had one hand resting on his thigh for balance and the other under the folds of her slinky, red, silk dress. Devlin's head was leaning back and his eyes were closed to slits. After a moment, he opened them and saw Anna's near naked form submissively posed, awaiting his pleasures.

"Mmmmmmmmmm," he sighed. He placed one hand on Elaine's head and pushed her back gently. "Enough for now, Elaine. I want to save all of my jism for Anna. Besides, we've got to get going." To Anna, he said, "I told you to get dressed. What are you waiting for?"

Anna cursed herself for forgetting how literal Devlin's instructions could be. She jumped at his reminder of her duty and walked over to where her panties were laying on the floor. When she bent down to pull her panties over her high heels, Devlin shouted at her.

"Are you really that stupid, Anna? Did I tell you to put on your underwear?"

Anna quailed at Devlin's hard, loud voice. "N-no, Mr. Devlin," she murmured back at him.

"Then why are you putting them on? Are you being purposely stupid or just disobedient?"

"Neither, Mr. Devlin," Anna squeaked back. "I just thought…"

"Your job isn't to think, Anna," Devlin retorted. "It's to do what I say. You've already earned three strokes of Vincent's whip before the night's over. You just earned two more. If you disobey me one more time, I'll have him take you up to the punishment room where you can spend the night. Is that what you want?"

Anna trembled at Devlin's threat and at the thought of the whipping she had coming. Tears filled her eyes. "No, Mr. Devlin," she answered. "I'll be good. I promise." She was standing in front of him, her panties still dangling from her hand. He was staring back at her expectantly. Panicked that she might have earned more punishment by her delay, Anna cast the soft, silken undergarment aside and picked up her dress. She quickly stepped into it and drew it up over her hips. She pushed her arms through the straps, shrugged her shoulders so that they could find their places, and then stood at attention before the man, her hands crossed behind her.

Her heart was pounding and her stomach roiled. It was just how she had felt when her father had ordered her around. His violence was random and drunken and she never knew when she would earn a blow from his powerful hands or a caustic stream of venom from his lips. She was helpless then and she was helpless now. She wanted to be brave, to steel herself against what Devlin was doing to her, how he was treating her, but something in her remembered how to act, recalled her unhappy tormented days of youth. It was like she was reliving them all over again.

Elaine had risen to her feet and, before they left, shot back the dregs of her scotch. The limo was waiting for them outside of the front door. The night was chilly, but the walk between the front door of the mansion and the rear seat of the long, warm, black luxury car was brief. Elaine got in first, then Anna, and then Devlin.

As the limo pulled down Devlin's long, meandering driveway, Elaine opened the bar and pulled out the bottle of scotch. It had some Scottish name that Anna was not familiar with, but she could see that it was very expensive. The model poured two inches of the dark amber liquor into a glass for Devlin and then two more, one for herself and one for Anna. Anna sat back and took a sip. The scotch was smooth and heavy, unlike any that she had ever had. She usually drank it with ice, but she admitted that it would have been a shame to dilute the rich, delicious flavor.

"Drink it all up, Anna, and then have another. I want you nice and loose. You're too tense."

Devlin's voice was soft and warm, almost friendly. She was surprised how quickly his moods changed. But she could not forget that it was the same voice that had promised her a whipping later tonight. She poured back the scotch obediently. It burned her throat had made her cough. She welcomed the rush of its effects, dulling her woeful thoughts, making her body tingle. Elaine quickly filled the thick, elegant tumbler with another two inches. "Bottoms up!" she toasted as she clinked her glass against Anna's. Anna took that as an order to quickly down her glass's contents and she finished it off in two, eager gulps. She handed the empty glass back to Elaine.

The rear compartment was flooded with the sounds of a classical symphony as they drove along. Anna welcomed its soothing tones, but she could not place it. Shuman? Schubert? Brahms? She couldn't remember. The turns of the violins were comforting, the rhythms of the percussions soothing. She leaned her head back and closed her eyes. She could feel the warmth of the bodies on either side of her. Her hands were on her thighs and the heat of her own flesh made her self conscious. Her loose breasts swayed as the limo made its turns along the country road. Her thighs were pressed together and she recalled that she was naked between them. Her skirt had ridden up when she sat down in the car exposing the tops of her sheer, silken stockings and the black straps of her garter belt. She hadn't had the courage to pull it back down. Available. That's how she felt. Either one of the people on either side of her could claim her flesh at any time. Her body was an instrument waiting to be played, just like the strings in the pleasing symphony flowing gracefully from the limo's speakers.

Anna felt herself slipping into slumber when she heard Devlin's harsh voice. "What are you doing, Anna?"

She was startled into immediate wakefulness. "Nothing, Mr. Devlin," she answered trepidatiously. What had she done now?

"Your, hands, why aren't they behind your back?"

Anna's heart sank. "I-I...," she started to answer.

"You better start listening to what I tell you, Anna, or I'm calling this whole thing off. Do you understand?"

"Y-yes, Mr. Devlin," Anna replied. Her lips were trembling. He couldn't call it off, not after what she had already been through! He just couldn't! She snaked her hands behind her and leaned back on them obediently.

"That's better," Devlin said calmly. He patted her thigh with his large right hand.

Anna tried to fight back her tears as she worried that she had earned herself more punishment. She remembered Vincent's cruel whip and the burning pain that it had caused her. She felt a tear roll down her check and she sniffled, trying not to cry. Devlin was staring straight ahead, disregarding her distress. Elaine, however, took pity on her.

"Oh, honey, you'll mess your mascara," she said sympathetically. She pulled a tissue from a dispenser built into the seat in front of them and gently daubed her eyes until they were dried. "There, there, now," she said softly. "You'll get used to it. Everything will be okay. I promise."

Anna welcomed the pretty woman's kind words. Would she get used to it? Would everything be okay? If only it were true. How could she ever get used to the chill that ran through her body every time that she heard Devlin's voice? The feelings that he had resurrected in her, of her inadequacy, her shame at her body's lusts and the meek and servile way that she had given herself over to his demands, it had taken years of therapy, oceans of tears, for her to suppress them, overcome them, once before. How would she deal with them now? What would be left of her after a year of service to this controlling man with an insatiable sexual appetite?

Elaine had poured Anna another glass of scotch. "Come on, honey," she said sympathetically, "it'll do you good."

Anna obediently opened her mouth to let the soothing, mind numbing liquid enter her. Elaine poured it slowly, but steadily over her lips, and Anna swallowed it gratefully. Elaine put the glass back down and dabbed Anna's lips with the tissue she had used to wipe away her tears. She caressed Anna's cheek gently and turned her face toward hers. "You're so pretty, Anna," she said, her voice husky, laden with lust. She pressed her lips to Anna's and gave her a soft kiss. Once, twice, she married them together, sucking at Anna's air. Anna felt her womb contract as the warmth of Elaine's lips transferred to hers. The third time that their lips met Anna felt the young woman's tongue gently beg entrance to her mouth. She spread her lips and let it slide between them.

Anna's head was woozy with the effects of the scotch. She let her body relax as Elaine's nimble tongue inflamed her. She swooned as the heat of her loins spread through her body. Her hands pressed against her back felt sweaty and hot. When she felt Elaine's hands take hold of the straps to the bodice of her dress and slide them across her shoulders and down her arms, lowering her bodice to her waist, she gave a small whine of protest which was converted to a moan when the young woman's hand took possession of her heavy, engorged breasts, one at a time, each in turn, massaging them lovingly, teasing and pinching her hardened nipples.

It was wrong. Anna knew it. She wasn't a lesbian. She had no lust for women. Nonetheless, a woman's tongue was driving her passions, her hand was fueling her lust. She moaned in half protest when she felt Elaine's hand slide down over her tummy and come to rest upon her thigh. A spark of resistance flamed within her. She remembered where she was, that Devlin was sitting next to her, that the coarse looking, Latino driver could certainly see her in the rear view mirror if he chose to look back.

Anna's brief inclination to resist Elaine's impassioned attack on her body faded quickly when she felt Devlin's heavy hand on her other exposed thigh. The two hands, one hard and firm, the other gentle and urging, spread her thighs apart. Anna felt her dress move higher on her thighs. She moaned with a combination of lust and self pity when the woman's hand slid up underneath it and began to probe the entrance to her moisture laden crevasse.

As her hand deftly and purposefully excited her quim, Elaine shifted her lips from Anna's mouth to her breast. Anna sighed with lust as the attractive young woman sucked on the nipple, flitting her expert tongue across it. Anna had her eyes closed, reveling in the exquisite sensations the woman was bringing her. A car passed them coming in the other direction and the headlights briefly lit up the interior of the limo. Anna opened her eyes reflexively and saw the eyes of the chauffeur peering back at her through the rearview mirror. A flood of shame passed through her even as the hand and mouth of her female tormentor drove her lusts higher and higher.

"You really are a slut, Anna," Devlin said tauntingly. "I think that I've done you a favor. How did you live with all of that lust penned up inside you?" The man's hand gave Anna's thigh a tight squeeze.

The cruel voice pierced Ann's haze of lust and booze. She knew that she had to answer him. He had asked her a question. Elaine had shifted her mouth to her other breast, sending a new wave of warmth through her body. "I, I don't know, Mr. Devlin," Anna answered softly. Elaine's finger was teasing her hardened love button. She felt the tell tale signs of her orgasm rising. Her hips shifted and she moaned again.

"I don't want her coming all over her dress, Elaine," Devlin said curtly. "Give it a rest."

Elaine's lips abandoned Anna's tingling, excited breast and gave Anna's pussy one last caress before she reluctantly withdrew her hand. "Okay, Mr. Devlin. I was just keeping her warmed up for you. She's hot." She gave Anna a kiss and leaned back in her seat. She picked up her glass from the cup holder and took a long drink of scotch.

Anna's blood was boiling with her arousal and her pussy yearned for completion. Her breath was heavy and she felt her face flushed. Devlin's hand was still on her thigh and its hot presence was tantalizing. Her thighs remained widespread and her loose, naked breasts swayed, their points tingling.

The rest of the ride was accomplished in silence but for the sonorous sounds of the unknown symphony. Each time a car passed them going the other way, Anna was conscious of her exposure to the eyes of the driver who looked back to take in her revealed womanhood. She wanted desperately to raise the straps to her bodice to cover her breasts, but she knew that she dared not move without Devlin's permission.

As the car sped through the night to their unknown destination, Anna leaned her head back and closed her eyes to block out her embarrassment and shame. Her mind, befuddled by the booze, began to wander. She wondered idly what Devlin's hold on the pretty model was. He had gotten her out of a jam, but what kind of jam? Did he have the same power over the lithe, beautiful, young woman that he did over her? Had Elaine at one time been put through the rigors of control and domination that she was enduring? Would she, Anna, someday be so corrupted as to act so free and easy while Devlin exploited and abused another hapless, female victim? Was Elaine her future?

She hoped not. She remembered the vision of Elaine squatting before Devlin in his library when she returned from the bathroom, blithely sucking his prick, her hand buried in her loins, her long, thin, elegant, brown hair falling down her back. Would Anna someday too take as second nature the idea that Devlin owned her body and soul?

Anna's unanswerable musings drifted away. Her lusts had cooled and she surrendered to the pressure on her thigh from Devlin's heavy hand. She let the rhythm of the traverse of the long, black limo over the country road lull her into thoughtlessness.

Anna perked up when she felt the car slow and heard the sound of its blinker clicking steadily, signaling a turn. They entered a narrow driveway bordered by two large, dark, stone towers. The driveway was overhung by tall, bare trees and they traveled along it for about a half mile before coming to a gate. The driveway split and they pulled up next to a booth staffed by a man in a brown uniform with a security badge on his chest. The area was well lit and

Devlin rolled down his window. The driver opened his window and showed the security guard some kind of pass. The guard peered into the limo. "Oh, hello, Mr. Devlin," he said politely. His eyes rested briefly on Anna's naked breasts. The man pushed a button and the gate rolled open. When the limo started to pull away from the booth he added, "Have a nice time."

They drove another quarter mile before pulling up to a large, sprawling mansion. The entranceway was lit by spotlights and Anna could see the Tudor like design of the building. It had three floors in the center and spread out to two story wings on either side. A middle aged man uniformed like a eighteenth century servant, his long, grayish hair pulled behind his head in a ponytail and topped with a bright red, tri-corner hat, opened the door to the limo. He was wearing a long, red coat with gleaming brass buttons. Anna suppressed a squeal as her bare breasts were exposed to him. Devlin seemed to recall her nakedness and before he stepped out of the limo he ordered her to, "cover your self up." Anna gratefully pulled the straps to her dress back up over her shoulders and followed her master out of the limo. Elaine got out last.

The entranceway was lit as if for a gala and Anna followed Devlin hurriedly up the steps so as to avoid the cold. She detected a knowing smirk on the face of the doorman as she passed him and, for a moment, she imagined that he was going to give her a lascivious pinch on her behind. Another servant, similarly clad, opened the large, heavy, solid wood doors to the mansion and Anna was glad to be inside. If Devlin's mansion was luxurious, the interior of this one was triple that. The walls were of dark, polished wood and large, colorful tapestries depicting medieval scenes were hung on the walls. The floors were covered with a plush, burgundy carpet so thick that she had to walk carefully on her high heels so as not to slip. A heavyset, rotund man dressed in a finely tailored, black tuxedo greeted them.

"Good evening, Mr. Devlin," he intoned respectfully, "your guest is waiting for you in the bar."

"Thank you, Owen," Devlin replied perfunctorily. He led the women past the cavernous entranceway a short walk down the hall and into a dark, wood paneled room redolent of cigar smoke and the odor of burnt wood. There was a large fire blazing in a fireplace and men sitting around it in large overstuffed, leather easy chairs. They had drinks in their hands and gave Devlin and his party a cursory glance before returning to their conversations. A pretty young woman dressed in a revealing, maroon, short skirted, cocktail dress, long, sheer stockings on her legs and wearing tall, bright red high heels, stood obsequiously by the side of the fireplace, apparently waiting to serve them. The girl, who had long, brown hair tied up in a ponytail behind her head, caught Anna's eyes for just an instant and then looked hurriedly away.

The bar was semi-circular and hewn from a dark oak. It had a brass rail a few inches from the floor and round, black, leather covered barstools. A silver haired man who looked to Anna to be in his late fifties was sitting on one of the stools and nursing a clear liquid in a martini glass. The bartender, dressed in a bright white shirt and a large, old fashioned red cravat, had been speaking with him. He nodded respectfully to Devlin. "Good evening, Mr. Devlin. The usual?"

"Why not, Henry," Devlin answered. "And Rob Roys for the ladies. Straight up."

"Right away, Mr. Devlin."

Devlin turned to the man who had been waiting for him at the bar.

"I'm glad you could make it Harrison. Let me introduce my two companions. The tall drink of water is Elaine. I've told you all about her."

"Nice to meet you, Mr. Harrison," Elaine said cheerfully as she extended her hand. "Mr. Devlin didn't tell me you were so handsome."

Handsome was a good way to describe him. His age wore on him well and he was fit and tall. His face had strong, sharp features and his suit bespoke culture and money.

"No, it's my pleasure, Elaine," Harrison returned. To Anna, he seemed to hold on to Elaine's hand just a little too long. His eyes wandered over her flesh appreciatively. "Mr. Devlin's description did not do justice to your charms."

"Why, thank you, Mr. Harrison," Elaine returned sweetly. "I've been looking forward to meeting you too."

"This is Anna," Devlin added once the other man finally deigned to release Elaine's, long, soft hand. "She's what you might call my protégé."

Anna's heart jumped into her throat. For a moment, she thought that Devlin was about to describe her as his whore. To be called a protégé seemed surreal after what she had been through with the man.

Harrison reached out his hand and took Anna's proffered one. "Happy to meet you," he said. He wore an ironic smile as he spoke. His hand clasped Anna's just a little too long, with just a little too much firmness. His eyes wandered down from her face to the tops of her breasts displayed by the low, loose bodice of her dress. Anna became conscious that, from where he stood, he was at least seven inches taller than her, he could see directly down her dress. His eyes lingered at her displayed beauties for a few moments and then continued downwards, taking in the swell of her hips and the long expanse of thigh revealed by her tight, short skirt. Anna pulled her hand away as gracefully as she could and murmured a polite reply. She had been given no instructions on how to behave while out with Devlin and she didn't want to commit any more crimes that would warrant further punishment.

The bartender brought their drinks and Devlin handed Anna hers. The liquor was a pleasing amber and sat in a tall, long stemmed, cocktail glass. There was a bright red cherry floating at the bottom.

"Drink up Anna," Devlin told her. "We're celebrating tonight. Mr. Harrison has been accepted by the membership committee of the club. He's to be inducted next week."

Anna raised her glass slightly in perfunctory congratulations and took a long sip. The vermouth gave the scotch a sweet taste. It made the mixture flow down quite easily. She welcomed the surge of numbness that followed it. If Devlin wanted her drunk, she was perfectly willing to comply. Even in this rarified, sumptuous atmosphere of Devlin's exclusive club, she felt demeaned and ashamed. She wondered what she would do if he ordered her to strip right here in front of everyone. Would she do it? A couple more drinks and she just might.

The high security of the club environs disturbed her. What was so special about it that it needed a security gate and a high, steel fence around it? Its size bespoke more than a bar and restaurant. She realized that she was as much a prisoner here as she was in Devlin's mansion. Never mind the fact that she had no idea where they were and had no car, she would have to pass through the gate in order to get out. Before that, she would have to get past the randy doorman. She shivered at the realization of her powerlessness and took another large sip of her drink.

Devlin and Harrison sat next to each other with the women on either side of them. They were engaged in an animated conversation about something or other. Anna wasn't paying attention. She was ruminating about her strange fate and how easily she had slid into abject obedience to Devlin and his servant. There was an odd comfort in it, as if having all of her decisions taken away from her had relieved her of the stress of adulthood.

The barstool was high and she had hooked one of her heels into a rung when she sat down. Her skirt had ridden up, exposing the top of her stockings and about an inch or so of her garter strap. She shifted her bottom in order to pull the hem of the skirt down. When she looked to her right, she saw that one of the men sitting by the fire had caught her gesture and was smiling lasciviously at her. She turned her head back away from him and concentrated on her drink.

Devlin was drinking a tumbler of neat scotch. He tossed it back and announced that it was time to eat. He led the party to the dining room across the hall from the bar. It was small for such a large club, with maybe twelve or so tables. About half of the tables were full. Out of the twenty people there, only a few of them were women. They were mostly young and fancily dressed, much like Elaine was. A tuxedoed *maitre d'* led them to a table in the corner. The table was lavishly set with elegant crystalware and fine china. Devlin took the seat in the corner and Anna sat to his right. Elaine sat across from her.

The dinner was first class all the way. After a round of elegant appetizers, Devlin ordered a fresh trout entree for her and Elaine and a thick filet mignon for himself. Harrison followed Devlin's lead. Their order was taken by the *maitre d'* but delivered by pretty, young women dressed in long, billowing skirts and tight bodices that exposed the upper portions of their breasts. There was something peculiarly servile about them. They never spoke and walked around the tables with their eyes downcast. Midway through their dinner, Anna thought she saw one of the men at another table caress one of the girls' thighs as she leaned over him to retrieve his empty plate.

Elaine fawned over Harrison throughout the meal. Having seen the pretty model in action throughout the day, Anna detected the false charm that she was emitting, but the man either did not or did not care. He seemed enthralled by the young woman's beauty. Elaine seemed to do everything she could to keep his attention, placing her hand on his arm when they spoke, smiling almost lugubriously at his efforts at witticism. Anna watched as his arm drifted under the table from time to time and Elaine's facial gestures gave evidence both that he had placed it on her thigh and that the familiarity was welcome.

Harrison apparently was well aware as to who Anna was. He asked her a series of questions about the work of the Center, where the girls came from, what they did while resident there. She answered him automatically. It disturbed her that he already knew so much about her. Making a deal with the devil to save the Center was one thing, but having everyone know about it was another. Anna had worked long and hard to win the respect of the powers that be, other social workers, the members of the Board of Trustees. The point of accepting sexual bondage to Devlin was to avoid the humiliation and shame of public exposure of the embezzlement at the Center. Had she exchanged one evil for another?

Her concern over how much Harrison knew was justified when Devlin explained exactly who he was.

"Harrison is the president of your bank, Anna. I've told him that you will be depositing $225,000 in cash in your account on Monday. He's arranged it so that there will be no problem. You wouldn't want too many questions asked, would you? Too many questions might result in an investigation and then all this would have been for nothing. We wouldn't want that to happen, would we?"

A cloud crossed Anna's face as she took in the fact that Harrison was aware of the theft of the money. Did he know the bargain she had struck to replace it, what she had become? Who would he tell?

Devlin took notice of the shadow that had crossed her visage. "Don't worry, Anna," he said. "If Mr. Harrison wasn't the very soul of discretion, he wouldn't have been accepted as a member of our little club here. What you need to think about is how you're going to thank him."

Anna's body experienced a chill as she tried to decode Devlin's meaning. The banker was looking at her with a gleam of expectation in his eye. "No way," she thought to herself. She rebelled at the implications of Devlin's statement. For now, she decided, she would play along. After the money was in her account, well that was another story.

She gave her best effort at a smile. "Thank you, Mr. Harrison," she said as sweetly as she could.

"Don't mention it," he replied.

By the time dinner was over, Anna was half in the bag. Devlin had ordered several bottles of wine and insisted that she drink her fair share. His hand had drifted to her thigh from time to time throughout the meal and taken owner-ship of it. It was a stark reminder of her obligations to him and a clear intimation of what was in store for her later. Despite the fine dining, the luxurious décor of the restaurant, the amiable, social company, Anna could not for a moment lose focus of the fact that she was here as

Devlin's prisoner, that she was his slave, that he could do anything he wanted with her.

After a rich dessert and cognac all around, Devlin announced that it was time to go. He signed the check that the *maitre d'* presented to him and the two couples sauntered out of the dining area, the glow of gustatory fulfillment over them. Elaine leaned heavily on Harrison's arm as they entered the hallway. Loud music was coming from behind a set of large double doors as they passed them. A plaque on the wall above them announced in bold, blue script that it was the entrance to 'The Blue Cantina'. Anna saw Elaine give a furtive glance at it and look away. A dark cloud passed over her face momentarily. The next second, she was gazing up at the elegant banker, all evidence of her momentary disquietude having passed.

Two men, laughing and with happy expectant faces, entered the apparent nightclub as Devlin and his group passed, nodding their greeting to the millionaire and his guests. When the door opened, a blast of heavy, pounding, rhythmic music was emitted. When it swung closed behind them, the music subsided into a dull, smothered beat.

There was a wide, heavily carpeted stairway further down the hall and Harrison and Elaine paused at the foot. Devlin reached out and shook the banker's hand. "Have fun," he said to him. And to Elaine he said, "I'll see you later in the week."

Elaine released Harrison's arm and stepped forward, proffering her lips to Devlin. They kissed and then she took Harrison's hand in hers urging him towards the stairs. Harrison gave a complicit smile to Devlin and followed her.

Back in the limousine, Anna felt frightened to be alone with her tormentor once again. While Elaine's presence had not been exactly comforting, it had at least given her the feeling of some protection against Devlin's worst impulses. For a while, they rode in silence. Anna had placed her arms back behind her as per Devlin's earlier instructions. She kept her knees pressed together and she leaned her head back against the seat. Devlin had taken out a cigar and was smoking it.

After a while, he seemed to be reminded of her presence in the car with him.

"Did you enjoy your dinner, Anna?' he asked her politely. His voice pricked at her through her alcoholic haze. She looked over at his expectant, handsome face.

"Yes, Mr. Devlin," she murmured.

"Then I think that you should show your thanks," he returned. "Come over here and suck my prick."

Jolted back into her new life as Devlin's whore, Anna moved to comply with his wishes. There was enough room on the broad, comfortable seats of the limo for her to kneel up next to him. His legs were spread but his fly was unopened. She looked beseechingly into his face for directions. She didn't want to touch him without permission.

"Go ahead, Anna. You can't suck it while it's in my pants. And if you need to use you hands for balance, you can put one of them on my thighs. But once you get my cock out, I don't want anything touching it except your mouth. Keep the other hand behind your back. And pull up your dress. I want to play with your cunt while you suck me."

Distressed by the man's polite but insistent demands, Anna pulled the hem of her dress up over her hips, exposing her bare bottom and the sex between her legs. She leaned over and eased down the fly to Devlin's pants and tentatively placed her hand in the gap that appeared there. He was wearing a pair of silken boxers and she was able to free his warm, soft tool. As she was preparing to place her trembling lips upon it, Devlin gave her another command.

"Pull down the straps to your dress in case I want to play with your tits," he said coldly. Anna obediently knelt back and dragged first one and then the other of the straps to her bodice over her shoulders and down her arms. Her pretty, flowery, earth toned dress was now bunched around her waist like a huge belt. Her breasts swung obediently free. She was conscious of the driver in the front seat and how she must appear to him. She resisted the impulse to look in the rearview mirror to see if he was watching her, and bent over to her task. She placed her right hand on Devlin's strong, muscular thigh and her left behind her back as she had been instructed. She drew his cock between her lips. It had been hardening in anticipation of her attentions and it was soon stiff and fully extended inside her.

Devlin gave a soft sigh as Anna washed her lips over his rigid pole. He had his cigar in his left hand and ran his right over Anna's exposed buttocks. Anna's head was swooning from the effects of the liquor she had consumed and the smell of Devlin's cigar. How much different was she than the tube of fine tobacco he was drawing on with his lips, she thought. She was a thing to be used, existing only for his pleasure. When he was done with her, would he cast her away, all used up, like the butt end of his smoke? The fact that he had made arrangements with the banker, Harrison, for the deposit of the money was reassuring, however. It made his promise to save the Center more real. She tried to concentrate on why she was here, why she was doing what she was doing and let all other concerns fade away.

The hard meat rolled over her active tongue and to the back of her mouth. She drew her lips up slowly, swirling her tongue over the shaft, conveying the warmth and delicate sensations of her lips and tongue to the fleshy spear. Devlin's hand was rubbing her sensitized skin on her rear mounds and her loins responded to his caresses despite her shame. She felt his fingers drift across her love lips which were pushed together by her closed thighs. She thought of the thin line of hair around them and of how they must appear, two long, rounded bulges of soft flesh between the rear of her naked, exposed thighs. Devlin's fingers probed at the entrance and rather than wait for instructions, she spread her thighs wider so that he could have full access.

Devlin chuckled. "That's a good girl, Anna. You're learning. Spread you thighs like a good whore so I can get inside you."

Anna cringed at the appellation, but did not interrupt her task of pleasuring Devlin's stiff joint. She felt his fingers slide between her tingling love lips and, taking advantage of the nascent moisture there, slip between them and enter her. She gave out her own sigh of pleasure as his fingers coursed gently over her needy pleasure bud.

"Don't let me come, Anna, no matter what," Devlin ordered as he stroked Anna's pussy. His thumb was implanted deep inside her, coursing in and out, and his fingers played with the hardened nubbin at her pussy's apex. She felt her juices flowing. It was hard for Anna to concentrate on the state of Devlin's prick as he drove her lust higher and higher. Every once in a while, when her breathing became heavy and her moans louder, he withdrew his hand and caressed her buttocks or slid his hand under her chest to caress and tease her breasts and nipples. The third time, when the hand returned, he pushed her on further and further until she felt her crises looming. "Mmmmmmmm!" she moaned, her voice muffled by the thick, stiff wad of flesh in her mouth. "Mmmm-mmmmmmmm!"

"That's it, come for Daddy, Anna. Let your cunt take hold of you," Devlin teased.

At Devlin's words, Anna's crevasse exploded into a series of hard, pleasurable throbs. Her thighs squeezed together, pressing her pussy's energized walls against the thick finger that moved inside. Her breasts ached with their fullness. Overwhelmed by the electrified jolts that passed through her, she ceased her efforts at Devlin's prick, unable to coordinate the strokes of her lips with the pleasure that flowed from her womb. She held the cock fast between her lips as she moaned and groaned at each fierce spasm of her flush, hot chasm.

"You're a hot piece of ass, Anna," Devlin taunted her once the more violent of her pussy's spasms had passed. He eased the teasing of her still vibrating cleft, letting her lusts subside to a low burn. "We're going to have a lot of fun together. Now get back to sucking my cock."

Anna's spasms of pleasure had subsided to mere echoes and she dutifully returned her attentions to the hard prick between her lips. Her body was filled with a suffusing warmth. When she was able to reestablish a rhythmic, dedicated pleasuring of the thick wand of meat, Devlin resumed his attack. He had softened his touch in deference to her spent orgasm, and now slowly, but surely, built to a more hastened pace as her passion began to build once more.

By the time they pulled up into the driveway of the Devlin mansion, he had made her come three times. Her body felt wrung out from her blasts of pleasure. She had been careful, while Devlin was plowing her pussy with his long, thick fingers, or teasing and pinching her stiffened, fat nipples, to gauge his build up of lusts lest she should err and make him come before he was ready. When the limo pulled to a halt before the front door, Devlin withdrew his hand from her loins. He placed the remnant of his smoldering cigar in the ashtray next to him.

"Okay, now, make me come, slut," he ordered her churlishly.

Anna obediently accelerated her attentions at his prick. Her jaw was tired as a result of her prolonged efforts and her arm was stiff from holding herself suspended over his lap. His hand pulled and squeezed her breasts as he got nearer and nearer to completion. His moans of pleasure were loud and undoubtedly easily audible by the driver who had remained in place in the front seat.

Anna knew that it was far past the time that she should be concerned about what he knew or witnessed. She had groaned and moaned loudly each time that she had come, unmistakable evidence of what was going on in the back seat. Somehow, however, his sitting calmly in the front seat, the car's engine idling, patiently awaiting his employer's signal, renewed Anna's sense of shame. Devlin had called her a whore right in front of him. Well, if she wasn't a whore, what was she doing blowing Devlin in the back seat of his limo, naked but for the bunched up fabric around her waist?

Devlin gave a mighty groan as his cock began to pulse and jerk within Anna's mouth. His spunk flooded it and she drank his jetting spume down dutifully while maintaining the strokes of her lips and the dancing of her tongue on the soft textured, stiff pole. Devlin's hand was on her head and he had grabbed a tuft of her hair. He pressed her head down hard and pushed his throbbing cock deep into her throat. Anna began to cough and sputter as her airway was cut off. She tried desperately to pull her head back, but Devlin's grip was too strong.

"Oooooooommmpf! Oooooooooompf!" she called out through her stuffed mouth in protest. Her air was getting short and she struggled to free her throat of the pulsing, throbbing mass that filled it. Her left hand, which she had obediently kept poised behind her throughout her ordeal, came forward and, using both of her hands, she tried to push herself away from her tormentor. But Devlin's grip was too strong. She cried and sobbed as her lungs screamed for sustenance. Finally, giving out a loud, prolonged, satisfied sigh, his forces spent, Devlin lifted her head from his crotch, pulling his tormenting cock free.

Anna strained to rush air into her lungs. Her chest heaved and she coughed and sputtered. Devlin still had hold of her hair in his strong, right hand. He shook her head violently. "Don't ever do that again, cunt!" he yelled. "When I shove my cock down your throat you'll keep it there and like it! You've got a lot of learning to do, bitch! You've just earned yourself another three strokes of Vincent's cane. How many is that now? Ten? You're going to be one sorry cunt in a little while! Do you want to earn some more?"

Anna struggled to gain enough breath to speak. She was overwhelmed with Devlin's onslaught of anger and violence. It was horrifying to her how quickly the man could go from a semblance of civility to cruel, vicious abuse. Ten strokes? "Oh my god," Anna thought. "I won't be able to stand it." She reached down inside her and managed a pitiful response to Devlin's question.

"No, Mr. Devlin, please no!" she protested, miserable at her callous treatment and the thought of what ten strokes of a cane would feel like.

"Put you hands behind your back where they belong!" Devlin shouted. Anna complied hurriedly. Her hair was aching terribly where Devlin had a hold of it, her nerve endings shrieking with pain. At some signal from Devlin, the driver arose from seat and opened the rear door of the limo. Devlin moved to get out, tugging Anna behind him. There was a blast of cold air on her near naked body as she struggled to follow him, her hair still in his angry grasp. He pulled her from the rear seat gradually until she was able to place first one and then the other of her feet on the ground. Then, keeping her bent over, her hands joined behind her, he dragged her up the steps to the front door.

Vincent was waiting there. After he closed the door behind them, Devlin gave Anna a shove and she tumbled to the cool, slate floor. She gave out a cry as she fell.

"Take off that stupid dress!" Devlin shouted.

Anna, afraid of further torment, rapidly complied. She turned on her hip and frantically pulled the dress down over her knees and then her high heel clad feet. Her lips were trembling and tears were flowing down her face. "Please, Mr. Devlin, don't hurt me," she whined. "I'll do whatever you want. Please."

"Shut the fuck up, Anna," Devlin returned. "Get up and put your hands behind your back!"

Anna quickly complied. She cringed before the angered, callous man. He reached to the floor and picked up her expensive, elegant dress. Taking it in his powerful hands, he tore a long strip from it. He quickly rolled it up into a ball, discarding the ruined remnant. "Open you mouth, slut," he ordered curtly.

Anna unhappily spread her lips. Devlin took the roll of fine fabric and stuffed it in her mouth. He pushed and prodded it until her oral cavity was fully packed. "When are you going to learn to shut the fuck up, cunt," he said angrily. "That's two more strokes. An even dozen. Want some more?"

Anna felt like her whole psyche was going to collapse. Her body was shaking from fear. Her knees felt weak and she felt like she was going to pee all over the floor. Her face was contorted with dismay. Her mouth was distended as wide as it could go. "Oh, i-er e-in," she moaned piteously through her gagged lips.

"Take her upstairs and mount her on my bed," Devlin order his servant. "I'll be up in a little while."

Vincent gave his master a small nod and turned to Anna. "Come," was all he said.

Knowing that she had no choice, Anna followed the tall, dark visaged servant up the stairs. Her chest was heaving from her sobs. "How will I ever survive?" she thought to herself miserably as she ascended the staircase.

Glad to be out of reach of the evil millionaire if even for a little while, Anna, naked now, hurried to stay up with the butler as he strode purposefully before her. It seemed unreal to her that she had voluntarily put herself into Devlin's cruel power, that she was moving of her own volition, if not free will, to whatever dismal experience the man had in store for her next. It was like she was on automatic, her mind having lost the ability to rebel against her treatment. Her pussy was still wet and oozing from his manipulation of her lusts in the limo and her breasts still tingled with the residue of her spent passion. Her stomach felt tight and queasy and her heart was pumping at a hundred miles an hour. Her hands were sweaty behind her back. Her mouth bulged from its stuffing and her weak knees were making her wobble on her pretty high heels.

When they reached the top of the stairs, they turned left and walked down to the end of the hall. A large, heavy wooden door stood at its terminus. Vincent opened it and stood back, inviting her in.

The room was cavernous and filled with manly, heavy furniture. There were 8' high, curtained windows and a dark blue, shag carpet. The bed was huge, with four finely carved dark oak posts at its corners. There was a tall, ornate headboard against the wall. Several elegant prints of luxuriant, erotically posed women lined the walls, which were covered by a light blue and gold wallpaper. A large chandelier hung from the middle of the ceiling and half moon, translucent sconces were mounted around the room.

Anna had only a few seconds to take in the sumptuous décor. Vincent pointed to a door opposite the bed. "Use the toilet," he said coolly.

Anna's bladder was near bursting and she happily entered the expansive, luxurious bathroom. The walls and floor were white marble and the fixtures were plated in gold. Keeping her hands behind her, she sat on the toilet and peed. Vincent, as was his custom, stood over her, watching, as if he needed to make sure that she complied with his command. Anna could not stop crying, although her sobs had subsided to sniffles. She looked up at the butler, hoping to see a modicum of sympathy for her plight. She saw none. Only the cold, hard face of the man who was going to, sooner or later this evening, administer twelve hard strokes to her body with a cane.

When she was done, Vincent wiped her pussy dry and flushed the commode. He had her stand next to him while he washed his hands. Anna could see herself in the large, gold edged mirror over the long, white marble vanity. Her lips were pursed and spread widely by her makeshift gag. Her jet black hair was mussed and her eyes were swollen and red. Her mascara had run and there were two dark lines descending from her eyes like a sad clown's makeup. Her golden earrings, dangling on each side of her face, seemed brassy and false. She was ashamed to be still wearing them. Foolishly, she had adorned herself with the bright baubles in the hopes of making herself seem more attractive, more sophisticated. Now they seemed just to accentuate her whoreishness.

The bright light made her olive brown skin seem wan and pale. She was a piteous sight although she knew she would not be shown any pity by these cruel men. Was that really her in the mirror, she thought sadly. Or was it someone else, someone who had been hiding in her for many years? Was the subservient, obsequious, servile Anna she saw in the mirror the real one, or was it the brave, independent, self actualized one that she had constructed? Something told her it was the former rather than the latter. Her life had changed over the last two days. Something had broken in her and she knew that she would never be the same.

Vincent ordered her out of the bathroom. Her heart heavy with dismay and shame, she obeyed and stepped back into the sumptuous boudoir. Vincent moved to the head of the bed and pulled down the covers, revealing a golden hued set of silk sheets. "Take off your shoes, your garter belt and your stockings and get on the bed," he ordered the frightened, young woman.

Anna moved immediately to obey his command. She quickly released the clips that had held her stockings aloft on her slender, well trimmed thighs and rolled them down her legs. She had to bend over to unbuckle her high heels and take them off her feet and her round, full breasts swayed and jerked as she struggled with them. When they were off, she unhooked the garter belt behind her and let it drop to the floor. Then, keeping her hands dutifully crossed behind her, she crawled up onto the wide expanse of the bed.

"Turn your head to the top of the bed and bend over on your knees," Vincent ordered. Anna turned her back to the cold, efficient man and bent over so that her breasts were crushed against her thighs, her hands slavishly crossed behind her.

"From now on, when I bring you here and order you on the bed, this will be the posture you assume," Vincent explained coolly. "Do you understand?"

Anna was overwhelmed with fear and unhappiness. She nonetheless managed a reply muffled through her stuffed mouth, knowing that failure to answer could bring down additional punishment. "Eh, ir," she answered, her voice whiny and child like.

"Stay where you are," Vincent ordered.

Anna kept her face pressed down in front of her, too afraid to look up and see what the servant was doing. She heard a cabinet opening and what she thought was the rattle of chains. When Vincent returned to the bed and leaned over it, she saw that she was right. A chill ran through her at the thought of being chained to the bed. "Oh, god!" she thought to herself desperately. "What is he going to do?"

The servant looped one end of the chain through a ring low in the middle of the headboard and then brought it up about three feet higher where he connected it to a metal clip embedded in the wood. The other end of the chain had a pair of steel handcuffs attached. "Give me your hands," Vincent ordered.

Trembling, her heart sinking, Anna moved her hands slowly from behind her back to above her head. She watched as Vincent locked each of her wrists in the handcuffs. When she looked up, she saw that although the chain could easily be released where it was connected to the dark oaken headboard above her, the fact that her hands were locked low near the ring at its base meant that she could never reach it. She gave out a whine as she saw how securely she was imprisoned on the bed.

Vincent disappeared for a moment more and returned with another length of chain. Reaching underneath her, he connected one end of the chain to the link in the middle of her handcuffs and ran it below her, under her breasts and down between her legs. The chain formed an inverted 'Y' and at each end of it was a bright, shiny, steel manacle. Anna whined when she felt her ankles encapsulated by them.

Vincent retreated from the bed and stood for a moment admiring his handiwork. Anna was panicked at her now helpless state. Her rear was proffered deliciously and the confinements on her ankles prevented her from extending her legs. Her hands were joined together in front of her, her elegantly decorated fingers inches from the head board. She tested the bonds, pulling at them sharply. They made a metallic rattle. The sound was harsh, cold, and bespoke the futility of struggle. She turned her head, whining her dismay, fully expecting to see a cane in the man's hand. Was she going to be beaten now? "Oh, god, please no!' she thought desperately.

But the man did not have a cane in his hand. Instead, he had a narrow, black cloth. Near the middle were two rounded indentations. It was a blindfold. Anna's belly turned over when she saw it. She was to be returned to the helpless darkness she had experienced that morning, a time that seemed like eons ago. She wanted to cry out in protest, but she knew that the man would pay her plea for forbearance no mind. Not to mention that her muffled mouth would only be able to produce a grotesque simulacrum of speech. She moaned nonetheless when he crawled up back onto the bed and placed it over her eyes.

After he had tied it off behind her head, he told her coldly, "Put your head down on the mattress and spread your legs."

Sniffling, her body trembling with fear, Anna placed her head between her outstretched arms and pushed her ankles as far apart as the 18" of chain between them permitted. Her breasts were squeezed against her thighs and her chin rested between her knees.

"Stay like that until Mr. Devlin comes," the man ordered. "You've already earned a dozen strokes of the cane. If you continue your disobedience, I'll think of something more painful to whip you with."

Anna sobbed at the threat. What could be worse than the cane? Her mind reeled with the dreadful possibilities. She decided that she would not do anything that would make her find out.

Anna's body gave an involuntary jump when she heard the door close. The room descended into a deep silence. She gave out a fierce, mournful moan of self pity. "Oh god! Oh god! Oh god!" she exclaimed to herself. The darkness and silence surrounded her like a suffocating blanket. The only real sensations were the harsh coldness of the steel bonds around her ankles and wrists.

The chain that ran from her handcuffs to the manacles around her ankles pressed into her forehead. She chewed unhappily on the large wad of insulting, demeaning fabric that filled her mouth, desperate to expel it, but made no effort to do so, knowing full well that if somehow she managed it, there would be a terrible retribution. Her mind reeled with the vision of how she would appear to Devlin when he entered the room, her pussy peaking out from her widened thighs, her rear posed in obscene presentation.

She wanted to cry out to someone to help her, to free her from the implacable confinements that Vincent had placed upon her and which rendered her, for all practical purposes, immobile. She thought of the clip above her that held the chain that was connected to her wrists. Anyone could come in and easily free her. But she could not free herself, could not lift her hands more than a few inches from the mattress. She shifted her hands slightly and was rewarded only by the dreadful rattle that they made.

Anna's sobbing soon faded into a dismal, hopeless state of fear. She hated her powerlessness, her reduction to a plaything for the heartless millionaire, her grotesque, demeaning confinements. How long would she have to wait before he came into the room and took advantage of her helplessness? His stiff, thick cock would pierce her proffered love lips. He would make her moan and shake with passion. She was filled with self detestation at the memories of how he had driven her to lust so many times in the last two days, how she had obsequiously sucked his cock and spread her thighs for him.

The waiting was the hardest part. When he finally came into the room and commenced his torment of her flesh, she would suffer shame and humiliation at her responses, rue her inability to prevent her desires from overflowing. But waiting, knowing what would happen once he put his hands on her, made her stomach churn, her heart ache with sorrow.

Anna had no way of telling how long it was when she finally heard the door opening. It seemed a long, long time, time that was spent by her in dreadful apprehension of the man's appearance but also in a lust driving anticipation of her upcoming use. All sensations of sight and speech denied her, her mind kept returning to her opened sex behind her and the use to which it would be put.

The heavy door deadened all sound from the hallway and she had not heard the man's approach. She gave a start when the latch to the door turned and suppressed a sob. She heard Devlin's footsteps cross the room and come to a halt at the foot of the bed. She felt his cold, hard eyes pouring over her naked, exposed rear. She expected to hear some taunt, some insulting reference to her sluttishness, her wantonness, but the man remained silent. The next thing that she heard was the sound of him stripping off his clothes, the light thud his shoes made when he kicked them off, the unfastening of his belt and the lowering of his zipper.

After a few moments, Anna felt the mattress shake slightly as the man crawled up onto it. She felt the heat of his body as he moved up next to her. She heard his heavy breath and smelled the manly odor of his flesh. A hand made contact with the taut, smooth skin of her back and slid gradually down it until it reached her plump, soft, rear mounds, caressing them. Slowly, with the confidence of ownership, it slid back up until it reached her shoulders. The hand felt hot on her skin and made her body tingle with expectation. She found that she was shivering and she yearned for the man to begin her torment, to take away the razor's edge of anticipation. She was surprised when he finally spoke.

"You have a beautiful body, Anna," he told her softly. "Your skin is smooth and hot. I'm going to enjoy owning you for a year. You've hidden your voluptuousness under your prim, social worker exterior, but you're nothing more than a lusty slut. Have you been thinking about my cock while you've been waiting here, Anna? Is your pussy hungry for it?"

Anna heard the questions, loaded with contempt despite the soothing, gentle tone in which they were rendered. She struggled over her answer, knowing that if she refused to reply, even though her voice would be muffled and faint due to the fabric that filled her mouth, the erratic, unpredictable man might explode into fury. The heat of his hand had stirred her desires and she had felt the sensation of her cleft moistening. If she lied and told him no, he might add to her punishments. All he had to do was place his hand on her quim to discover her falsity. But by admitting her slavish yearning to be filled, wouldn't she be admitting everything that he was saying about her, that she had always been a sluttish whore just waiting for someone to claim her?

Her heart breaking with shame, Anna decided to tell the truth. Her pussy did yearn to be filled. She had been thinking of his conscienceless cock all the while she had been kneeling here, prone and helpless.

Tears filling her blinded eyes, Anna murmured a disconsolate, "Eh, i-er e-in."

"Good girl, Anna," Devlin responded. His hand was still wandering her distended back. The sound of his genuine approval brought Anna a wave of relief. She felt like a burden had been lifted from her. Her wantonness was no longer a secret. She had admitted it to her owner, her master, and to herself. She could give in to it now without remorse or shame. It was who she was, that's all, and there was nothing to be done about it.

"I'm going to fuck you, Anna," Devlin said gently. His hand drifted over the roundness of her buttocks and descended to the gap between her thighs. "I'm going to give you what you want and you're going to moan and cry out with pleasure. You're my whore now, Anna and I'm going to make the most of it."

Devlin's hand had passed over Anna's needy crevasse and she gave out a soft sigh as she felt the strong, thick fingers tease its opening. Her whole mind was concentrated on the meeting point between Devlin's body and hers: his insistent, rigid fingers and the outer surface of her proffered, near hairless slit.

"Raise yourself up a little bit, Anna," Devlin told her. He slid his left arm under her torso and pushed her body up. She had to shuffle her confined feet forward so that she could straighten herself. Her hands were pulled down in front of her, limiting her ability to kneel straight, but she was able to rise far enough so that her heavy, blood filling breasts swung free.

"That's it, Anna," Devlin told her. "I want to caress your breasts." He cupped her left mound and squeezed it gently with his free hand. His finger played across her stiffening nipple and then he pinched it lightly. He shifted his hand to her other breast and did the same, drawing a low moan from the confined, sightless woman.

"Do you like it when I play with your breasts, Anna?" he asked. "Does it make you hot, make your pussy water?"

His fingers had penetrated between Anna's tingling, engorged labia. The invisible hands that were manipulating her flesh were stoking her needs. Each time Devlin pinched her stiffened nipples a wave of excitement flowed through her. The fingers of his right hand, buried in her pussy, teasing her nubbin of pleasure, had created a suffusing warmth from her loins that was spreading through her body.

"Eh, ih-er e-in," she sighed through her filled mouth. Her effort at speech reminded her of how her face had appeared in the mirror in the bathroom, her lips spread and pursed like a fish, the wad of cloth distending them clearly visible. Was she still a human being? Did the cruel millionaire perceive any aspect of her humanity, her right to self determination, to preserve some part of herself, some remnant of dignity? She doubted it. But did she deserve any considerations for her individuality when she succumbed so readily to his demands, fulfilling his pernicious descriptions of her? Devlin gave her right breast a hard squeeze, sending a twinge of pain to her and she moaned with sexual excitement.

Devlin maneuvered himself behind her. She could feel his strong, muscular thighs on either side of hers. His hands reached around her torso and grabbed her breasts. His chest was hot up against her back and she could feel his hardened manhood, his meaty weapon, laying amidst the divide between her soft, rear globes. While his left hand continued to massage and squeeze her breasts, his right hand drifted over her belly, the inside of her widespread thighs. He ran his thick fingers along the separation between her engorged, excited love lips and then back over her thighs and belly again, driving the confined young woman's passions to an intense need.

He kissed her neck and back as he explored her body. His hot tongue and lips brought a thrill to Anna's skin. She pulled, involuntarily, at her bound hands below her in automatic need to seize and attenuate the hands that were tormenting her. She was being driven wild with desire, a desire liberated by Devlin's scurrilous treatment of her.

Devlin retook possession of Anna's plush, dilated quim and began to stroke her parted love lips, dragging two thick fingers along their divide and teasing and rubbing on her pleasure bud. Anna began to moan as she felt her lusts rising to a crest. Her breath had become heavy and her body was quivering in anticipation of her impending explosion. Devlin placed his mouth next to her ear. Through her lusty fog she heard him whisper conspiratorially.

"Have you ever been fucked in the ass, Anna?"

The nonchalance of his statement startled her. She hadn't considered that use of her body and her mind revolted, amidst her impassioned fog, in silent protest.

"I'll bet that you'd enjoy it," Devlin continued in a deep, soft voice. "I'm going to fuck you there now. Do you want me to fuck your little brown star, Anna? Would you like that?"

A wave of trepidation passed through Anna at the man's question. She had never been fucked there before. In spite of all that had happened to her in her youth, that was one indignity that she had not suffered. The thought of it appalled her, the idea of being used like a boy, her femininity ignored, a pathway chosen solely for the pleasure of her abuser. Through her impassioned state, her pussy yearning with the need of completion, she revolted at the man's coarse, callous expression of his intent.

"Oooooooh!" she moaned plaintively past the moist, demeaning mass of fabric in her mouth. "Eeeeeease ont! Eeeeeease!" She pulled desperately at the chain that bound her hands in place. "Eeeeeease ont ooo at, eeeeeease!"

"Oh, I'm going to fuck you there, Anna. I love ass fucking and we're going to do a lot of it. Do you like being my whore, Anna? Did you think it was going to be like this?"

"Ooooooooo!" Anna moaned unhappily. Devlin's hands were still tormenting her body, his hot torso pressed up against her. She tried to fight off the excitation that he was bringing her to no avail. He had withdrawn his hand from her pussy and was stroking her inner thighs and belly while massaging her breasts. She teetered on the edge of explosion. Her blinded vision, the darkness that surrounded her, made it seem that her tormented flesh and the hands and body that were exciting her were the only things in the world.

"You know that you are a whore, Anna, don't you?" Devlin continued to taunt her. "A whore gets paid for sex. You're getting paid to fuck me. That makes you a whore. An expensive one, but a whore nonetheless. You are a whore, aren't you Anna?"

Anna burned with shame as she realized the truth of what Devlin was saying. She was a whore. "...es! ...es!" she moaned miserably.

"If I fuck you 10 times a week for a year, Anna, that makes about 500 fucks. At \$225,000 that makes it over \$400.00 a fuck. That's fair, isn't it? For 400 bucks I should be able to do anything that I want, shouldn't I?"

The truth of Devlin's perverse calculations was self evident. Anna could do nothing but moan at the thought of submitting to the millionaire's coarse, insistent demands over 500 times. But the thought that he was about to perform an act upon her she considered perverse and illicit permeated her mind. She rejected his salacious equation. "Eeease ont uck eee ere! Eeease!"

"Oh, its coming, Anna. I'm going to fuck your pretty little ass and there's nothing you can do about it," Devlin answered. His hand had resumed its torture of her quim and Anna could not prevent a moan of pleasure escaping as her clit reverberated at the callous man's touch.

"First, I'm going to get my cock good and wet, Anna. Bend over and give me your tight cunt to fuck."

He placed his hands on her shoulders and forced Anna to resume her prone posture. He pulled her knees back until the chains that confined her ankles were stretched to their limit. Keeping one hand firmly pressing down on her back, forcing it into an arch, he took hold of his thick, rigid meat and guided it to her moist hole. He pushed his hips forward and his cock slid easily inside her puss.

Anna gave out a great sigh as she felt the hot prick pierce her sopping, needful divide. The rasping of it's movements across her bud of pleasure made her body quake with need. Devlin fucked her with long, hard strokes. Her hands twisted in their confinement and she bit down hard on her messy, mouth filling gag.

The callous man had kept her tottering on the edge of her orgasm and the relentless thrusting of his hard wand pushed her over the edge. "Oooooooooh! Oooooooooh! Oooooooooh!" she moaned as her pussy contracted hard on the insistent cock. Her body tightened into a compact mass as the pleasure of her pussy's spasms shot through her. Devlin's hot hands were on her back wandering over her taut skin. She could feel his hips slapping against her firm, round rear globes. "Oooooooooooh! Oooooooooooh!" she moaned again.

Devlin slowed his thrusts as Anna's orgasm faded. Her heart was pounding and she was snorting through her nose to catch her breath. "Good girl, Anna," Devlin said. "You've got a nice hot, tight cunt. It's a real pleasure to fuck it." His cock's movements within her were now languid and easy, giving her pussy small, sharp echoes of her climax. But while the cock's torment of her sex slowed, it did not stop. Gradually, the pace picked up again and Anna's passions began to burn anew.

"Here we go again, Anna," Devlin said mockingly. 'I'm going to get you all steamed up again and then I'm going to sink my dick in your ass. Get ready for it."

Anna wailed at the man's expression of intent even as the increase of pace of his thrusts within her pussy made her body yearn for more and more. "Uuuuuuuummm! Uuuuuummmm! Ummmmmmmmm!' she moaned as she felt her need grow hotter and hotter. His rock hard prick went on and on, scouring the walls of her canal, rasping along her hardened, tingling clit. Suddenly, the thick cock vacated her steamy space. She moaned and yanked at her bound wrists in protest. Devlin's powerful right hand pressed her hips down, while his other spread her rear cheeks, readying his target. She felt the fat, bulbous head press against the virgin opening.

"Here it comes, Anna," Devlin announced. He had taken hold of his piece and he pressed against the small, brown opening. "It's going to hurt like hell, but you'll get used to it."

Anna gave a loud moan of dismay as she felt the head of Devlin's cock begin to breech the entrance to her bowels. It slid along smoothly, coated by her cunt's mucousy discharge. But its ease of passage did not assuage the tearing of the tissues that surrounded the tiny entrance and Anna howled behind her gag as the pain emanated from her delicate anal ring and coursed throughout her body.

"Ooooooh, eeeeeease! Ih urs! Ih urs!" she screamed through her gag.

"Of course it hurts, Anna," Devlin retorted. "But once we get your asshole nice and stretched, you'll find out how good it can feel."

The cruel millionaire slowly sank his cock deep with Anna's tortured bowels. When he was encapsulated to its hilt, he slowly eased himself back out again until the head of his cock was just poised within the entrance. "Ahhhhhhhhhh," he said. "You're ass is tight, Anna. And it's so hot inside." He paused his exploration of her bowels for a moment and then slowly and steadily eased himself forwards once again. "Ohhhhhhh yeah," he moaned as he sank deep back inside her.

Anna was mortified by his perverse possession of her. She could feel her tears flowing from her blinded eyes. She had never experienced anything like the feeling of the thick, long, conscienceless prick in her ass. It was a strange, unignorable presence. Her anal ring burned as the cock brushed along it. "Ooooooooh!" she moaned.

Satisfied that he could come and go with ease, Devlin began a rhythmic thrust within Anna's small, rear entrance. "Oh that's good, that's good," he kept exclaiming. He reached his hand around Anna's hip and took repossession of her quim. He began to rub her sensitized clit, spreading her cunt's moisture over it, flicking it with his fingers, pinching and squeezing it. To Anna's dismay, she felt her juices begin to rise once more. The friction of the steely cock over her anal ring had started to produce a strange tingling sensation. As the hand continued it work between her outspread thighs, she felt like she was going to come.

"Oh, no! No!" Anna thought. She didn't want to come this way. Devlin would never let her forget it. It was too perverse, too strange.

But the pleasurable sensations continued to grow. "Uhhhh! Uhhhhh! Uhhhhh! Uhhhhhh!" she moaned at each hard, now frantic thrust of Devlin's cock. Her face had been pressed down on the mattress. The strength of the passions flowing through her caused her to raise herself up on her elbows and tilt her head back. He hips involuntarily thrust back at the cock that was driving her lusts. She tried to press her pussy down on the knowledgeable hand that was teasing her sex. She felt it coming, her climax, and her body shook. She bit down on the balled up fabric in her mouth. "Mmmmmmmmmmmmmmm!" she called out loudly. "Mmmmmmmmmmmm!"

Devlin's moans had turned to grunts and her moans were a signal for him to release his passions. "Oh, yeah! Yeah!" he yelled as his cock began to spurt and jump inside Anna's bowels. His hands seized her breasts and squeezed them hard, using them to anchor his thrusting loins, as if they had been put there just for this purpose. His torso was draped over her back. It felt to Anna as if a demon had taken possession of her. His climax sparked Anna's own release and she shuddered and quaked as her pussy throbbed and pulsed. It was like nothing she had ever experienced. Her whole body felt like it was coming. She could feel the pulsing of Devlin's cock as it slipped back and forth across her sensitized anal opening. "Mmmmm-mmmmmmm!' she shouted. "Mmmmmmmmmm!"

Devlin's motions behind her began to slow and Anna's orgasm started to fade into echoes. A mesmerizing haze enveloped her. Devlin's body was limp and she could feel the heaving of his lungs and the beating of his heart on her back. When he had regained his senses and his cock lost its hardened form, he rose and slipped it from her. She felt her rear opening gaping in memory of her recent possession.

Devlin rubbed his hot hands the length of her taut back. "That wasn't bad, Anna. You really got into the spirit of the thing," he said coolly. His voice was calm and collected, but Anna could hear the satisfaction in his voice, the rise and fall of his recovering breath.

Giving her ass a friendly rub, he eased himself off of the bed. Anna heard him go to the bathroom and begin rinsing himself clean at the sink. Her rear opening burned from its defilement and her heart was still beating wildly. She had placed her forehead back down on the mattress, resting it between her outstretched, confined arms. Her thighs were tired and aching and she longed to stretch them out. The man had, at least temporarily, ceased his assault on her, but she was still his bound, blinded and silenced prisoner.

CHAPTER FIVE

Anna felt shame and was filled with self recriminations for her wantonness. The man had used her in a profane, perverse way and she had delighted in it. Devlin had been right. When she had agreed to his salacious bargain, she had never imagined that she would be chained and gagged on his bed, that her abuse would be so total, that she would feel so demeaned and humiliated. It was as if she had fallen into a nightmare from which she could not awaken. The cold, steel bindings on her ankles and wrists bespoke a stark reality incongruous to her dreamlike state. Two weeks ago, if anyone had suggested that she would willingly submit to being anyone's sexual slave, she would have bristled with ire. She was overwhelmed with how fast her life had changed, how quickly had been the descent into her baser nature.

From her confined position on the bed, Anna heard Devlin using the toilet. While he was pissing, the door to the bedroom opened. She heard Devlin's voice echoing from the bathroom. "I'm done with her for the night, Vincent. Take her upstairs and give her her punishments before you put her to bed."

Anna experienced an icy chill at Devlin's words. The dreaded punishments that Devlin had prescribed for her were finally at hand. She clasped her tiny hands into fists and emitted a woeful whine of self pity.

Wordlessly, Vincent crawled on to the mattress and unclipped the chain from the headboard. He drew it though the ring in the wood just above Anna's hands. A knot formed in her stomach as he guided her off of the bed and to her feet. Her body was tired and worn from her sexual ordeal, but her mind was alert, her senses heightened by the knowledge that she was soon to experience suffering at the butler's hands.

Devlin had come out of the bathroom. Anna's hands were still bound by the handcuffs in front of her and her blindfold still blocked her sight. Her knees were weak and her throat had become dry. She wanted to beg and plead with the man to spare her. She knew though that talking, or attempting to talk, since her mouth was still obscenely stuffed, would worsen her fate. Devlin stepped up to her and seized one of her breasts in his hand.

"Are you frightened, Anna?" he asked mockingly. "You should be. Vincent is an expert with the cane and twelve strokes is a lot to take. But don't worry, he'll take his time so that you can feel every one. Maybe tomorrow, you'll do better." His voice changing from a taunting tone to one of command, he said to Vincent, "When you have her mounted, bring down the other one."

"Yes, Mr. Devlin," Vincent replied.

Anna burst into sobs when she felt the pull of the chain on her hands signaling her duty to follow the butler to her fate. Why did she have to be beaten? She had done everything she could to follow Devlin's rules. She would be good! He didn't have to punish her!

But no one asked Anna for her opinion. She blindly followed Vincent's lead past the door to the bedroom and down the hall. Her feet were bare and the rug below them was soft. Her chains rattled and clicked together as she walked. She had to adopt a shuffle to her steps to avoid tripping on the chain that led from her ankles.

"Bring down the other one," Devlin had said. Anna recalled the footsteps she had heard in the hallway outside her room. They were indisputably from someone wearing high heeled shoes. During the day, she had wondered idly if they had belonged to Elaine. She had never gotten up the courage to ask, put off by Elaine's statement that she shouldn't ask too many questions about Devlin's activities.

But Elaine was back at the club with the banker. So it must be someone else. Some other woman was also serving time as Devlin's abject prisoner! The realization that she was sharing the house with another woman who was suffering as she was, treated as a sexual toy, a lowly whore, brought no relief to the frightened woman. What kind of man was Devlin, she thought. Did he have a whole bevy of women in his power forced to serve his sexual whims? What did that portend for her? Maybe it meant that her abuses at his hands would be limited. After all, if he had other women to torment and rape, maybe his use of her would be assuaged.

He had said that he would fuck her 500 times over the next year. If he had other women to play with, maybe his interest in her would swiftly wane. She could only hope. In the meantime, she recalled as she was propelled blindly down the hall, she was on her way to be whipped.

When they reached the stairs to the upper floors, Vincent slowed so that Anna could manage them without falling. Her vision blocked by the dark, black cloth over her eyes, she had to estimate the distance between each stair. Her bare breasts bobbed and swayed as she struggled not to fall. She made careful, deliberate steps to avoid tripping. She could hear the lose chain between her feet dragging on the wooden steps. The higher they went in the mansion, the greater grew her fear. When they reached the top floor, her stomach was in knots and her heart was beating wildly. They passed down about fifty feet along the hall, past where the door to where her room should have been. When they came to a stop, she heard Vincent fiddling with some keys and then the unlocking of a door. A moment later, he pulled her into the room on the other side.

Anna shivered when she heard the door closed behind them. She was led a few feet deeper into the room. The hardwood floor was cool on her bare feet. Vincent released the chain that connected her ankles to her handcuffs and she sensed him stepping on up on what had to be a stool. There was the sound of the links in her chain running through some kind of a ring and then her hands were pulled up over her head. When they were fully outstretched, the steel of the handcuffs biting into her wrists, she heard Vincent move the stool and the sound of him clipping the end of the chain off to something.

When Vincent returned to where Anna was standing, her arms outstretched above her, he took the end of the chain that led to her manacled ankles and ran it through a ring in the floor between her feet. That too was pulled taut until her feet were drawn together and immobile. The butler returned to where Anna was standing helpless and untied her blindfold from behind her head.

The room was large, about fifteen by twenty and the walls were covered with mirrors. Anna saw her abject reflection all around her. The steel of her handcuffs and manacles glinted in the mirror. Her breasts were drawn tight by her outstretched posture. She could see the terror in her eyes.

Vincent's reflection was everywhere. He walked over to the wall where Anna saw an array of whips and what looked like riding crops and canes mounted on hooks. He seemed to study them for a moment and then picked off of the wall a three foot long cane with a shiny, dark brown, leather handle. It was about an inch and a half around and made of finely polished, light colored wood. He brought it over to where Anna stood.

Anna felt her knees weaken and her stomach rebel when she saw the implement of her upcoming abuse in the man's large, boney hand. She moaned from fear. She could feel the sweat starting to pour off of her body. Her throat was dry and tears were running down her face. She had never been so frightened in her life.

"This is the punishment room," Vincent announced matter-of-factly, his voice echoing off of the cold, reflective walls. "This is the cane I am going to use to beat you with. I will be back in a few minutes. In the meantime, you can study it and think about the costs of disobedience."

Vincent took the stool and stepped up to the ten foot high ceiling. There was a hook there and he looped the leather handle of the cane onto it. When he stepped back, Anna could see it swinging back and forth in front of her. The tip of the cane was about level with her eyes. She stared at it with fear in her heart as Vincent stepped quickly from the room.

The sound of the closing door echoed through the mirror encased room. A feeling of deep sorrow and loneliness spread through the frightened woman. She tried frantically to free her bound hands, but could not slip the handcuffs over the heels of her hands. She pulled at the bindings on her feet. Out in the hall, through the door, she heard another door open and close. A minute later there was the sound of Vincent's footsteps followed by the unmistakable sound of a pair of high heeled shoes negotiating the wooden floor of the hallway. Her mind quickly calculated how much time she had before her ordeal would begin. Two minutes, three? Maybe five at the most.

Anna looked around the room frantically. Her own eyes peered back at her from the mirrored walls. Her face was distorted by her gag, her eyes were red rimmed. She could see the ends of her chains running along the ceiling and floor behind her to their termini. Her body, curvaceous and appealing, was reflected everywhere she looked. She could still see the three red stripes Vincent had placed upon it this morning and wondered, fearfully, what she would look like when he was through with her tonight. The cane that Vincent had selected appeared in the mirror a few feet in front of her. It had stopped swaying and hung there motionless like a harbinger of her fate.

A chill ran through her body as she looked at herself and the cane reflected together. Then, up near the ceiling, in the corner of the room, she saw a small camera, a copy of the one in her bedroom. Its red light was on and it peered down at her. Her miseries were to be recorded. No doubt to be played later for the amusement of Devlin and his friends. There would be a permanent record of her agonies. It was doubtful that the cruel butler would shirk his duties to apply excruciating pain to her body when he knew that his boss might be watching.

A wave of dreadful fear overwhelmed the young woman and she renewed her futile efforts to free her self. The echoes of her whines of fear and the clattering chains bounced off of the mirrored walls. She was still desperately struggling when she heard the sound of Vincent's steps on the stairs.

As the steps drew closer, Anna began to cry. When the door opened and Vincent stepped in, closing it behind him and locking it, her sobs turned into wails. He looked at her dispassionately and then removed his jacket. He hung it on the hook from which he had taken the cane and turned back to her. Deftly, he took hold of the dangling cane and lifted its handle free of the hook in the ceiling.

Seeing the cane in Vincent's hands again caused Anna to lose all control. "Eeeeeas on't eat eee! Eeeease!" she called out through her gag. "'ll ooo nytin! Eeeeease! Eeeeease!"

Vincent's face showed no reaction to her pleading. He stepped up to her and took hold of the gag that filled her mouth, pulling it free. He placed the balled up fabric in his pocket. Anna coughed and sputtered as her mouth was liberated. She returned to her piteous imprecations.

"Please, Sir! Please don't beat me! I'll be good! I'll do anything you say! Please!"

Vincent raised his free hand and placed it over Anna's mouth, stifling her pleas. "In this room, you are allowed to beg and plead all that you want, Ms. Addunizio. Feel free to scream as loudly as you like. It will help you remember the pain and your suffering."

When the cruel servant removed his hand from her mouth, Anna resumed her pleas. Her voice was lower now, supplicative. Somehow, the butler's use of her last name made her surroundings and what was about to happen to her more surreal. Was she Anna Addunizio, or some abject sex slave? Or was she both? She hated herself for her weakness and servility. Her mind raced with the hope that she could say something, offer anything, that would make the cold, passionless man deviate from his master's instructions.

"Please, Sir," she whined. "Please don't beat me. I'll suck your cock. I'll let you fuck me. I'll do anything you want. Please, just please don't beat me."

Disregarding Anna's plaintive words, Vincent stood back from her and swung the cane through the air. It made a fierce 'whoosh!' as it sped rapidly in an arc. The sound made Anna even more frantic. Her voice was raised now.

"Oh, please don't do this! Please! Please!" she called out. Vincent's only response was to begin to circle around her. She turned her head and saw his reflection in the mirrored wall as he passed behind her. She saw his hand draw back and saw the cane begin to rush towards her flesh.

"Oh, god, no!" Anna called out. The collision of the sturdy, thin cane on her flesh made a 'cracking' sound that resounded throughout the room. A line of fiery pain erupted across her plump, round buttocks.

"Awwwwwwwgh!" Anna called out. "Oh, god, that hurts!" she screamed. "Please don't do it again! Please!"

"One," Vincent announced. He waited a few moments and then raised his arm again. "Ohhhhhhh!" Anna yelled in anticipation of the pain to come. This time the cane landed on the backs of her thighs. "Oh! Oh! Oh!" Anna screamed. "Oh, that hurts! Please stop! Please!"

"Two," Vincent intoned.

Anna sobbed and cried as the pain from the strokes of the cane burned into her flesh. She saw Vincent circle around to her front. When his arm reared back, she closed her eyes and clamped her mouth shut to try and suppress her upcoming cry of pain. The cane crossed the front of her thighs. It felt like a knife had been drawn across them. Anna's mouth burst open and an involuntary scream poured out. "Ahhhhhhhhh! Oh! Oh! Ohhhhhhhh!"

"Three," Vincent stated coldly.

Anna's body was trembling and shaking in her bonds. Burning pain emanated from where she had been struck. Her muscles carried the aching memory of the weight and speed of the cane where it struck her so forcefully.

Vincent waited until Anna had recovered a small degree of equanimity. Her face was contorted with anguish. It was wet with tears and her mouth turned down in a pitiful frown. Devlin had cruelly suggested that she would be given time to enjoy each blow she was to receive and she saw that his servant was insuring that his prediction would come true. She wanted it to be over, wanted the pitiless man to assail her in a flurry of repeated, rapid blows so that her suffering would be foreshortened. It was not to be.

Vincent waited calmly for about a minute before he prepared himself to deliver another blow. Anna was surrounded by grotesque images of herself, distended and helpless. She closed her eyes to try and blot them out, but could not keep them shut, fearful that she would not receive warning of the next, cruel insult to her flesh. He was standing in front of the distraught woman and slightly to her right. Anna saw where his eyes were directed. "Oh, god, please! Not my breasts! Please don't beat my breasts! Please!" she yelled frantically. Disregarding her frantic request, Vincent swung the cane behind him and brought it forward rapidly. It landed across the very tips of Anna's outstretched mounds.

"Ahhhhhhh! Ahhhhhhhh! Ahhhhhhhh!" she screamed. "You bastard! You cocksucker! Ohhhhhhhhhhh! Ohhhhh-hhhhhh!" The pain from the blow had driven the poor young woman past the point of all rationality. As the immediacy of the pain subsided, she suddenly regretted her outburst. What was she thinking? Calling him names and cursing him would only make it worse. "Oh, I'm sorry! I'm sorry! I didn't mean it! I'm sorry!" she pleaded frantically.

"Four" was all that Vincent replied. He brought his arm back and landed a blow across Anna's tender, flat belly.

Anna continued to scream and plead for mercy as the beating continued. After each stroke, Vincent called out the number loudly and coolly. He proceeded in sets of three, giving the dismally unhappy woman time to recover after each set. Anna alternated between screams and pleas and curses and deprecations against her assailant. Each time that she caught herself denigrating his ancestors, his birthright, asserting his subhuman status, she corrected herself and begged for forgiveness. Whatever she said, how loudly she screamed, how much her body contorted and struggled to free herself or avoid the blows, Vincent's demeanor and pace remained exactly the same.

By the time the twelfth blow landed, Anna's mind had gone somewhere else. She was blubbering and moaning and, despite Vincent's careful pacing, oblivious to its effect. It took her a few moments to realize that her ordeal was over. She looked at herself in the mirror and saw her body covered with long, red stripes. She had peed herself at some point and she noticed the wetness of her inner thighs and the puddle around her feet. Her throat was sore from the effect of her screams. She hung almost lifeless in her bonds, disregarding the painful burning in her wrists as they supported her weight.

Vincent quietly and coolly removed his jacket from the hook on the wall and replaced the cane. He put his jacket back over it. His shirt was drenched with the sweat of his exertions. His face, however, remained dispassionate. He stepped away from the dangling, young woman and entered a closet that had been built into the wall. The door had been covered by the mirror and was almost imperceptible to a cursory glance. Anna heard the sound of water flowing into a pail. A moment later, Vincent emerged from the room with a plastic pail filled with sudsy water in one hand and a large, coarse cloth in the other. He placed the pail by Anna's feet and, sinking to his knees, proceeded to sop up the spillage from her bladder.

The pungent smell of disinfectant rose from the floor to Anna's nostrils, arousing her partially from her stupefied state. When Vincent was satisfied that the floor was clean, he took each of Anna's feet and carefully washed the bottoms and swiped the outline of where her feet had been placed on the floor. Anna almost laughed amidst her misery at the butler's punctiliousness. Of course he wouldn't want her soiled feet to walk about spreading germs and dirt. He was the master of the house and all that occurred there fell within his domain, even to the tiniest speck of dust.

After returning the pail and the soiled cloth to the closet, he retrieved and redonned his jacket. He then stepped behind Anna and released the chain that held her ankles in place. Standing on the stool, he released the end of the chain that held her hands aloft from its hook. Anna felt her body sag as the tautness in the chain was relieved. She would have fallen had Vincent not held on to the chain, keeping her hands above her until she was able to regain her balance. He then slowly let it run through the ring in the ceiling until it was free.

Anna's mind was dull from the results of her torture. A heavy tiredness flowed through her as if all of her energy had been discharged through her screams and yells of pain. As if in a dream, she followed Vincent's lead as he pulled on the chain that led to her confined wrists and guided her to the door. He unlocked it and she shuffled after him out into the hallway and down to the door to her room. He unlocked it and led her in.

He took her directly to the bathroom. She stood there listlessly as she heard him start the shower. He waited for the water to become hot. He then turned and, with a small key he drew from his pants pocket, unlocked the bindings around her wrists and ankles. They clattered as they fell to the cool tile floor.

Anna obediently stepped into the hot flow of water in the shower. At first, the water stung her in the places where she had been kissed by the cane, but soon the warmth of the water began to sooth her. She was surprised when Vincent, stripped to his shirt, his sleeves rolled up, leaned in and took the head of the shower from its mounting. It was connected to the wall by a three foot long hose. "Put you hands on your head," he ordered.

The tired, dispirited woman complied obediently. Vincent ran the warm water from the hose over her head and then all over her body. There was a large, soft sponge and he squirted some soap into it and proceeded to wash her. His hands were gentle and tender. He spread the soap over her body with the sponge and then caressed and massaged her skin with his bare hand. He cleaned her pussy thoroughly as well as the crevasse between her rear cheeks.

Anna let the sensation of his ministrations to her body begin to comfort her. The man took care to pat her wounds softly with the delicate sponge. He had her turn around and did her back. Anna closed her eyes and tried to imagine herself somewhere else, that someone else's loving hands were caressing and massaging her body. She knelt dutifully, her hands behind her, while he washed and rinsed her hair and proffered her face so that he could wash off the remnants of her makeup.

When he was done, Anna stepped from the shower and stood docilely while he dried her body. Again, he was careful to deal delicately in the areas of her bruising. He dried and combed her hair. Placing the comb down on the vanity, he opened the medicine cabinet and withdrew a tube of antiseptic cream. He carefully daubed it over her wounds. Making her bend over, he spread the soothing cream around the cracked and torn membranes of her anal ring. The manacles and handcuffs had left raw, red circles around her wrists and ankles and he worked the cream into them as well.

Anna's body felt warm and renewed by her bathing and the burning pain from where the man had beaten her had subsided. She was grateful for the attentions the man was giving her, even though he had been the source of her misery. She watched as he rolled down his sleeves and put his jacket back on. He took hold of her arm and pulled her in the direction of the bedroom.

Anna let herself be led from the bathroom to her bed. She had placed her hands behind her back automatically. That had been one of the points of her 'lesson' hadn't it? She would never forget it now.

Vincent turned down the sheets. Anna expected him to allow her to lie down on the bed, but he was not done with her yet. He stepped over to the dresser and opened a drawer. She gave out a slight, dispirited whine when she saw that he had her leather bindings in his hands.

"Turn around," he ordered.

Anna felt a renewal of her sorrow as the man fastened her wrists together behind her. When he turned her back to face him, her lips were trembling. "Sit down on the bed," was all he said.

The unhappy woman sat own on the mattress. She looked up at her torturer piteously. Her stomach turned as she watched him lower the fly to his pants and draw out his long, thick cock. "You know what to do," he said.

Yes, she knew what to do. Was she going to be expected to service this tall, callous, dark man as well as Devlin? She recalled the camera over the mirror in her room. Clearly, the man felt that he was within his rights. Who else would she have to submit to? Harrington? Devlin had practically said as much. The leering, fearfully visaged driver? Who else? Elaine? Tomorrow was Sunday. She would be freed to go home. And the next day was Monday. Once the money she had sacrificed herself for had been paid, she would be free to do what she wanted. She could run away, somewhere where Devlin would never find her. The Center would be saved and all would be well.

She looked at the thick meat proffered to her by Devlin's cruel servant. He had beaten her with no compunction for her suffering. Now she was supposed to bring him pleasure. She knew how much more she would suffer if she refused. Tears forming in her eyes, she leaned forward, her useless hands bound behind her, her heavy, wounded, bare breasts swaying out from her body, and took the heavy, fat cock between her lips.

Vincent's prick hardened quickly between her lips. His hands were on her head, guiding her movements, clamping her finely trimmed, jet black hair against her scalp. The fat, fleshy helmet of his cock slid over her tongue and against the roof of her mouth. Her back was arched and her hands writhed unhappily behind her. The meat was salty with the man's sweat and Anna fought back her revulsion at its invasive presence. As the man drew her head back and forth, she kept her lips pursed firmly around the thick shaft, washing it with her tongue and giving his member a gentle, pleasure giving suckle.

Vincent was in no rush. He plowed Anna's mouth slowly and deliberately. She could hear his soft sighs as he reveled in the hot moisture surrounding his cock and the energetic tongue that caressed it. His hips were moving gently, timed with the movements of Anna's head. Anna did not know when it started, but she suddenly realized that her lusts were rising. There was something right about the way that the man was using her, something that reverberated in her psyche. She had been beaten cruelly, but wasn't that something she deserved? Devlin had shown her her true nature. She was a whore, a being to be used for other's pleasures. Everything happened for a reason. Wasn't that what people said? Fate had led her to be Devlin's slave. Wasn't that what she was supposed to be if fate decreed it?

And wasn't it right that she should serve those who served him?

Anna began to earnestly suck and caress the stiffened manhood between her lips. She felt a yearning between her thighs. With every push of the cock across her lips and over her tongue, her excitement grew. She remembered the liberation she had felt when she had admitted her lust earlier tonight while chained on Devlin's bed. It had felt so true, so right.

When Vincent's grip on her head became tighter and his hips started to thrust more insistently at her mouth, Anna felt a wave of pleasure flow through her. When his essence began to spill over her tongue, his cock jerking and spasming within her mouth, she was filled with pride. She rejoiced in each groan and moan of passion that the cold, seemingly emotionless man emitted.

As she had been taught, when Vincent's ejaculations eased and his cock stilled, Anna kept her lips pursed around it. She relented only when she felt the man's large, strong hand ease her head back and he pulled his cock from her lips. Without a word to her, Vincent drew his manhood back inside his trousers. He went to the dresser and returned with the ball gag and hood that she had worn that morning. Anna quailed at their sight, but held her incipient rebellion in check, certain now that the men had the right to do with her whatever they liked.

She opened her mouth obediently as the large, round, rubber ball was inserted. She leaned forward compliantly to enable the man to fasten it behind her head. She suppressed a sob when the dreaded hood was lowered over her face, shutting out all light. When Vincent had pulled the string at its base tightly around her throat, he pressed against her shoulders until she was lying on her back. Her bound hands pressed uncomfortably into her and she was grateful when she felt the strong hands urge her over on to her belly. She crossed her legs in anticipation of their binding.

When they were fastened together, Vincent ran his hands up along the back of her thighs and over her firm, round rear globes. Anna felt the renewal of her desires as the strong, hot hands glided over her flesh. He placed his hands underneath her hip and torso and guided her to her side. Her joined hands behind her slipped towards her right hip, propping her up. She was leaning back onto them, her breasts, belly and pussy exposed. She felt the comforting warmth of Vincent's strong, capable hands sliding along her thighs, over her taut belly and her breasts.

Since she could not see what the man was doing, she had to imagine his face, his clothes, his demeanor as her handled her body. Her sightlessness accentuated her consciousness of the contact between their skin. Vincent was kneeling on the bed next to her and he used his hands to spread her thighs. Her knees bowed out as far as her crossed ankles would permit. His hand delved lightly over her bearded quim and over the insides of her tender, well formed, olive brown thighs.

To have the man's hands caressing her tortured flesh felt wonderful to Anna. For the umpteenth time today, she felt her juices rising. The fingers on her loins parted her tingling love lips and traced the line between them. When satisfied at her state of lubrication, they descended within and began a slow, gentle agitation of her canal.

Anna sighed with pleasure. This was the reward for her sluttishness, her wantonness. She had been living a life of relative sexual deprivation for years. Now, in two days, she had rediscovered the joy in intense, sexual release at the hands of others. How could she deny it after this? It didn't matter who was teasing her cunt, whose cock was in her mouth, whose prick plowed her canals. Her body cried out for pleasure.

Anna felt Vincent's fingers pry open her love lips, spreading them. A moment later, she felt his breath on her loins. A hot tongue washed over her stiffened clit, sending an electrified surge of pleasure through her body. It played with the little nubbin and then lashed along the inner surfaces of her distended labia before plunging inside her.

The sensuous butler carefully and deliberately gemauched her burning slit. Each time that her thighs began to quiver with her impending crisis, her hips starting to gyrate, her moans becoming long and anguished, he would stop, letting her passions cool and then begin again. When she finally came, her ankles pulled desperately at their bindings and she bit down harshly on the gag in her mouth. Her moans of pleasure filled the room. The hot tongue tormented and teased her throbbing cleft. Her spasms seemed to go on and on. Anna tried to close her thighs, to terminate the agonizing pleasure the tongue was bringing her, but Vincent's hands kept them forcibly apart until he was satisfied that he had wrung every throb of pleasure from her gaping crevasse.

Anna was still giving off soft moans at the echoes of her climax when Vincent rose from the bed. In her postorgasmic reverie, she could hear him cleaning up the bathroom. She heard the rattle of her chains that he had left there on the floor as he picked them up. He came out of the bathroom and stepped past her bed. A drawer to the dresser opened and she heard him placing the chains inside. They made a dull, clanking sound as they settled against the wooden bottom of the drawer. The drawer was shut. The cruel implements of confinement would be available for use at any time.

She heard the unlocking and opening of the door. She felt a flurry of panic as she realized that she was to be left bound, hooded and gagged for the night. A moment later it closed again and the deadbolt was shot home from the outside.

Anna was exhausted from her ordeal. Her pussy continued to burn in afterglow from Vincent's oral attentions. She writhed her confined hands as she experienced a need to caress and comfort her well used portal. But her body was denied her. The men could do what they wanted to it, but she was to be denied the simple right of access. She squeezed her thighs together in frustration.

Her thoughts turned to the camera in her room and she wondered whether Vincent had turned out the lights. She had no way of telling through the blinding hood that she wore. The fact that Vincent had not pulled up her covers told her that they were probably on and that whoever monitored the other end of the camera was watching her. She thought of how she must appear, her bruised and battered, naked form, her cruel bindings, her hooded, featureless head. She strained at her bound ankles and wrists, testing them. A cloud of sadness enveloped her.

So much had happened to her over the last twenty four hours. What would tomorrow bring? What would it feel like to be able to walk out of the front door of the mansion, get in her car and drive to her apartment? How would she feel on Monday, when she had to resume her life as the executive director of a busy social service agency? Would the other staff members and the young residents of the Center be able to discern the subservient slut that she had become? Would her ability to rationalize her plight fade and she become immersed in inner contempt for her easy slide into abasement?

Anna quickly slid into sleep. Several times during the long night she awoke with a panicked start, unable to fathom why she could not move her hands or feet. She peered into the jet black darkness of her hood frightened at the cloying substance over her face. Her heart beat wildly and it took her several moments to remember where she was and why. When she did, she ceased her struggling and, with a heart full of sadness, succumbed to her condition. She soon drifted off again to a light, fitful slumber.

* * * * * * * * * * * * *

When she awoke in the morning, Anna discovered that someone had come in during the night and covered her. She was surprised that the entry of a person into her little prison had not disturbed her sleep. Although she was sure it was morning, she could not tell why. Utter darkness still surrounded her. She discovered that she had to pee and she hoped that Vincent would soon come and see to her needs. During her long wait, she wondered what was in store for her this day. She rubbed her naked thighs together self consciously, knowing that undoubtedly it included the possession of the sexual folds between them.

When Vincent finally came, he drew back her covers and untied her ankles. She knew it was him from the sound of his steps on the stairs. Anna had expected and hoped that he would untie her hands and remove her hood, but he did not. He urged her up from the bed and guided her into the bathroom. The tiles were hard and cold on her feet. He sat her down on the toilet and she obediently and gratefully emptied herself in it. After he wiped her and washed his hands, he led her back into the bedroom and ordered her to kneel on the bed facing the headboard. She waited patiently there until she heard the sound of her chains being removed from the dresser. She hated being tied, but dreaded being chained. The cold strength of the handcuffs and manacles were impersonal and especially cruel.

She suppressed a sob when she heard the chain being drawn through a ring in the headboard and clipped above her. Yesterday, the callous butler had fastened her hands to the headboard first, but now he first drew the chain that terminated in the steel manacles between her knees and captured her ankles in them. He then untied her hands and ordered her to bring them in front of her. When she did, he pulled them down, one after the other, and locked her hands in place. Before leaving the room, he paused for a moment. Anna felt his hard, boney hand run over her proffered buttocks. His touch reminded her in a very direct way of the availability of her twin portals behind her. Apparently satisfied, he left the room.

Anna was hungry and thirsty. She knew too well that he personal needs and desires were secondary to the whims of the men that controlled her. The ever present bonds on her body and the constant darkness that surrounded her filled her with an oppressive misery.

The worst was the large, pliant, round ball in her mouth. It was a constant reminder that she no longer had the right to ownership of her bodily orifices. They belonged to her masters, Devlin and Vincent, and whomsoever they would give the right to violate them.

She bit down on the rubber monstrosity in her mouth and pulled sharply at the bonds that held her wrists in place. She was poised for her masters' use, and would remain so until they deemed otherwise. She was conscious of the fact that the camera above her mirror was capturing her demeaning pose and the awareness of the exposure of her proffered rear and sex shamed her. She bent her shrouded head to the mattress between her outstretched arms. She had only one option, to wait.

When you can't act, you think, and Anna's mind swam with the recollections of her cruel abuse and the damage to her psyche they had inflicted. She never wanted to be beaten again the way she had been last night. Vincent had been right about letting her scream and plead for mercy. Nothing emphasized the implacable will of her controllers than the futility of her assertions of her humanity. Her supplicative entreaties for surcease of her torture echoed through her mind. She would have offered her soul to have the whipping end. Maybe she did. She couldn't remember everything that she had said. She did know that she had been stripped of all pride, all self respect. It was devastating to know how easily your self image could be destroyed.

Silence reigned on the fourth floor of Devlin's mansion for a long time. She wondered if Devlin was having a luxurious breakfast. Had Elaine returned to join him? Were they laughing and joking at the elegant table in the beautifully appointed sun room downstairs while Devlin related to her how he had taken her anal virginity. And what had happened to the woman who she had heard walking in the hallway last night? Was she ensconced in a neighboring room, bound and deprived of all volitional rights as she was? Who was she? Was she young and pretty, like Elaine?

Anna knew that she was at least attractive since she doubted Devlin would have deigned to even turn his head for her unless she was. Had she committed some crime that Devlin held over her? Or had she traded her soul for the achievement of some ambition like Elaine apparently had. Would she ever meet her, perhaps be forced to engage in a Sapphic tryst with her for Devlin's amusement?

The question as to where the woman was was answered when Anna heard the sharp sound of her high heeled footsteps on the stairs. Vincent's heavy, deliberate steps preceded them. The footsteps passed her door without pause and then she heard a door opening and closing. About ten minutes later, the door opened and closed again and Vincent's footsteps returned. He did not stop at her door as she hopefully expected. She would have gladly exchanged his use of her for the lonely, dark bondage she was subsumed in. But the steps continued to the stairs and Anna dolefully listened while they faded away.

Knowing that another woman was a prisoner down the hall from her somehow assuaged her feeling of self hatred for how easily she had succumbed to Devlin's mastery of her. If other women willingly subjected themselves to him as obsequiously and totally as she had, then her surrender seemed less despicable. On the other hand, it highlighted the impersonal, demeaning essence of her slavery to the callous millionaire. She was just another body to be used, another female existing only to titillate his passions. How could she hope for some moderation of his cruel indifference to her feelings and the remorse she felt at her self debasement if she was just one of a collection of female bodies that he owned?

When she finally heard the distinctive tread of Devlin's energetic steps on the stairs, Anna felt a chill run through her body. What would he do to her? Was he coming for her or the other one? Her heart skipped a beat when the footsteps stopped at her door and she heard the lock being turned.

"Ahhhh, Anna," Devlin's deep, amiable voice pronounced after he entered the room and locked the door behind him. "I see that you've been waiting for me. You're such a good little girl." Anna felt the bed depress next to her and felt the warmth of Devlin's body. His hand ran over her arched back and then over her well presented, round, firm buttocks. "I don't have a lot of time to spend with you this morning, Anna. I'm going out for a while. But I did want to see how pretty your body was with all the marks Vincent put on it last night. I see your bottom is all black and blue. And there are long, dark bruises on your back. Vincent really knows his work."

Anna had been wondering dolefully what evidence of last night's abuse would be displayed on her body. She was disturbed and ashamed at the news that they were so prominent. Devlin placed a hand in her short, black hair and pulled her head up. Kneel up, Anna," he said. "I want to see your tits."

Anna obediently shuffled her knees forward so that she could raise her body. It chagrined her to hear Devlin's amusement at the evidence of her torture, but she had learned a hard lesson on obedience the night before and she harbored no inclinations to do anything but what her callous master said.

When her torso was raised, her hands still fastened below her at the base of the headboard, Devlin positioned his body towards her front so that he could get a good view of her breasts. She felt the soft cotton of the robe he had worn yesterday morning brush up against her skin.

"Oh, they're all black and blue too, Anna," he said with feigned surprise. "I'll bet that hurt." He reached out his hand and took possession of first one breast and then the other. Anna suppressed a sob while the man rudely manipulated her flesh.

"I watched the video this morning, Anna. You said some pretty nasty things to Vincent. I'm surprised he didn't give you a few more strokes to teach you better manners. I hope for your sake that you never speak that way to me."

A chill ran through the distraught, bound woman. She couldn't stand the thought of another trip to the punishment room. And the idea that Devlin had watched her torment on tape, his passions undoubtedly stirred by the visualization of her abuse, disturbed her deeply.

"So, the $64,000 question is, Anna, did you learn your lesson? Did you, Anna?"

"...es, ih-er e-in," Anna moaned unhappily through her gagged mouth. She really did.

"That's good, Anna. I'm happy to hear it. Now, like I said, I have somewhere to go. Vincent will, I'm sure, keep you well entertained until I come back. So I'm just going to give you a quick ass fucking and I'll be on my way."

Ann quailed at the idea that he was going to use her rear portal again. It had been painful to be penetrated there by his thick, hard cock. She felt Devlin's hands on her thighs and she fretfully allowed herself to be brought back to her former position. She sensed him standing next to the bed and discarding his robe and slippers. The mattress gave a little shake as he climbed on it behind her.

"I don't have the time to get your pussy all wet, Anna, So I guess some spit will have to do," Devlin informed her as he ran his hands over her proffered ass. Anna moaned with unhappiness at the thought. A second later, she felt a trail of warm liquid spill over her rear entrance. Devlin's fingers rudely entered her there and spread it over her anal ring. The cracks and tears in her flesh had not fully healed and she experienced a fierce burning as the membranes were stretched. "Ohhhhhh," she groaned unhappily.

Her master's thighs pressed up against her rear haunches and she felt the tip of his cock press against the entrance to her bowels. It was one thing to be fucked there while in the midst of passion and after a night of consuming an ocean of alcohol. It was another to be used so without any chance to prepare herself for it. She moaned again as she felt the cock begin to slide home.

"You'll get used to it, Anna," Devlin said. His hot hands had spread the cheeks of her rear. "Ohhhhhhhh, that's nice and tight," he exclaimed as his cock delved deeper and deeper into her. "I may just give up on your pussy until its better trained, Anna. Your ass is a real treat."

Anna hung her head in shame and sorrow as the man began to pump himself along the ring of her small, tender entrance. The cock filled her bowel and its presence was a hateful reminder of how slavish she had become. Her pussy felt abandoned and useless. She absorbed Devlin's callous assessment of her fucking skills with despondency.

Although Devlin had stated that he was in a rush, he took his time plowing Anna's rear hole. He eased his cock out until the head popped free and then pushed it in again, as if seeking to reexperience the thrill of entering her tight ring.

Each time the stiffened wand punctured her, Anna gave a little wail of dismay and pulled dismally at her cruelly bound hands. Gradually, though, the pain and burning of the tight little hole began to give way to a tingling that spread from her rear entrance down to her disused, ignored, crevasse. Despite her unhappiness at this use of her, her juices started to seep and she felt her needs begin to rise. She felt horrified that she could experience pleasure from a cock in her ass. She gripped her bound hands together tightly and she bit down hard on the offensive mass in her mouth.

"No! No!" she thought in anguish at her sluttishness. She dreaded Devlin's discovery of her lustful responses to his assault. If he found out that she liked being cornholed, he might never use her any other way again. But her mind was unable to fight off the pleasurable sensations that the thick, steel hard wand was giving her. She moaned again in frustration and despair.

Devlin picked up his pace as his own passions began to envelope him. She could hear his heavy breath and felt the slap of his hips on her rear. His hands had hold of her hips and she felt them tighten as he gave out a great groan of pleasure. "Oh, yeah!" he called out. "Oh! Oh! Oh!" Anna felt the warmth of his discharge flood her bowel. Her lusts had been raised by the man's callous use of her rear opening but she realized, unhappily, that they were not to be brought to fruition. Devlin slowed his thrusts as his orgasm waned. When his spasms finished, he slowly pulled his meat from her rear passage.

"That was good, Anna," he said, his voice reflecting his satisfaction. His hands wandered over her burning rear globes and along her hips. One hand drifted between her legs and Anna felt a thick finger trace the line of her labial lips. They were protruding from between her clamped together thighs.

"You're wet, Anna!" the man exclaimed. "I told you you would get to like it. Don't worry, Vincent will take care of your whorish pussy later. I've got to get going."

Devlin bounced off of the bed and stepped into the bathroom. Anna heard him washing himself off at the sink. He returned a few moments later and redonned his robe and slippers. Without saying more to her, he unlocked the door and let himself out.

Anna hung her hooded head and cried. She had been afraid that the man would discover how her body had succumbed to his impassioned stuffing of her rear and it had become true. She yearned to crawl up into a little ball and hide under the covers of the bed, but the chains held her implacably in place.

About an hour later, Vincent finally came and released her. He removed her hood and chains and let her use the bathroom. He had brought a tray with him containing a fresh fruit salad, a carafe of coffee and a crisp, light croissant with butter and raspberry jam on the side.

"You have forty-five minutes to eat and bathe," Vincent told her. "Be sure to trim your pussy. When you're done, I want you to assume your position on the bed and wait. Do you understand?"

She nodded her head dolefully. "Yes, Sir," she murmured. Vincent waited a moment, making sure for himself that she understood her duties and then left.

Anna welcomed the sustenance even though her heart was filled with sadness at her treatment. It was glorious to be freed from her bonds. The morning light sparkled through the small window of her room. The tray had a stand at its bottom and she sat on the edge of the bed and quickly devoured the fruit salad and croissant. The coffee was hot and had a hearty, deep taste. It felt good going down her throat. Her belly welcomed ease from her hunger.

It was Sunday and some time today she would be freed from Devlin's clutches. She had but to endure the next few hours and she could go home. Tomorrow, all her troubles would be over, at least as far as the Center was concerned. The idea that she would be able soon to drive away and put her experiences here behind her brightened her mood. So what if she had been brutally and callously used. She would have the last laugh when the money went into the Center account. She would refuse to come back here. That's what she would do. What would Devlin do about it anyway? There were laws and even he was subject to them. His threats did not mean anything to her.

But then his words came back to her. He knew people who would do worse things to her. What did he mean by that? Would they kill her? Kidnap her? Torture her? She experienced a shiver through her body. Well, she didn't have to decide today. She could put it off.

Anna finished her meal and stood to go into the bathroom. As she did, her image appeared in the mirror opposite her bed. She saw on her body the bruises that Vincent had put there the night before. They were ugly and terrifying. She recalled the suffering she had gone through. It was one thing to be courageous and defiant when not confronted by the prospect of unbearable pain. It was another once you had gone through it and knew what it did to you.

Tears fell down her face as she took in the sight of her disfigured body. Her breasts carried two long lines of deep purple bruises that had begun to suffuse over them. Her belly and thighs were marked too. Fear ran through her as she thought of Devlin's threat. She did not want to suffer like last night ever again. Disconsolate at her dismal options, being Devlin's slave or suffering the unknown, cruel torment that would be inflicted on her if she reneged on her deal, Anna trudged to the bathroom to take her shower.

Anna finished her ablutions and then returned to the bed to perform the careful denuding of the short, raspy stubble of pubic hair that had grown up overnight on her loins. After returning the razor and small bowl of soapy water to the bathroom and casting a hateful glance at the camera on the wall, she mounted the bed and positioned herself on her knees with her hands behind her back. She leaned over and began to wait obediently for the return of the butler.

He was not alone when he returned. Although Anna's head was pointed away from the door and could not see who had entered, she distinctly had heard two sets of male steps come up the stairs and into her room. Who could it be? Devlin said he was going out!

Her question was quickly answered. Vincent ordered her to kneel up and turn around. When she did, she saw the scarred face and taut, muscular body of the limo driver. He was already in the process of removing his clothes. Anna's face collapsed into a dismal frown. A whine escaped her lips. Devlin had said that Vincent would make sure her pussy was taken care of. She had thought that he meant that Vincent would make use of her, much like he did last night when he put her to bed. But this is what he meant. The driver was going to fuck her!

Vincent had moved towards the dresser and opened one of the drawers. He brought forth a band of leather with a large, circular hole in the middle. It was made of some kind of rubberized plastic. Anna knew what it was at once. It was a ring gag. She had seen pictures of women wearing them and getting their faces fucked by huge, domineering men. The very idea had appalled her at the time. Now she would be wearing one. There could be only one reason for it and the knowledge that the Latino driver would soon be forcing his stiffened cock between her helpless lips horrified her.

Vincent presented the infernal device to her mouth. Sorrowfully, her hands crossed slavishly behind her, Anna opened her lips and accepted it. Despite her revulsion, she had no thought of resistance. Her lips trembled as the plastic circle was pushed past them and lodged behind her teeth. The plastic circle distended her lips into a wide 'O'. Her jaw was distended and the pernicious intrusion of the device in her mouth was immediately uncomfortable and distressing. Tears filled her eyes as the man buckled the leather straps behind her head.

She knelt there dismally while Vincent returned to the dresser. He took out a wide leather belt. He stepped back to Anna and circled her waist with it, fastening it tightly behind her. It had loops on its sides and Vincent efficiently trapped each of her wrists in one so that they were held securely just above her hips.

"Carlos is going to give you some instructions on how to take a cock down your throat," Vincent said coldly.

Anna looked up at the grinning face of the limo driver. It was heavily whiskered. His teeth gleamed in his mouth. He was naked and he was caressing his growing cock with one hand. "Oh, god!" Ann thought. She remembered the distress she had experienced when Devlin had shoved his long, thick member in her throat in the limo last night. She had felt like she was going to suffocate. And now the driver was going to do it to her again. She looked up unhappily at Vincent as if she could dissuade him from forcing this ordeal upon her by a dismal glance.

"When he's done, he will fuck you," was all that the emotionless servant said. He turned and let himself out of the room.

Carlos watched him go and then turned his eyes on the bound, naked young woman on the bed. His grin expanded as he surveyed her delights. "We're going to have a good time, *conchita*," he said. His chest was barrel shaped and covered with a mat of thick, black hair. He had a slight paunch to his belly. His thighs and arms were heavily muscled. The hair on his head was black and stringy and reached down to his shoulders. He looked about 30 or 35 years old. His nose seemed like it had been broken several times and his brown eyes were set wide apart. His skin, like Anna's, was dark, but with a tanner hue than hers. Anna's hands squirmed in their confinements and she let loose a wail.

"Don't cry, *petita*," Carlos said as he approached her. His cock was hard now and Anna saw that it was thick and long. "You'll like my prick. After you take it down your throat, I'll make you come with it. All the *putas* love it."

He sat down on he bed next to where Anna knelt, helpless and disconsolate. He took hold of her heavy breasts and caressed them softly. "Ohhhhhh, what pretty titties you have," he said, his voice heavily accented. His tone was an approximation of sweetness, which did nothing to allay Anna's distress. "It's too bad they're all marked up like that. You'll have to learn to be a good girl from now on, eh?"

His face was inches from Anna's and she caught a whiff of his coarse breath. "Oh, god! Oh, god," she thought. He leaned over and captured one of her nipples in his mouth. The pull of his broad lips caused her breast to tingle and her teat harden. He slurped at it hungrily before shifting to the other. His large, hairy hand held the breast firmly, squeezing it tightly as he suckled on the stiffened nubbin. "Mmmmmmmmmmm," he moaned. "Your titties taste good, my little whore," he said when he emerged. "Yesterday, when you sucked off Mr. Devlin my cock was as hard as a rock. I couldn't wait to get the chance to stick it in you. I'm going to fuck you until your eyes roll over. But first, I've got to give you your cocksucking lesson."

The strong Hispanic man took hold of Anna's arm and pulled her from the bed. "Get on your knees," he told her.

Miserable at her fate, Anna sank obediently to the floor. He swung his legs out so that he was sitting on the edge of the bed. She was poised between the man's thick, hairy, muscular thighs and his cock jutted out towards her face. He took hold of her finely trimmed, jet black hair and pulled her mouth towards his prick. Anna looked up at him dolefully, her lips distended in a grotesque, circular grimace.

"First we need to get all warmed up," he said. He positioned his manhood in the middle of the ring that distorted Anna's mouth and guided her head forwards. Anna's hands strained at the loops that held the tight to her waist. Her stomach roiled and her heart started to pound in her chest. She felt the cock roll past her tongue and she braced herself for the piercing of her throat. She whined and her body stiffened.

"Not yet, pretty birdie," he said, noting her reaction. "I'm going to enjoy your pretty, little mouth a little first." The man began to slowly urge Anna's head back and forth over his cock. "Mmmmmmmmmmm, that's nice *petita*. Your mouth is good and hot."

Anna was squeezed between the man's powerful thighs. Her head was tilted slightly downwards so that the man could have ease of penetration. The thick rod slid back and forth over her tongue. She tried to calm herself, but all she could think of was the fact that he was shortly going to subsume himself in her to his length and she would choke and sputter. His right hand had a relentless grip on her hair. His left ran over her head, down her neck and over her shoulder. It was rough and calloused. He shifted it under her torso and took hold of her breast, squeezing it hard. It was painful and Anna gave out a whine of unhappiness as she absorbed the pain. He took her nipple between his fingers and pinched it until she moaned. "You like that little birdie? You like it rough?"

Anna tried to give an answer refuting the man's suggestion, but the cock in her mouth and her distorted lips allowed her only to make a piteous moaning sound. She tried to pull away from the hand that held her head prisoner, but his grip was like a steel trap and she only managed to strain the nerve endings of her hair.

"Calm down, whore," the man said as he continued to plow her mouth. "You don't want me to have to slap you around do you? Or maybe you would, eh? Does that get you hot?"

"Mmmmmmmmmm!" Anna moaned. She knew that violence simmered just below the surface of the man's veneer of pretended politeness. She ceased her struggle and gave in to the force of his powerful paw.

Carlos had picked up his pace and the cock was banging against the entrance to her throat. He had freed her tortured nipple and now had hold of her head with both hands. "Here it comes little whore. I'm going to slide it in nice and easy. Just relax and let it happen."

Anna felt the cock pass the end of her mouth and into her throat. The bulbous head felt huge inside her. She balled her hands into fists and her body shook with fear. "Ga-ahhhhhh!" she moaned as the cock blocked her air passage. "Ga-a –ahhhhh!"

"Relax, *putita*," the man said. "You're going about this all wrong. I'm going to leave it in for a minute and then I'll pull out and let you have a breath."

Carlos left his cock lodged motionless in the back of her mouth. The head was just past the opening and Anna felt like she was going to throw up. She tried to calm herself like she had been told. There was no use, really, struggling. The man was going to do it anyway. And struggling just made it worse.

A full minute passed, at least, and Carlos slowly drew his cock back until it was just out of Anna's mouth. She gasped for air. "Good work, *putita*," he congratulated her. "You'll get the hang of it. Here it comes again."

The cock passed through the circular opening that was her lips and moved slowly but surely across her tongue and again to the back of her mouth. She felt the fat head push her throat open and enter it. He went a little further than before. Anna choked and sputtered. "Ga-a-aaaa!" she moaned. He held her still for a long time. This time, she had taken a deep breath before he entered and she was able to tolerate it a little better.

"Goooood! Goooood!" the man exclaimed. "Let's leave it in a little longer, eh? See how much you can take."

Anna quailed at the man's statement. She had already been running out of air. Her eyes were clamped tightly shut and her hands jerked and strained at their bindings just above her waist. The cock was a heinous presence in her mouth, hot and soft and hard all at the same time. Her jaw ached from its forced extension and not being able to close her lips to manage the use of her mouth made her feel sick with despair. She began to get desperate for air and moaned and groaned while the man held her head firmly pressed down. The thick intruder filled her passageway. Her mouth was overwhelmed with his hot, salty taste. She strained to keep her position, but her lungs were screaming and her body was rebelling against its strange invasion. ""Mmmmmmmmpf! Mmmmmmmmmpf!" she pleaded. She tried to pull her head back, but the man's grip was too strong. "Mmmmmmmmmpf! Mmmmmmmmpf!" she moaned again.

Suddenly, the man pulled her head off of his loins. The cock sprang free and Anna took a long, desperate breath of air. Tears were streaming down her face. The man allowed her two deep breaths and then entered her again.

Her lesson continued on and on. Carlos alternated between short, tolerable lodgments in her throat with long, agonizing ones. After a while, the passage of the cock past the end of her mouth became easier, the presence of the huge mass of flesh in her esophagus more tolerable. He began a steady rhythm of slowly exiting her mouth and then thrusting firmly back into it until her face was pressed against his belly. He began to moan with pleasure. "Ahhhhhh, you're doing good!" he called out. "You're a natural! I'm going to come in your throat now. Take it like a good whore!"

Anna braced herself for the man's discharge. He pressed his cock down as far as it would go, further than he had pierced her yet. She felt the hard roundness slide into her throat. The man's cock was long and she found it difficult to believe that he had fit it all inside her. His hands held her head down firmly and he pushed his loins against her face. "Aaaauuuuugh!" he called out. "Aaaaaau-uuuuugh! Aaaaaaaauuugh!" Anna could feel his meat pulsing and jerking in her throat. It was as if the cock had come alive inside her. His hot spume coated her throat and slid down into her. She gagged and choked, but resisted the urge to try and pull away, to escape his grasp. She had done that yesterday and it had resulted in a beating. If Devlin used her mouth again this way, she wanted to be able to avoid his ire.

It took a long time for the man to come. He continued to announce his pleasure in deep, throaty groans. Anna was frantic with the need to breathe. Her head began to swim and she felt like she was smothering. Finally, the man, having reached the end of his ejaculations, pulled his meat from her. He drew her head back and peered into her face. She was panting wildly in an effort to regain her breath.

"*Buena, putita!*" the man yelled out. "You fucking did it! Now that wasn't so bad was it? You're a good little whore!"

Anna felt a strange sense of accomplishment. Her cheeks were awash with her tears and her body was still shaking from her ordeal. But she had done it. She had taken the whole thing and made the man come. The next time that Devlin fucked her throat, she would be able to accommodate him.

Carlos was rubbing her head gently. The heat of his hands was comforting. Anna looked up into his face. Now that the worst was over, she was able to see the man in a different light. He didn't look so bad after all. He was just doing his duty. Maybe he wasn't all that mean.

"Now get up on the bed so we can have a good fuck, *petita*," he said to her. He took her by the arm and helped her to her feet. She crawled up onto the bed. He took her in his arms. He began to stroke her body. He ran his hands over her hips and thighs and over her back and neck. He leaned over and took a nipple in his mouth, suckling it tenderly. Pushing her down on her back, he kissed her breasts and then took hold of them in his mighty, scarred hands and massaged them while he shifted his lips back and forth between her nipples, teasing them with his teeth and running his hot tongue over them.

Anna felt her passion rising. A part of her wanted to revolt against his manhandling of her flesh, but the rest of her wanted desperately to have the man's cock inside her. Hadn't she earned a good fuck? Wasn't that her reward for taking his cock down her throat?

Carlos paused long enough to release the infernal device that had held her lips distended so grotesquely. When he pulled it free of her mouth, he placed his fat lips upon hers and slid his tongue inside. Anna welcomed the intruder passionately. She pulled at her bound hands, wanting to draw the man's body onto hers, to clutch at his broad shoulders . He ignored her efforts and continued with their impassioned kiss while his hands roamed freely over her body. She felt his hand run across her belly and slide over her love mound. He took possession of it, tracing a line along the interior of her labia until her moisture allowed him to ease a thick finger inside. She spread her legs in welcome as he caressed the inner lining of her crevasse. His body was laying against her and she could feel that he had resumed his hardness. She wanted his cock, but was afraid to say so. Silence was ingrained in her now.

The man continued to caress her loins while kissing her fervently. He rubbed her stiffened bud gently until she moaned. He drew his lips back from hers. "You ready for me, *petita*? You ready for my cock, eh?"

"Yessssss!" Anna moaned. "Oh, yes, fuck me, please!"

The Latino shifted his bulk until he was between her outstretched thighs. He used a hand to guide himself to her portal and slid his fat cock home. Anna groaned with pleasure as he filled her. He gave a deep, satisfied grunt and began to thrust himself madly. Anna raised her knees and circled her legs around the man's thighs, pulling him deeply into her. "Oh, god! Oh, yes! Oh, yes!" she called out to the little room.

Anna had never been fucked like this. Carlos pounded his hips into hers, stroking his cock along the depth of her crevasse, drawing it across her pleasure bud. His hands grabbed her head and he retook her lips. When his tongue was inside her, fervently scouring her own, he reached his arms down and lifted Anna's thighs until she was almost doubled back against herself. His cock plunged deeply inside her.

She came at once. Her pussy throbbed and spasmed and she screamed her pleasure into Carlo's mouth. The man paid her groans and shouts of excitement no mind as he continued to slam away at her electrified hole. Her first orgasm was followed quickly by a second. She waived her heels in the air while he continued to pump away. He pulled his lips from hers and his body tensed. "Here it comes, whore!" he shouted. "Here's something for you! Take my spunk, whore! Take it!"

Ann's eyes rolled back in her head as the cock began to pulse and jerk inside her. She could feel his spume spilling into her womb. Her pussy's fierce contractions began again and she moaned loudly. "Oh, yes! Oh, yes! Yes! Give it to me! Give it to me!"

When the man's motions slowed to a stop, Anna's pussy was still reverberating from her orgasms. Her heart was thumping in her chest and she struggled to regain her breath. Carlos's chest was heaving. She looked up to see his broad, toothy grin. "Now that's a fuck!" he called out to her. "You're a hot little whore. We'll have to do this again, eh?"

Anna did want to do it again. She cursed herself for her wantonness, but she could think of nothing better than fucking the strong, coarse Latino man over and over. She remembered suddenly the camera on the wall and she realized that her lascivious display would be on film. What would Devlin say? He would undoubtedly laugh and taunt her. She began to rue her outburst of passion.

Carlos ignored Anna's sudden sullenness. His limp manhood slid out of her quim and he released her uplifted legs. "Time to go, *petita*," he said. "We'll do this again some time, eh?" he repeated.

Anna lay there sullenly as the man began to dress. When he was finished her ordered her to get up. He released the belt around her waist and freed her hands. Anna felt wobbly on her feet. "Turn around," he ordered her.

Anna realized that the man was going to tie her back up. She wanted to beg him not to. It was heaven to have the use of her arms and legs. But she knew better than to protest.

The man retrieved her leather bindings and joined her wrists together tightly. "Get on the bed," he ordered her curtly.

Dispirited at the resumption of her servile status, Anna obeyed. She lay on her belly and crossed her legs in anticipation of he man's demand. He joined her ankles together. She heard him rooting around in the dresser and looked over. He was searching for something. He pulled out a leather belt with a thick, leather prong attached to it. It was shaped just like a penis.

"Now this is a gag!" the Latino exclaimed. "You don't want that little ball thing when you can have this!' he said gleefully. He showed it to Anna. She grimaced at the thought of having it in her mouth.

"Please don't," she whined in a little, plaintive voice.

"You'll like it, *putita*," he retorted. "It's just like a real cock."

He leaned over the prone woman and proffered it to her mouth. Anna turned her head away in protest. "Please don't put that in me," she whined. "Please."

Carlos took hold of the hair on her head. "If you don't want a whipping, you'll open your mouth like a good little whore," he said. His voice had a hard edge to it. Anna sobbed and turned her face to him. She didn't want a whipping. Nothing was worse than that.

The callous Latino pressed the tip of the penis like gag against Anna's lips. She opened them sadly and he pushed the cruel device home. Anna felt it fill her mouth and moaned. He buckled it tightly around her head driving the leather prong deeper into her mouth. "How's that feel, eh *putita*," he asked her mockingly. "It's not as good as mine, I know, but you can think about the next time you blow me while you lay here. I was gentle this time. Next time we'll have some real fun."

Anna moaned in misery. The ball gag had been bad, but this was much worse. The man was right. She would be thinking about cocks and blowjobs and how the men had callously used her mouth all the while she laid waiting for someone to free her. When she saw the black hood in the man's hands, she moaned again. She would be in darkness once more.

When the hood was pulled tight around her neck, Anna heard Carlos open the drawer to the dresser. He came back to the bed and she felt her bound legs being lifted and drawn up towards her head. He tied something to her joined ankles. He then took them and fastened them to her wrists. He was hogtying her!

Anna's shoulders strained as her arms were pulled back behind her. "Ooooooooom!" she called out from behind her hood in protest. "Eeeeeeeeeeeeou!"

"Now that's the way to tie up a whore," Carlos announced happily. He pushed her over to her side with his strong, calloused hands and ran them over her breasts playfully. "See you later, *putita*," he said.

CHAPTER SIX

It was about an hour later that Vincent came for her. The time had crawled by slowly and Anna's shoulders and hips ached from her confinement. Carlos had been right. This was definitely worse than merely having her hands and feet bound. There was no comfortable position. Having the faux penis in her mouth was a constant reminder of the cocks that had visited it over the last two days. She cursed the Hispanic limo driver for his unnecessary cruelty.

"This is how a whore should be tied," he said. Well, she was a whore wasn't she. Why shouldn't she be treated like one. But even whore's had rights, didn't they? Why she had to be treated so dismally, she didn't know. She had done everything that was asked of her. She wondered miserably if she was going to be constantly available for the driver's use. It was another reason to take Devlin's money and run. She had a couple thousand dollars saved up. She could make a new life somewhere, somewhere where Devlin would never find her. Couldn't she? But he seemed so powerful. Wouldn't he find her eventually? And what would happen then? Her treatment so far told her that the consequences of running would be severe indeed. Hobson's choice, that's what she had: no choice at all. Suffer now or suffer later.

Vincent did not comment on Anna's grotesque and cruel bindings when he came into the room. He paused for a moment as if considering them. Anna gave out a whine of self pity at his delay in freeing her. When she felt his hands at her ankles releasing the straps, she was overcome with relief.

Once she had been freed and her offensive gag removed, Vincent gave her some instructions. "Mr. Devlin wants you to come downstairs. Wash your body off and make up your face. When that's done, put on these stockings, this garter belt and your high heels. Be standing at the end of the bed when I come in. You have fifteen minutes."

Fifteen minutes? That wasn't much time at all. Anna nodded unhappily at the servant. When he had left the room, she sprang to her duties. She stepped in the shower and washed herself in haste, careful not to get her hair wet. Her arms and legs were cramped and tired, but the warm water seemed to refresh them. She dried herself quickly and stood before he mirror over the vanity and used the makeup she had been bought yesterday to adorn her lips and outline her eyes.

There was a very light rouge the sales girl had picked out for her and she daubed it on her cheeks. The final touch to her face was a light blue eye shadow. She brushed her hair until it was straight and neat. Last, she took hold of the small spray bottle of expensive perfume that she had been given and she gave her neck and the hollow of her breasts a little spritz. She was about to put it away when a thought occurred to her. She took the small bottle and lowered it to her belly. She gave the bottle a pump, spraying it lightly over her loins. When she looked back in the mirror as a final check on her appearance, she was satisfied.

She wondered what Devlin had in store for her. One thing she knew was that if she was not ready when Vincent came back, she would be in big trouble. The purplish bruises she saw on her breasts as she was painting her face were a stark reminder of what could happen. She was disgusted with herself at how she had jumped at the butler's command, but what alternative did she have? Until Devlin set her free later today, she lived under the cloud of Vincent's cruel cane.

Anna had just slid her stockings up her finely toned legs when she heard the sound of Vincent coming up the stairs. She quickly snapped the clasps from the garter belt in place and slipped on her shoes. She had just finished buckling the second one when she heard the key in the lock. She stood up straight and put her hands behind her back.

She was out of breath and her heart was pounding when the door opened. She stood as straight as she could to present herself to her master's lackey. Being in Devlin's presence would be no picnic, but at least it was a chance to get out of her room and avoid being tied up for hours and hours on end. She was afraid that if she was not ready, not only would she suffer a punishment, but she would lose the opportunity to be freed from her room.

Vincent gave her the once over. He seemed happy with what he saw. He opened the door and led Anna into the hall.

Anna wondered whether the other female prisoner could hear the clatter of her high heels as she walked down the passageway. She felt a minor pang of guilt as she followed Vincent down the steps. Apparently, only one of them was permitted downstairs at a time. Since it was Anna's turn, the other woman would have to remain in her room. Was she cruelly tied like Anna had been or was that something reserved specially for Anna? Was she a more or less permanent resident of the house or would she too be looking forward to the end of the weekend so that she could resume her other life? But why should she worry about the other woman? She had enough troubles of her own. She put the thoughts of any sisterly obligation she might have for her out of her mind.

Devlin was sitting in the sun room. The room was bright and, looking out the massive windows, Anna estimated by the position of the sun that it was about two o'clock. He was on the telephone. He was dressed casually, with a pair of well pressed dark green slacks and an aqua blue sports shirt. There was a pair of tan bucks on his feet. He was sitting in one of the easy chairs and on the phone. Anna stood before him dutifully, awaiting his command while he talked. Vincent had left as soon as he saw to it that Anna was presented to his master.

"Yes, I'm very interested," Devlin was saying. "It should be fun. I haven't been down to the islands in over a year....Yeah, I have my own gear....Two weeks? No, I don't think I can get away for that long. A week at the most....Ha, ha, ha, ha, yeah, I'll bring one for you. I've got a couple extra...."

Devlin was caressing Anna with his eyes while he talked. At one point he snapped his fingers and pointed to the floor. Anna took this as a signal for her to kneel in front of him and she sank to the carpet.

His conversation went on for a few more minutes. When he rang off he took a sip from a tumbler of amber liquid that had been on the table next to him and then spoke to her.

"Have you ever been to Aruba?" he asked.

Anna was somewhat surprised by the casual nature of his question. "N-no, Mr. Devlin," she answered.

"I'm going down in a few weeks with some friends. Maybe I'll take you with me. Would you like that?"

Anna was not sure how to answer him. She would love to go to Aruba, but certainly not with him. But if he was away for a while, that would be a good thing, no? What should she say, yes or no? She hesitated.

"You don't have to answer me now. We'll talk about it some more. Did you have lunch?"

Lunch? What did he think she was doing all day? "No, Mr. Devlin she answered.

"We'll be having dinner in a little while. Can you wait?"

"Yes, Mr. Devlin," she answered. The truth was that she was starving. But she didn't want any favors from the cruel man.

"Stand up and turn around slowly, Anna. I didn't get a real good look at you this morning. I want to see your bruises."

His reference to the disfigurements from her beating made Anna quiver. Every time she thought of her ordeal, her stomach flipped over. She rose slowly and turned in a small circle.

"Vincent really did a job on you, Anna. I told you that he was skilled. Come closer to me."

Anna stepped over until she was next to his chair. He leaned forward and ran his hands over her belly and breasts. "You've got a fine body, Anna," he said. He slid his hands over her hips and down her thighs. Anna began to get aroused at the feel of his hot hands. She knew that at any moment he could decide to make use of her. Standing near naked before him, her trimmed love lips clearly visible, her full round breasts swaying, she knew that she made a lascivious sight. Hadn't she made herself all up for him, doused herself with perfume, painted her face? She was wearing a black garter belt and a pair of sheer, black stockings. Her red high heels pushed her breasts up and made her legs seem long and languorous. She had been prettied up for his delight. She was his slave, at least until she left, and the knowledge that she would be soon panting with lust as he plowed her with his cock made her pussy tingle. She cursed herself for it.

"But I think that you could use a little exercise, a little toning up. Do you belong to a gym?"

"No, Mr. Devlin." Anna responded. She tried to hide her developing lust from him, but her voice quivered slightly.

"I'll make arrangements for you to join one of the spas near the Center. I want you to work out every day. Understand?"

"Yes, Mr. Devlin," Anna answered. She felt like an idiot. "Yes, Mr. Devlin. No, Mr. Devlin." She was like a child in front of the schoolmaster.

"Turn around and let me feel your butt," Devlin ordered.

Anna turned and presented her buttocks to the callous man. He rubbed his hands over them and then gave them a little pinch.

"Yeah, you have to be careful at your age, Anna. You don't want to get big butt-itis, do you?"

"No, Mr. Devlin."

His hands left her ass and Anna turned around again to face him.

"So, did you enjoy your day as my guest, Anna?"

Anna definitely knew the answer to this question. And she knew better than to lie. "No, Mr. Devlin." The memory of being hogtied for what seemed hours was still with her.

"Don't you like being all tied up, Anna?"

"No, Mr. Devlin."

"I took a look at the video. Carlos knows how to treat a whore, doesn't he?"

Anna felt a wave of shame pass through her. She had been afraid that he would see the film of her session with the limo driver. And being reminded that she was now no more than a whore as far as Devlin was concerned filled her with unhappiness. "Yes, Mr. Devlin," she eked out.

"I have to say that he gave you quite a fucking. Being a whore does have some advantages, wouldn't you say?"

"Yes, Mr. Devlin."

"And I was very impressed at your cocksucking lesson. Are you ready to take me in your throat now?"

"Yes, Mr. Devlin," Anna answered. At his mention of it, Anna recalled the feel of Carlos' cock filling her throat. She felt queasy as she thought of it.

"Well, lets see how you do," he said.

Anna moved herself between Devlin's muscular thighs and sank to the floor. The plush carpet gave way under her stockinged knees. Her hands were still crossed behind her as she had been taught and she looked up at her master for permission to take out his fleshy weapon.

Devlin nodded and Anna leaned forward. She slowly lowered his zipper and fished inside his pants for his cock. She took hold of the still soft tube of flesh and, when it was clear of the opening, bent over and took it in her mouth.

The long, rubbery snake soon began to take form. Anna suckled it gently with her lips until it was hard and fat. She fought off her revulsion at the prospect of pushing it past the back of her mouth. When it had grown to full protuberance, she pressed her head down and felt the bulbous head slide into her throat.

"Ahhhhhh, that's good, Anna. That's the way to do it. Keep at it. I want you to play with your pussy while you suck me. From now on, whenever my cock is in your mouth, I want you to caress yourself. Unless you're all tied up of course." He gave a little chuckle.

Anna knew better than to answer the man. She spread her thighs, slid her right hand from behind her back and put it between them. She had already started to get hot as a result of servicing Devlin's cock. There was something about being subservient to him, a shameless slut servicing her lord, that raised her passions. The smell of his loins and the taste of his cock set something off in her. She guided her fingers to her already slightly parted love lips and began to stroke them. Within a few moments, her puss had dilated and her moisture had begun to flow. She moaned when her fingers delicately rubbed against her clit.

"That's the good girl, Anna. Get your pussy nice and wet," Devlin said in response to her sigh of passion. "But don't come unless I tell you to."

Ashamed at her easy lust, Anna continued her attentions to Devlin's cock. She rode up and down it with her pursed lips, terminating each downward stroke with the helmet lodged in her throat. At each upbeat, she washed it with her tongue. Her breasts had grown hard and she felt her face flushed with desire. Her left hand had remained behind her back and she balled it up into a little fist to try and control her lust.

She could hear Devlin sigh and moan his enjoyment of her oral attentions. He stroked her head with one hand while she serviced him. Her pussy was quivering with need and she had to resist the urge to drive her passions past the boiling point. She imagined the stiff, thick cock that was in her mouth plowing her hungry cleft and a wave of desire passed through her. Her thighs were shaking and her breath was growing heavy. It made it difficult to time her gasps of air.

"Come on, suck it like you mean it, Anna," Devlin spat out.

Anna bristled at the insult to her skills and began to obediently quicken her pace. The cock passed in and out of her throat rapidly and she was beginning to feel sick. She didn't know how much more she could take. Finally, the thick wand began to throb. Devlin gave out a mighty groan. She took a deep breath and plunged her head down on his cock. The meaty wand passed deeply into her. It jerked and spasmed and jetted Devlin's come into her belly. It seemed to take forever. Her hand at her loins had unconsciously stilled at the initiation of Devlin's crisis and she resumed her stroking of her puss as she realized her default, fearful that Devlin might punish her for defalcation.

When the cock came to rest, Anna let it sit there for as long as she could. Her chest was screaming for air. She whined as her body protested and she fought off the urge to pull free. She relented her throat's grip on the expended tool only when Devlin pushed her head back gently.

"Not bad, Anna," he said. Anna looked up, her chest heaving with new air. Her eyes were soft and watery from the ardor of her completed task. His face was flush and relaxed. His head was leaning back and his eyes were closed. After a moment, her opened them and looked down at her. She had continued to rub her pussy since he had not ordered her to stop. It was flush and hot.

"Lie back and finish yourself off, Anna," Devlin ordered her. "I want to watch you make yourself come."

Anna blanched at his command. He had asked her about her self administrations of pleasure Friday night and whether she would do it in front of him. She had answered, 'yes'. She hadn't thought about it since then. She was shamed and embarrassed at performing this private, special function in front of him.

Seeing her reluctance, Devlin took hold of her right nipple and squeezed it harshly. "Do it, Anna," he spat at her. "Or would you like to be whipped?"

Anna moaned from the pain. "No, Mr. Devlin," she answered plaintively.

"Then get down on the floor and do it!" he responded angrily.

Anna leaned back and lay down before the callous millionaire. She spread her thighs and raised her knees. She closed her eyes in an attempt to stop her tears. How low could the man make her go, she thought dismally. "Will he leave me nothing?"

Her passion had gone off the boil at Devlin's crude demand, and it took her a while to push out the feelings of shame and humiliation that she felt. She tried to think about better times, lovers that she had, fantasies of romantic interludes. But it was when her mind turned back to where she was and what she had become that her juices started to flow once more.

Anna rubbed her bud of pleasure with her thumb as her fingers darted in and out of her soft, luscious purse. She was a slut. She had always been a slut, even when she was a young girl. Men used her and they had the right to do it. It was right that she should be punished, tied up and gagged. Her flesh needed to be debased, used, despoiled. She was conscious of the eyes of her master, her owner, burning into her. She had a vision of her delicate, black shrouded, stockinged thighs, her swaying breasts, her trimmed, flush pussy, as his eyes must be seeing them. Chance had brought her to him. Who would have thought that he would bring out all these feelings, reawaken her lustful, sinful soul? She felt her desire heightening. Her breath was growing short. She pressed her heels deeply into the soft, plush carpet and moaned.

"Play with your tits, Anna," she heard her master order. Her other hand was behind her back and she dutifully removed it and took hold of her blood filled mounds. She caressed and massaged them, pulled at her stiffened teats, pinched them. Her legs were splayed as wide as she could get them as she rubbed and stroked her fiery pussy. And then it was upon her. Her pussy's walls clenched and spasmed. Her body tightened and her thighs shook. "Ohhhhh! Ohhhhhhhh!" she called out. Wave after wave of electrical pulses of pleasure passed through her. Her hand was rubbing her clit furiously. "Oh! Oh! Oh!" she yelled.

When her pussy's convulsions slowed, Anna let her hand follow it. Her clit was sensitive to the touch and her body gave a little jerk as her fingers passed over it. She stroked her engorged labial lips and then ran her hand over the inner portions of her thighs, reveling in the softness of the silk coverings. Her other hand caressed her soft mounds gently.

"Very good, Anna," Devlin said. "I enjoyed that very much. You're a passionate slut. You looked like you were going to pass out."

Anna heard the deep, approving voice of her master amidst her foggy reveries. Should she thank him for the complement or be shamed at her lasciviousness? She did feel satisfaction that she had pleased him. Somehow, his approval meant a lot to her. He was her master, the one who determined and prescribed all that happened to her. If he was pleased, he might treat her better. If he was not, she knew all too well what would happen.

"Come here and give me a kiss, Anna," Devlin ordered.

Anna roused herself from her stupefied state and rose to her knees. The man had his arms spread and was inviting her onto his lap. She rose and climbed up into it. He put his strong arms around her and she presented him with her flush lips. When his matched hers, she parted them and let him slip his hot tongue inside.

Devlin gave her a long, passionate kiss. His arms felt good around her. It was like she had a new home, something she had been unconsciously looking for for many years. She wrapped her arms around his sturdy neck and pulled him towards her. She felt proud that she had endured all the man's abuse, all of his cruelties. His hand ran along her hip and over her smooth, dark thigh. She reveled in the feel of it. When he took hold of her breast, she felt like she could come all over again. She wanted his cock inside her. But only he could advance that cause. She had no right to make any demand of him other than to be her lord.

Devlin broke their kiss. He gave her hard nipple a little pinch. "Vincent has all the dresses you bought yesterday down in the library. I want you to try them on for me so I can see how you look."

Anna, happy at being deigned worthy of more of her master's time stood up from his lap. She put her hands behind her as he rose and she followed him from the room. He paused at the door and took one of her hands in his. Anna felt pleased at the affectionate gesture. Keeping her other hand in place, she walked with him down the wide, sumptuous hallway to the stairs to the ground floor. His hand was hot and firm in hers and she was comforted by its strength and force of will.

As they descended the broad stairway, she felt like she was being given a treat by a kind uncle or, heaven forbid, her daddy. But her father had never been like Devlin. He was a drunken lout with a mean streak a mile long. She had never held hands with him in her life. She hadn't had any contact with him or her drunken sot of a mother since she was sixteen. Devlin was what a family felt like, she thought as she looked at him.

The dresses were spread out on a large rack in the study. Her lingerie was spread out over one of the sofas. Her shoes were lined up like obedient little soldiers. One by one, Anna modeled the outfits for Devlin. He sat in a large, overstuffed chair, the same one she had been bent over and fucked by him in front of the day before. Anna felt giddy and child like as she pranced in front of him. He commanded her to curtsey and laughed when she dipped her head and lifted the short skirt that she was wearing. She playfully edged it up until the lacy black panties were showing.

Some of the dresses he liked, some he didn't. He had poured himself another glass of scotch and presented one to Anna for her to drink. As was his custom, he urged her to drink it all down at once and her head was cloudy and suffused with the warmth of the alcohol as she stripped and redressed again and again.

There was a long, dark green, satiny gown that he liked best. It had a low bodice and he told her to put it on again without a bra or panties. Her breasts quivered as she walked back and forth for him. The long slit in the gown's side revealed her naked thigh all the way to her hip. It gaped open when she walked and anyone who saw her could observe that she had on no underpants. Her sex felt strange and free under the voluminous, soft, smooth fabric.

"You look lovely, Anna," he said. "I'll have to give Elaine my complements on her taste. There's a party I have to go to on Wednesday and I want you to come with me and wear that dress. And I have something special for you to go with it."

Anna stood silently, her hands poised behind her, as Devlin got up from his chair and opened a drawer on one of the little coffee tables. He took out a small, black jewelry box with scriptive, gold lettering. He brought it over to Anna and opened it. Inside were a pair of glittering, diamond earrings.

Anna gave a gasp when she saw them. The jewels sparkled in the light. They looked like they were worth a fortune.

"Put them on," he told her.

Anna took the earrings from the box one at a time. They were more like studs than earrings. She cocked her head slightly, smiling as she slipped out the cheap, tawdry, gold plated rings that she had been wearing. Devlin took each one as she removed it and put it in his pocket. "You won't be needing these," he said. "I want you to wear your diamonds all of the time."

When the diamond studs were in place, Devlin ordered her to step back and display them for him. She smiled at him appreciatively. She wanted to thank him but knew better than to speak without permission.

"You look wondrous in them. Say thank you, Anna," he told her.

"Thank you, Mr. Devlin," she said beaming.

"You're welcome. Raise your skirt. I want to see how it will look when you're naked."

Anna leaned over and took the hem of her long, dark green dress in her hands. She lifted it up, gathering it as she went until her loins were displayed. She looked back at her master proudly.

"Very nice," he said. "But we'll have to get something down there to go with them. Maybe a stud in your belly button or something."

Anna had never gone the route of getting body piercings. She considered it paganistic and crass. But if Devlin wanted to give her more diamonds, that was okay with her.

"Come here," he told her.

Keeping the folds of her dress in her hands, Anna stepped over to him. He took her head in his hands and kissed her passionately. Anna felt her knees weaken as his hot tongue explored her mouth. After a moment, he dropped one hand and seized her nether lips. He caressed and stroked them while they kissed until her cleft began to soften and dilate. When it had grown moist, he ran his fingers along the slit gathering her moisture. He spread it over her tingling clit, massaging it softly.

Anna moaned with desire. Devlin broke their kiss. "Get down on the floor on your elbows and knees," he told her. His voice carried evidence of his lust. She turned and dropped to her knees obediently. She heard his zipper opening and then he knelt down behind her. His hands lifted the hem of her dress and he pulled it up until her soft, round rear globes and the length of her lower back were exposed. He caressed her smooth haunches and then ran his hands over her bare back.

Anna shivered with the pleasure of his hot touch. She lowered her head to the floor. She had wanted his cock and now she was going to get it. Her pussy was burning with the need for his penetration and she spread her legs wider in invitation. He passed his hand between her thighs behind her and captured the feverish slit. He stroked it and buried his fingers within, casing Anna to sigh with pleasure. She delighted in their hot presence and her lusts began to build as they coursed back and forth along her pussy's walls.

She was squirming with need when Devlin pulled his fingers back. A moment later she felt the head of his cock begging entrance to her womb. Devlin inserted the head just within her hot folds and then, taking hold of her hips, eased himself slowly in.

Devlin commenced a steady, rhythmic stroke of his cock in her crevasse. Anna sighed and moaned with pleasure as it scoured the inner walls and rode over her enflamed clit. Her lust rose steadily. When her fevered cunt began to throb with delight, she felt it grip the thick, stiff, manhood hard. The rush of pleasure made her head dizzy.

He body shook and she groaned. Devlin kept going past her first climax and through her second. She had just begun her third when he grunted and, solidified his grip on her hips. In her throes of passion she felt his cock come to life inside her. His spunk flooded her and she cried out, "Oh, god! Ohhhhhhhh! Oh! Ohhhhhhhhh!"

Devlin let his cock soften in her belly. He rubbed her back and ass while his cock detumesced. Anna felt a warm glow of sexual satisfaction flowing through her body. She was Devlin's whore. All that she had suffered, the beatings, the bindings, the terrible isolation of being hooded and gagged in her little prison on the fourth floor faded away when compared with the satisfaction that she felt at that very moment. Little more than an hour ago, she had been planning how to escape from Devlin's demonic domination of her. Now she wasn't so sure. She knew that she should be rebelling against his callous use of her, but she had never experienced the sexual exhilarations that she had this weekend. What was she to do?

Devlin rose to his feet once his cock finally slipped from Anna's messy quim. She heard him zipper up his pants. She was still crouched on the floor, the bottom of her dress pulled up over her head. As she had been for many hours over the weekend, she was sightless.

"I have some more calls to make before dinner, Anna. Just stay where you are until its ready," he told her.

Anna heard Devlin walk from the room. She was alone again and bound in a position that she had become intimately familiar with, not with leather or chains this time, but by Devlin's words. She had shifted again in Devlin's estimation from a person to tease and flatter to a thing to be left behind when he was done with it. It was strange to be half draped and half exposed, her bare back and naked rear and loins brazenly displayed for anyone who came in the room to see. But, after all, it was what the men considered the important part of her, the part they could vent their lusts on. Her face, her mind, they were really of no value in her new life.

After about a half hour, Anna heard the door opening. Someone, she assumed it was Vincent, had come in and begun to clean up the clothes that she had left strewn around the room. Although the emotionless butler had seen her naked many times by now, had forced her into similar lascivious poses, she felt self conscious now. Perhaps it was the slavishness with which she was obeying Devlin's instructions. What self respecting woman would allow herself to be treated like this? All she had to do was stand up to cover herself. She could get up, demand her car keys, toss Devlin's baubles back at him and walk out the door.

But she knew she wouldn't do that. There was still the issue of the money. It wouldn't be paid until the morning. And did she want to leave? If Devlin had absolved her of her bargain and paid the money into the agency anyway, would she beg him to let her stay? She would not know for sure until she left. The confusion and conflict she felt about being Devlin's slavish slut would be clearer when she was able to get out of here. Until then, her thinking would be suspect and any decision she came to would be provisional and indefinite.

Vincent, or at least the person she hoped was Vincent, she dreaded the thought of being exposed as a slavish whore in front of any more people, completed the task of straightening out the room and left. There was so much mysterious about Devlin's mansion. Where were the other servants? There must be more. And who was the woman in the room upstairs? The implements of her subjugation, the chains, the leather bindings, the gags, had all been readily available whenever her users had found a need for them.

Her room seemed specially outfitted for its function: holding a female captive. If she continued on as Devlin's whore, stayed the course instead of fleeing, would she learn more than she wanted to know about his activities? And once she knew, would he ever set her free?

When Vincent came to call her for dinner, he first stood wordlessly over her, taking in her abject form. Humiliated at her slavish posture, she wanted to cover herself, but knew that she needed to await his signal. Her mind filled with a vision of how she must appear to him, her bare back and ass, her lavender garter belt stretched across it, her black encased, stockinged legs, her pretty high heels on her feet, the green dress spread over her upper half as if she was hiding herself, ostrich like. His signal, when it finally came, consisted of the curt, cold command to "Get up."

Anna raised herself from the floor and smoothed out her dress. Looking out of the tall, arching windows of the study, she saw that it was dark outside. Vincent led her to the hallway and the clacking of her heels on the stone floor reminded her of her when she had first arrived to become Devlin's 'guest'. If she knew then what she knew now, would she have run screaming out the door? She realized that so much of what had happened to her over the weekend, the long, boring hours of blind and silenced confinement, the deprivation of the use of her limbs, the chains, even Vincent's infernal cane, had all be done with a calculation of inculcating in her the very slavish obedience she was exhibiting now.

Devlin was not yet in the small dining room when she arrived. Vincent pointed out to her the same chair she had sat in on Friday night. She sat in it, carefully spreading her long, dark green skirt around her and crossed her arms behind her.

Devlin arrived a few moments later. He had changed and was wearing a dark suit. She wondered if he always dressed for dinner or whether he had donned the finely tailored clothes so that he would be simpatico with her elegant gown.

He sat in the chair opposite her and, a few moments later, Vincent emerged from the kitchen with a cart. Like Friday, the meal was sumptuous and refined. The salad consisted of mixed arugula and romaine lettuce with a tart vinaigrette dressing. There were small baked mushrooms stuffed with crabmeat and covered with a light, creamy sauce. Dinner was a large roast, cooked until its shell was dark brown but juicy and succulent on the inside. It was accompanied by fluffy, brown wild rice and crisp string beans mixed with slender slivers of almonds. The tall, obsequious butler kept Anna's wine glass filled with a tangy California pinot noir.

As on Friday, Devlin was loquacious. They talked more about the Center and the work that Anna did on a daily basis. There were several important issues she had to deal with soon. One was a replacement for Carol. It was funny, but Anna had hardly thought about her all weekend. She was the whole reason that she had become Devlin's slave. Anna wondered where she was, if she would ever turn up. $225,000 was a lot of money to abscond with and even a junkie in the throes of her addiction could make it last a long time. Anna fretted about her friend in spite of the fact that she had done her so much harm. Would she turn up dead somewhere from a drug overdose? Would some other junkie, finding out how much money she had, murder her for it?

"I have someone I'm going to send by on Monday for you to interview to replace your assistant," Devlin said. "She has very good experience."

Anna assented to considering the woman but she had to wonder if it would be someone who, like her, had fallen into Devlin's clutches. It would be hard to explain why she didn't want to hire her. Devlin had supreme authority over her now and she realized that a suggestion from him was tantamount to an order.

The dinner passed quickly. Anna was slightly inebriated from all of the wine. She drank a cup of black espresso to try and sober up for her drive home. Devlin insisted, however, that she have a small glass of anisette with it and the creamy, cherry covered cheese cake that Vincent served for dessert.

When the dinner was over, Devlin pushed himself back from the table. His mood seemed to shift. "I want you to take off your dress and wait here. Vincent will take you upstairs. He will bring you your clothes and you can go. Before you do, we'll have a little chat in my office."

Anna felt joy at the prospect of finally being freed. Devlin's change of attitude reminded her of the cruelty that he was capable of. She was amazed at how swiftly and without warning his moods could change. The sooner she was out of there the better.

The young woman rose from her chair and removed her dress. It zippered down the back and she had to reach her hands behind her to gain access to it. Disrobing before her owner, she recalled making the same motion on Friday night when he had ordered her to show him her breasts. Then, as now, the arching of her back caused them to swell out. It was strange to remember how ashamed she was to show off her naked breasts and how unhappy she had been at his rude order. Now she was almost inured to displaying her naked body to him and his servants. How much she had changed in three days.

When the dress was off, Anna carefully folded it over the back of her chair. When she was stripped, Devlin tossed back his anisette and stepped from the room.

Anna stood silently, her wrists crossed behind her, dressed only in her garter belt and stockings, while waiting for Vincent to arrive to escort her. In the silence of the dining room, alone and naked, or nearly so, she tried to push from her mind her feelings of helplessness. She was bound in position as firmly and decisively as if she had been chained in place. Devlin's command was as unbreakable as the steel chains she had been adorned with earlier. The only noise in the room was the ticking of a small clock mounted on the wall. Its repeated, inexorable machinations became a drumbeat in her mind, driving home at each click her abject and utter servility

About ten minutes later, the staid butler emerged from the kitchen and ordered her to follow him. She trailed dutifully behind him as the ascended the stairs. In her room, her clothes were laid out on the bed. There were no panties or bra.

Dressing in front of the butler was oddly disconcerting. She kicked off the red pumps that she had been wearing and stepped into her brown skirt. She left on the garter belt and stockings since her former ones were not present. When she pulled her burgundy sweater blouse over her head and had redonned her high heels, she was ready to go.

As they left the room that had been her prison cell, Anna gave a passing thought to the anonymous woman down the hall. Was what to be her fate? Would she be permitted to leave tonight? Anna felt sad for her, whoever she was.

When they arrived on the ground floor, Vincent led Anna into Devlin's office. He was on the phone again and she waited patiently for him to finish, her hands crossed behind her. He concluded his call, put the phone down, and looked up at her. He had removed his jacket, which was draped over the back of his chair, and was in his shirtsleeves.

"Tomorrow morning at 8:15, Carlos will pick you up at your apartment," he told her. "He will have the cash and he will take you to the bank. You will see the manager there who will have full instructions. There will be no problem. Once the money is put in your account, you will give Carlos the receipt so that I have proof that the money was deposited. He will then drive you to the Center's bank and you will deposit your check into its account. You will give him a copy of your check and the deposit ticket as well. Do you understand?"

"Yes, Mr. Devlin," Anna answered. It was true. It was really going to happen. The Center and her life's work would be saved. She had been worried that all of this had been a ruse to obtain her sluttish, slavish services over the weekend. She was relieved that she had not gone through all of her humiliation and abuse for nothing.

"As I told you on Friday, Anna," Devlin continued. "Once the money is in your account, our deal is sealed. If you renege, you will wish you had never been born. Got it?"

A tremor of fear passed through the young woman. "Yes, Mr. Devlin, I understand," she returned.

Devlin sat quietly for a moment. He was tapping the desk with a pen that he was holding in his hand. His eyes wandered over Anna's form. After a few moments, he resumed his lecture.

"On Friday nights, you will present yourself here at 7 p.m., sharp. Don't be late like you were this time. I won't tolerate any excuses. And if you come here again dressed like some whored up real estate agent I'll whip you myself personally, understand?"

Anna shivered at the thought. She indicated her understanding.

"Vincent will bring some of the dresses and other things that you bought yesterday to your apartment. On Monday, before Carlos drops you off back at your apartment, you will stop at a hardware store and make a copy of your key and give it to him. Although you will be here primarily on the weekends, you belong to me and I don't want any barriers between us. You will not leave town without permission and you will carry your cell phone on you at all times. I don't care what you're doing or who you're with, when I call, I want you to answer. And if I want you here, at my office in the city, or anywhere else, you'll come immediately. Is that clear?"

"Yes, Mr. Devlin," Anna answered dolefully. She thought dismally of what her life would be like for the next year if she did not run away or decide to challenge Devlin's enforcement of their devilish bargain.

"I want you to keep your pussy shaved like it is now. Do it every day. You'll never know when I'll decide I want to use you. I don't want your pussy all rough and scratchy. When you come here, unless I have Carlos pick you up, park in the back and use the servant's entrance. When you walk in, you're to strip and wait out in the foyer. Someone will come and tell you what to do. If not, you just wait there for me. As for sex, you are not to have sex with anyone, at any time, under any circumstances, without my permission. You are to masturbate every night before you go to sleep, starting tonight. And throw away all your old bras and panties. Vincent will deliver the new underthings I bought you to your apartment tomorrow."

The young woman meekly expressed her assent to the man's terms. Time would tell. She would agree to anything so that she could leave.

"And finally, and most importantly, you are not to tell anyone about our arrangement. Not your coworkers, your friends, your priest, anyone. And nothing about what you've seen or heard here. If I find out that you've talked, well, lets just say that you won't. Okay?"

Anna nodded. The thought of being ever at the man's beck and call at every moment of every day was dismally depressing. She would have to fuck him at his office and anywhere else he decided to have her. And she would have no life of her own. She wondered how he would know if she jilled herself off every night. She knew that if she didn't somehow he would find out. She couldn't imagine herself lying to him.

"Okay, now bend over the couch over there. I want to fuck your ass once more before you go."

A wave of misery passed through Anna at Devlin's coarse instruction. She had thought that she was finished with his abuse of her. Unhappily, she turned and walked over to the couch that divided the room. Its back was low and when she bent over it her ass was raised high. Her hands remained dutifully crossed behind her. One of the massive windows of the huge office was right in front of her.

She could see the well lit parking area in front of the mansion. Her car was out there waiting for her. Soon she would be in it and driving home. What would it be like to be free after all she had gone through, she wondered unhappily. She heard Devlin get up from his desk and walk over to her. He lifted the back of her smooth, tan skirt and placed it on her hips.

"Spread you legs wider," he said churlishly. His hands were hot when he began to caress her rear globes. He stroked her presented pussy between her legs. To Anna's unhappiness, the attentions to her pussy began to stoke her arousal. In a short while she was wet and he was plunging his fingers back and forth along the walls of her sexual tunnel while she moaned.

"You are a slut, Anna," he said, laughing. "Maybe you should be paying me for getting you so much cock."

Anna gave out a low whine at the insult. She couldn't help her arousal. She didn't want it. Something inside her just clicked when she thought of being penetrated by the strong willed man. She heard Devlin's zipper fall and she tensed, preparing herself for the callous piercing of her anal ring. Devlin took swipe of her pussy's moisture and wiped it over her rear entrance. The round, fat head of his cock pressed against it and she felt it slide over the delicate membranes of her small, back hole. Her ring was still tender and she gave a moan of pain as the cock passed over it.

Devlin make a quick job of it. He plunged himself back and forth in rapid, almost violent strokes. Anna felt like she was being battered by him. His thick cock filled her bowel like a malicious, evil presence. Her pussy, spurned, burned with unwanted lust.

About a minute after he started, Devlin's body tensed and he began to jet his juices deep into her bowels.

When he was finished her released her. "Okay, you can go," he said. He retreated to his desk where he produced a moist towelette from a dispenser and cleaned off his cock before restoring it to his pants. Anna rose slowly from the couch. Her ass burned and her pussy was unsatisfied. Tears were rolling down her face. She should have expected one last humiliation form the man, but she had been excited at the prospect of leaving. Remembering the literalness of his commands, she forwent any thought of a goodbye or a by your leave, straightened her skirt and walked to the door.

Vincent was waiting for her in the foyer holding her long, black, woolen overcoat over his arm. In his other hand were her kid leather gloves and her small, black purse. This is where it had all started. Little had she know that the act of removing her gloves and coat in front of the staid servant was but a harbinger of what awaited her. As she donned the heavy coat, she glanced at the broad, carpet covered staircase and thought of her room on the fourth floor. Would she ever see it again?

If she returned she knew that she would. She would be bound and gagged there awaiting use or abuse by any one of the three men who had tormented her flesh over the last three days. How many more men would be added to the list of those she would be required to service? The thought of it made her shiver. She felt more tears coming, but held them back, unwilling to show the cool, emotionless butler her sorrow and weakness. When her coat was buttoned, Vincent handed her her gloves. She put them on deliberately, stretching the thin, fur lined leather over her hands. He then handed her her purse.

Anna stood silently for a moment. Here she was, dressed essentially the same way she had come in. But so much had changed. Parts of her that had been long hidden had been revealed during her weekend of abuse, her voracious appetite for sex, her ease at sliding into submissiveness, her tolerance and even hunger for abuse. But if you had taken a snapshot of her on Friday when she arrived and compared it to her now, the only difference that you would see was the finely trimmed hair and the sparkling diamonds in her ears. Devlin wanted her to wear them all of the time. She realized that they were not really a gift to her, but the bestowal of his emblem of ownership on her. Every time that she looked in the mirror she would see them. People would remark on them. She would be reminded time and time again of her submissive slavishness to the cruel millionaire and his right to the use of her at any time and at any place.

She had half expected some words of parting from the fearsome butler, but he opened the door silently and gave her a cool, dispassionate gaze. She stepped out into the cold night.

As on her arrival, the stones of the parking paddock crunched as she walked over them. She had spent the bulk of her weekend in high heels and crossing the loose stones was not as difficult as when she arrived. The bright lights that flooded over the entrance to Devlin's mansion and the parking area before it made her feel like she was on stage and she was self conscious as she walked, imagining that Vincent, or Devlin, was watching her as she made her retreat,

Her car was still where she had left it. She took her keys from her purse and beeped the locks open. When she got in the driver's seat she turned on the engine immediately, wanting the car to warm up as soon as possible. She sat there for a few moments, gathering herself. A heavy weight was on her heart. Why had Carol stolen the money? How could she have done this to her best friend? It was a betrayal of the worst sort. A part of Anna cursed her and hoped that, wherever she was, the tall, attractive, blond woman would suffer for her crime, pay as severe a penalty for it as she was.

Her mind turned to the issue of what she would do once the money Devlin had promised had been paid. Should she return, Devlin's dutiful slave, for a year of abuse and torment, or should she flee once the money was in the Center's bank account and risk the terrible consequences he had threatened? If she fled, she would lose all contact with the Center, a place that had been to most important thing in her life for many years. The girls there depended on her and she considered them as family. And what would she do? Waitress? She would not be able to use her social security number or her real name for fear that Devlin would find her. No, running would not be the answer.

She felt a surge of sorrow pass through her body. Determined to be strong, she took hold of the gear shift and placed the car in reverse. It obediently backed up until her front end was clear and she turned the wheel to direct the car to the roadway some half mile down the long, sinewy driveway.

At the end, Anna turned the car to its right to head towards her apartment. The country road was dark and lonely and there were no other cars. After driving for about a mile or two, she felt overcome with grief and shame at what she had done, what she had become, what had been done to her. She pulled the car over to the side of the road, placed it in park and began to cry.

* * * * * * * * * * * * * *

Back at the mansion, Devlin was in his office on the telephone.

"Everything went well," he was saying. "She doesn't suspect a thing....Well, it'll take a little while to work the whole thing out, but all should go according to plan....Yes, I'll keep you apprised. Just make sure you're ready when the time comes....Okay. Goodbye."

Devlin put the phone down and leaned back in his large, cushioned, black chair. He was not a contemplative man, but he was relishing his memories of the sweet body parts of the young woman who had just left. It had gone better than expected.

He was interrupted by the buzzing of the intercom on his desk. It was Vincent.

"Yes," he said.

"The men are here, Mr. Devlin. The van is out back."

"Okay. Bring down the girl and have them wait in the foyer. I'll be out in a minute."

He poured himself a shot of scotch into his large, round tumbler and tossed it back. Life was good.

When he emerged from the office, Vincent was leading a tall, thin, thirtyish woman with long, blonde, thin hair down the stairs. Her hands were bound behind her and she wore a ball gag in her mouth. She was naked and Devlin admired her long, languorous legs and her small but well formed breasts. Her sex was shrouded with a pale covering of yellow hair. She was wearing a pair of red high heels and was peering down at her feet as she walked, careful not to make a misstep.

When the woman reached the bottom of the stairs, she looked up nervously.

Two men had entered from the rear of the mansion and were waiting in the foyer. Between them was a big, black, rectangular, steel box. It made a soft clattering sound on its rubber wheels as it rolled over the slate floor.

The woman looked over at the men fearfully and then back at Devlin.

"Ahh, Carol," Devlin said, placing his hand between her thighs and capturing her dainty, shrouded sex. "You look lovely. You really are a wonderful fuck."

The attractive woman looked disconsolately back at the millionaire. Something was happening now and she looked like she wasn't looking forward to it.

"It's been a fun couple of weeks, Carol, but I'm afraid that our time together has come to an end. You're going on a little trip. I'll see you again, I'm sure, once your training is over."

The woman gave him a panicked look.

"Don't worry, everything has been taken care of. It's a good thing that you came to me. As I promised, the money you stole will be replaced. There will be no prosecution. The charges from your drug arrest will be dropped. I don't know why you had so much on you. Ten years in prison is a long time."

Carol had not been told that her friend had sold herself to cover up the theft of the money from the Center, nor would she be. It was better that she be kept in ignorance.

Devlin laughed to himself over the irony that Anna had spent the weekend with him totally ignorant that her best friend, the cause of all her misery and abuse, was being held prisoner only twenty feet away from her. Devlin had enjoyed shuffling them back and forth unaware of each others' presence or that they were succeeding each other in pleasuring his cock. Now that Anna was firmly entrapped in his web, he had no reason to keep the other one around. It was time to get her up to speed in her new life.

It had all been a set up, of course. He had waited patiently for Carol, the former heroin addict, to crack under the temptations that he continuously, surreptitiously, put before her. It had just been a matter of time. One of his men, playing the role of an ardent lover, had convinced her to take the money so that they could run off together. After spending a few days with her, living high off of the hog, he had absconded with the ill gained loot and brought it to Devlin.

Carol had been arrested after a staged raid of the hotel room and found with two ounces of heroin in a gym bag in the closet. The detective in charge, as per their prior arrangement, notified Devlin and he went down to the station and secured her release, assuring her that it was only due to his powerful police connections and his connections to the Center that the whole thing had been kept out of the papers.

Disconsolate and remorseful, she begged him to help her make things right. He had laid out, more or less, the same perfidious conditions he had later proposed to Anna. She believed that she was trading herself so that she would be spared a harsh prison sentence and so the Center, and her friend Anna, would be saved. The fact that the woman had made herself disappear without a trace had made everything else so easy. It was doubtful that she knew exactly what she was agreeing to when she made her bargain with him to be his sexual slave, but that was just too bad. He had pumped Carol for all the intimate details of Anna's life and he was well prepared for his campaign to seduce and corrupt Anna when she came into play. Once Carol was in his clutches, Devlin knew that Anna, his ultimate target, would follow.

The funny thing was that most of the money that Anna would deposit in her bank account Monday was the same money Carol had stolen from the Center. It was just the kind of twisted irony that Devlin enjoyed.

Carol's eyes started to tear and a supplicative moan passed her gagged lips. She looked like she was going to faint.

The men who had come in were wearing dark blue t-shirts and jeans and heavy work boots. They were both tall, young and muscular. They were staring at the naked form of the blonde woman appreciatively. The black box had been opened at its end.

"You have to get in the box, Carol," Devlin said coldly. Unlike Anna, Carol was a whirlwind in bed and he would miss the use of her. Well, there were others and, after a few weeks, Carol would again be available, although he would have to share her.

The woman stared at the beckoning enclosure. Her eyes had grown misty and her fear was written across her face. She looked up at Devlin. "Eeeease, on't!" she moaned fretfully past her gagged mouth.

"Oh, I'm afraid you have to Carol. These are the consequences of your actions. Everybody has to accept the consequences of what they do." Except me, he thought. He removed his hand and stepped back from the trembling woman. He nonchalantly took a whiff of it. There was nothing like the smell of an excited pussy. "A bargain is a bargain," he continued. "If you don't get in willingly, Vincent will beat you and then you'll get in anyway. Or these men will force you in. Either way, you're going in the box."

"Ohhhhhhhhh!" the woman moaned. Her body was shaking. Tears had escaped her eyes and were flowing down her cheeks. "Eeeeeeease, ih-er eh-in! Eeeeeeeas!" she screamed

Devlin just glared at her coldly. She looked around once more as if calculating the amount of physical force around her.

"Come on, honey, we haven't got all night," one of the men said. He was grinning, obviously enjoying the spectacle of the unhappy, forlorn woman.

Carol gave a great sob and lowered herself shakily to her knees. Her nipples had stiffened from fear and her small, firm breasts made little points at the end. She looked up at Devlin anxiously, obviously seeking a reprieve from her fate. Seeing no hope of dissuading him, she moaned and began to crawl on her knees to the box.

The opening was just about big enough for her to squeeze through. The dismal, naked woman shuffled her knees towards it on the cold, hard, slate floor and, bending her neck, placed her head inside. Her long, blonde hair fell loosely about her shoulders. Her bound hands were clamped into nervous, desperate, little fists on her back. Sniffling and whining, she edged first one knee and then the other over the lip and onto the padded interior. Her noises made little echoes from inside as she sadly coaxed the rest of her body in. It was just tall enough so that she could fit with her back bent over and her thighs scrunched up under her. She was crying disconsolately now, her sobs emerging from the baffles built into the box's sides. Her lightly veiled, blond sex was visible, squeezed between her clamped thighs, and her well used, dainty, brown tinted rear access peeked out from behind her.

The tips of her high heels jutted out from the opening. One of the men stooped down and, grabbing her ankles, removed her pretty shoes one by one. He handed them to Vincent. The other pushed her feet further inside and then swung the small doorway to her tiny prison closed. It snapped shut with a loud 'click!'. At the sound, Carol gave out a loud wail of unhappiness that sounded strange and distorted as it emerged from the cruel, black enclosure.

Devlin and Vincent watched the big, black, steel box being rolled away by the men. Carol's sobs could be heard faintly as it receded. Devlin turned to Vincent.

"I'm going to the club. Have one of the other sluts, Irina, the little Russian girl with the passport problem, here by ten o'clock. Give her a good whipping and then have her ready on my bed when I get back."

"Yes, Mr. Devlin," the tall, obedient servant replied.

Devlin turned and walked towards the front door.

* * * * * * * * * * * * *

Carol's little prison was wheeled down the hallway towards the servant's entrance. The men pushed open the steel covered door and pulled the box over the transom. The rear entrance had a loading dock and their van was backed up to it. One of the men opened the doors while the other slid the box over the end of the dock and into the back of the van. He got inside after it and fastened its bottom to clamps on the floor so it would not roll during transport. There was a double hose leading from a small air tank built into the side of the van and he snapped it into place on the box's top. Carol could still be faintly heard wailing and bemoaning her cruel imprisonment. When the man slid the slots over the baffles closed, all noise from the little enclosure ceased.

The men got into the passenger compartment and started the grey van on its journey. On its side, inscribed in large, scriptive, blue letters, were the words 'The Blue Cantina'.

To be continued.